Sea of Darkness

Sea of Darkness

ROLAND
HUNTFORD

Charles Scribner's Sons
New York

Copyright © 1975 Roland Huntford

Library of Congress Cataloging in Publication Data
Huntford, Roland
Sea of darkness.

1. Colombo, Cristoforo — Fiction. I. Title.
PZ4.H949Se3   [PR6058.U58]   823   75-17690
ISBN 0-684-14418-2

Copyright under the Berne Convention

All rights reserved. No part of this book
may be reproduced in any form without the
permission of Charles Scribner's Sons.

1 3 5 7 9 11 13 15 17 19 V/C 20 18 16 14 12 10 8 6 4 2

Printed in the United States of America

La verdad adelgaza, y no quiebra.
(Truth can be stretched, but it does not break.)

                                                  SPANISH PROVERB

Pero porque segun tengo entendido, que cuando determinó buscar un principe cristiano que le ayudase e hiciese espaldas, ya él tenía certidumbre que habia de descubrir tierras y gentes en ellas, como si en ellas personalmente hubiera estado (de lo cual cierto yo no dudo)...

(For, as I understand, when he [Columbus] decided to seek a Christian Prince who should help and support him, he was already certain that he would discover lands and people in them, as if he had been there personally (of which I certainly do not doubt)...)

                              BARTOLOMÉ DE LAS CASAS,
                                  Historia de las Indias (1527)

CONTENTS

PART I · PROLOGUE AT LA RÁBIDA   9

PART II · GENOA   15

PART III · TERRA NOVA   85

PART IV · LISBON   175

PART V · LA RÁBIDA   209

I

I HAVE been told that I cannot speak the truth, but perhaps I can write it.

Like Pontius Pilate, I can reply: what is truth? That my name is Cristóbal Colón, Christovão Colóm, Christoforo Colombo or, as the English say, Christopher Columbus? That I was born on such and such a day in such and such a place? Or that I am a beggar, a wanderer in Spain and an exile wherever I go?

But this is no time to quibble. The fulfilment of ambition draws near. Before me lies the voyage which has become the obsession of my waking hours. I am waiting at the Convent of La Rábida, while my ships are being made ready in Palos at the foot of the hill. From my window as I write, I can see the muddy channel down which I soon will sail to cross the Ocean and discover new countries in the West.

I know - none better - the hazards I will have to face. Before I leave I must put my affairs in order. I have decided that in the time still left to me in Spain I will set down the truth about myself.

If I do not return, it is to be published immediately; otherwise, it will be hidden for posterity to read. For, whatever the result of my enterprise, I do not want deceit to be my only monument. I want to be seen as I really am; the only question is when. The time will surely come for my reputation to be mauled by men bereft of all passion save curiosity. When that happens, I wish to speak in my own defence. Until then, I claim the privilege of appearing before history in the manner that I choose.

I propose to go down as the great precursor, the man who demonstrated the existence of new lands across the Atlantic by sheer force of intellect; and sailed out to prove it himself; navigator, explorer and philosopher in one. As Seneca said more than a thousand years ago:

There will come a time in the long years of the world, when the Ocean Sea will loosen the shackles that bind together and a great part of the earth will be opened up and a new sailor such as the one who was Jason's guide, and whose name was Thypis shall discover a new world, and then shall Thule be no longer the last of the lands.

Wearing a mask, however, can be an unhappy business. Sometimes the craving to reveal the true self can be well nigh unbearable. And I have not dared to do so to a single human being; even those closest to me. The compulsion to declare myself has come as a blessed relief.

But the prospect of 'stirring up the heart so that it may not sleep in desperation', as St Augustine says of confession, is marred by the injustice I have had to endure.

It is now the Year of Grace 1492. It is six years since first I laid before Isabella, Her Most Catholic Majesty, a simple plan for sailing westwards to annexe certain territories, and was rewarded with a Commission of Inquiry: six years of futility, disappointment, and the purgatory of inaction; years that have achieved nothing for me but the age of forty, and the privilege of surveying a herd of younger men already where their ambitions have driven them, while I have not yet started my life's work.

Think of waiting, always waiting, for the answer that never comes; fobbed off with excuses, suffering elegant procrastination; always a little more time, to hear this opinion, to consider that idea. Never mind; history, if I win, will pronounce the Commission a pack of obscurantists that almost succeeded in strangling my enterprise.

But all the obscurantism, if the truth be known, has not been on one side. The circumstances were justification enough. I could not trust my interrogators.

The Commission's avowed purpose was to investigate my plans and judge if I was worth supporting; I feared that its real intention might have been to worm my secrets out of me so as to give someone else the reward that is my due.

The Ocean is not the *Mare Tenebrum*, the Sea of Darkness, of popular superstition. We all know that the world is round. We all agree that if you sail west you must necessarily reach land.

Whether it is India, or a country hitherto unknown, is beside the point. There is no lack of plausible schemes to explore it, whatever it may be. Everybody seems to be a discoverer now. Anybody could steal my ideas. And what would poor Colón be then? - a poor, neglected wretch, his only hope some future scholar seeking the man behind the myth. I will not be a footnote to history, I want to be history itself.

So I have suffered a nightmare of everlasting subterfuge. I have had to parry every question. I had to persuade the Commission that I alone was qualified for the task of westwards exploration, while concealing what I really might have known.

But all this is behind me now. The Commission has spoken; the Queen has given her consent. I can at last devote myself to my Atlantic islands, instead of dissipating my energies on overcoming contumacious adversaries. My work is done, I have laid my plans; I have helpers on the quays. The time remaining before departure is virtually my own. I can concentrate on the task of baring myself to posterity.

But when I think of the questions with which I have been bombarded, these past few years, I hardly know where to begin.

Who am I? they ask. Where do I come from? Why am I called Genoese, when my loyalty is not to the Republic? If I come from Genoa, why is my Italian so poor? I speak Castilian, but it is not the Castilian spoken today. And why does my mother tongue appear to be a form of Catalan, when I don't come from Catalonia?

I must explain all this, and more. Unless I drain the cup of truth to the dregs, I shall not achieve the peace of mind for which I am searching.

PART ONE
Prologue at La Rábida

PART TWO

Genoa

II

'BEHOLD my infancy is dead long ago', as St Augustine says, and out of that limbo I retrieve my first memory. It is the return of the Genoese fleet after the fall of Constantinople. I want to describe this, because in that event lay the beginnings of the voyage which now, almost forty years later, is on the verge of fulfilment.

I seem to be suspended high above the ground. Beneath me spread the harbour of Genoa and the bay. It is early morning and the water is rippled by the sea-breeze. Ships far below, like walnut shells bobbing in line ahead, make their way slowly down the roadstead to the mole. I look down on to stubby decks drifting by into the harbour. Like maggots on a morsel, onlookers cluster round each vessel as it berths.

Suddenly I am on a quayside. Men are walking down a gangplank from a ship. Some are brightly dressed; clearly merchants or men of rank. Others are wearing the dun-coloured jerkins and rough hose of common sailors. A stretcher is unloaded and placed on the flagstones. Ignored by the passers-by, it stands alone, until a brown-clad monk appears. He bends over, and draws back a blanket to show a figure covered in bandages, like someone gored by a bull, which a man in a scarlet coat proceeds to inspect. My uncle Antonio, who has been standing by, steps forward to look closely and talk to the monk and his companion.

But is this memory? The year is 1453, and I was not yet two, scarcely old enough to understand what was happening. Certainly what I have told has so often and intensely been described to me that I have come to believe that it is what my infant eyes actually saw.

My uncle Antonio showed me the fleet that day; he told and retold the story afterwards. He rarely did so without airing his views about the fall of Constantinople; and his views were nothing if not decided. He despised the Genoese fleet for refusing to fight. He told me time without number, passionate indignation never failing to erupt, how the Genoese had betrayed the Greeks to save their own skins. He believed implicitly that it was Genoese cowardice alone that allowed the Turks to win.

'It was disgraceful,' I remember Antonio once saying, 'the Genoese were poltroons every man jack of them. Their excuse for not fighting was that they were neutral. And afterwards they had the effrontery to pretend that, by being neutral, they had been particularly virtuous. They even gave the impression that they had somehow been the real heroes of the siege. It makes you sick; and to think that I'm forced to acknowledge those disgusting creatures as my fellow-citizens.'

From this, it will appear that my uncle did not really consider himself Genoese; nor, although I was born in Genoa, do I. I seem to have plunged into the middle of my story. To make everything clear, I had better begin at the beginning.

III

SHE who is honoured as the founder of my family was burned at the stake or, if you prefer the modern euphemism, 'relaxed in person' almost three hundred years ago by the Inquisition in Southern France. Her name was Beatrice Vidal. She was a Cathar. In other words, the Colóns are not of Genoese origin, and they began as heretics.

There seems no harm in admitting that, for we have purged our errors now. We accept that Catharism was anathematized by the Church, doubtless with perfect justification. On the other hand, it was our spiritual cradle. Its influence cannot be denied. Its mark remains on the Colóns. To understand me, you must understand the Cathars, and I must therefore begin by explaining Catharism.

Catharism is the correct name of what is now vulgarly called the Albigensian heresy. But although suppressed in an earlier Inquisition, it was not entirely exterminated. It has survived in the shadows until our own times.

If Catharism is mentioned at all nowadays, it is usually in disgust, as some loathsome creed of which infant sacrifice and other lurid rites are held to be the ingredients. At best it is presented as a witches' brew of occult heresies.

I suppose there is some justification for this view. The Cathars denied the humanity of Christ. They considered him no more than a phantom. They denied the doctrine of the Trinity. And, for good measure, they rejected the omnipotence of God. They looked upon the Devil as coeval and coequal. To them, the material world lay entirely in the kingdom of evil, only the things of the spirit being good, that is, belonging to God. Earthly existence was to them a form of purgatory, each soul undergoing successive reincarnations more or less vile, until, purified by suffering, it was released from the circle of life, and admitted to Heaven. A few souls, however, were predestined never to do so; condemned to wander eternally on earth.

But all this is just a shell of philosophy and speculation. At heart, Catharism was extremely simple. It was a return to original Christianity. Indeed some say that it was the only legitimate successor of the primitive Church, and that Rome is the impostor. The Cathars rejected the mountains of interpretation thrown up by generations of priests. They insisted that the Bible was the only source of faith. They denied the proposition that reading Holy Writ was the prerogative of the Clergy; they maintained that it ought to be open to all, translating it into the vernacular. They reviled the worship of saints, relics, and images as heathen abominations. Their own churches, like those of the early Christians, were plain, white-washed, undecorated, lacking even a crucifix. In fact, the Cathars regarded the crucifix with particular loathing. In their eyes, it was a detestable monument to the triumph of Evil, a symbol of gloating over the sufferings of Our Saviour. They also rejected infant baptism, holding that it meant imposition on a helpless creature, and that it ought only to be performed on those in full possession of their faculties. They copied the first Christians in ruling their Church through a lay council of elected Elders. They accepted women priests. The Cathars were, indeed, heretics on a grand scale.

Such were the people among whom Beatrice lived. She was born in 1181 at Carcassonne and married a fellow Cathar of Catalan origins called Philip Colón or, as it then was, Colóm. They moved to Toulouse, for Philip was a weaver, and Toulouse was famous for its cloth trade. It was also a Cathar citadel. The one concerned the other, for weaving was then notoriously a Cathar occupation. 'Weaver' in fact was slang for heretic – as it still is in Catalonia, I am told.

Beatrice gave birth to her only child in Toulouse. It was a boy, called Bernard. He came into this world of ours in the year of the Incarnation of our Lord 1203. Soon afterwards began the Golgotha of the Cathars.

Cathar and Catholic had subscribed to the doctrine of live and let live. But in the long run it was more than Rome could swallow and in 1208 the Holy Father Innocent proclaimed the Holy Albigensian Crusade for the extermination of the heretics of the Languedoc.

> 'De Montfort cried in his tent at Mass,
> While faggots outside were aglow,
> "Smell of heretics' burning flesh,
> Is the sweetest incense that I know".'

So runs a verse of a Colóm family song, about Simon de Montfort, the Leader of the Crusade. Dare I confess that I regard him as a little lower than the angels?

But he did win the war. He did not, however, succeed in exterminating Catharism. Now it was the turn of the Inquisition. And that, as far as the Colóms were concerned, is a story on its own.

It was the duty of certain Cathar families to maintain small hospices for their fellow-Cathars. Beatrice and Philip ran such an establishment, together with their weavers' workshop and once, during their early years in Toulouse, they entertained a certain Dominic de Guzmán. He was the future St Dominic. But he was then just one more itinerant Spanish evangelist trying to save the land from the heretic. And he was such a queer fellow, forever shouting at strangers, having fits in the middle of the streets, and muttering to himself. He was poor into the bargain; no innkeeper would take him in. But Cathar charity knew no bounds, and the Colóms gave him shelter.

Dominic repaid their hospitality by leaving in a huff after unsuccessfully trying to convert them, announcing that force would prevail where gentle persuasion had failed.

And force was duly invoked. Soon afterwards, Dominic founded the Order which bears his name, to convert the heretic by argument. That failing, the Dominicans resorted to the Inquisition and turned to systematic persecution. We Cathars were not only the first victims of the Inquisition, but its first cause. It is a melancholy distinction, but one that we have never allowed ourselves to forget.

After years as a miserable fugitive in her own country, Beatrice was finally arrested and sent to the stake. I have a vision of her agony. It is the first auto-da-fé. Beatrice is marched through the streets of Toulouse together with three hundred unrepentant Cathars. They are led outside the city to a hill where, on a sacrificial platform of charcoal and pitch, stakes are massed in ranks like an army on parade. They are bound to the stakes with wet thongs, the purpose of which is to hold them upright until the flames have done their work, so that as charred mockeries of themselves they may be a warning to the world.

It is still not too late to repent; one word will avert the ordeal. Nobody accepts the deliverance thus offered. The pyre is lit and the words of prayer rise above the crackle of the kindling.

The platform gradually transforms itself into a gently burning mass, with little blue flames rippling like waves across an incandescent sea, for the terms of the sentence are execution by *slow* fire. Evening comes, and the light reaches far out from the hilltop, like a beacon on the shore.

Meanwhile, Philip and Bernard, who have eluded capture, are fleeing the country. It is easy to reproach them for not sharing Beatrice's agony, but we are not all born to be martyrs. They wait near Toulouse as long as they dare, believing, no doubt, that by remaining they can somehow help. They wait until there is no hope left. Then they escape and, as a boy, when I used to pretend that I was Philip evading the persecutors, I imagined that they fled the same night that Beatrice perished, guided in the dark by the glow of her embers.

*

Colóms, father and son, fled to Barcelona. There they set up looms and began a new life. They were not alone. Cathars had long found asylum in Catalonia; the Inquisition had to wait until our time to cross the Pyrenees. They persevered in the error that had been the cause of so much unhappiness in the past. But experience had taught them circumspection.

They now sought safety in disguise. They dressed like their neighbours, avoiding the excessive sobriety which had made them so conspicuous in the Languedoc. They went to church. They were enabled to do so by one of their rules, which said that the effect of an alien religious ceremony could be warded off by a private reservation.

The Barcelona Cathars then, went to Mass, but continued to hold their own service privately in the privacy of their homes. It was not really as serious as it sounds. The strict observance of Catharist austerities, while encouraged by persecution, somehow lost its urgency before the toleration of Catalonia. By the time of my great-grandfather, Diego Colóm, the much-anathematized Cathar rite had degenerated into something not much more than reading the Bible in a Catalan translation. The Cathars were distinguished from their fellow-citizens not so much by religious doctrine as by rules of cleanliness, honesty and hard work. Work had become their highest virtue; sloth the most degrading sin.

The Cathars assumed that, since they were now Catholics, albeit with a difference, they were at last safe. They forgot that difference of any kind produces dislike and envy. When persecution of the Jews erupted a hundred years ago, they too were in danger, for the hatred of the outsider overflowed on to them.

I can remember how intensely excited I used to feel as a small boy when my father told the tale of those days. He was anything but an inspired narrator, but there was something compulsive about that episode, which overcame all deficiencies in the telling. It fascinated me more than all the magnificent tribulations that had gone before. It was the end of the story, and from it I learned that I was one of the last of the Cathars. I learned that I was different from my neighbours, and that I had a capacity to maintain ideas against the hostility of the world. I might even say that I felt an obligation to do so.

I was taught to remember Easter, in the Year of Our Lord,

1390, as the agony of the Barcelona Cathars, although it is of course usually associated with a famous slaughter of unrepentant Jews and the wholesale baptism of the survivors.

On Good Friday, some cleric preached a frenzied sermon on the Agony of Our Lord, ending with a clamour for revenge. He ran out into the street, waving a crucifix, howling for the blood of the unbeliever. The populace, already whipped by the priests into a fury against the Children of Israel for murdering Christ, and now inflamed by celebrating the Passion, needed only this to be unleashed. They descended on the Jews, but some turned aside to massacre the Cathars as well.

And so history, alas, repeated itself. As the Cathars of Toulouse had perished a hundred years before in the flames of the Inquisition, so did their descendants die at the hands of a Barcelona rabble. As Philip Colóm and his son had fled, leaving Beatrice to burn at the stake, so was Diego and *his* only son, Juan, my grandfather, forced to escape, while the rest of their family was butchered.

Diego gathered the Cathar survivors, and managed to reach the port. There he found two Genoese ships, with whose owners he had had dealings. The captains were so moved at what they saw, that they agreed to carry the pathetic company to Genoa, and the Colóms now re-enacted the grim comedy of the refugee.

*

Genoa, ever generous - or lax - in matters of faith, gave asylum to the fugitives from Barcelona. Settling in the quarter known as the Portoria, between the inner and the outer city walls, they re-established themselves as weavers.

But Diego had lost the energy or desire to succeed. His spirit broken by remorse at having left his family to their fate in Barcelona, he sank to the deplorable state of an impoverished artisan. Devoid of ambition, he accepted a shadow of the life to which he had been accustomed. That he had fallen was melancholy enough; what was worse, he bequeathed to his successors the blight of humble station that had come upon him.

Colóm became Colombo. It was Juan who assumed the Italian form, following the Cathar principle of avoiding unnecessary distinctiveness. The immediate reason was, however, political rather than religious. Catalan corsairs were then harrying Genoese shipping, and Catalan mercenaries pestering Genoese colonies in Naples and the Levant. To be Catalan in Genoa at the time was not therefore in the best of taste. Juan and most of the Portoria community found it tactful to veil their origins.

Diego would not have approved, but he died before the change was made, a patriot to the last. The unpleasant episode in Barcelona had not succeeded in erasing a pride in all things Spanish. It may seem odd that he persisted in feeling affection for a country that had treated him so callously. But he reasoned that what had happened was a kind of fever that would disappear one day, leaving Spain once more a happy place to live in. He imbued the Colombos with a sense of their origins, which they have never lost. Spanish the Colóms were, he used to say, and Spanish they would remain. He always believed that the family would eventually return to Aragon and, even although granted Genoese citizenship, he maintained towards the Republic an attitude of temporary attachment. He transferred this feeling to Juan. Juan was just over ten years old when he arrived in Genoa, but he felt like a Spanish expatriate to the end of his days. It is an attitude that I, too, have inherited. Language had much to do with it.

With appropriate discretion, the Cathars preserved their religion in Genoa as they had in Barcelona. They also maintained their native tongue - or more correctly tongues. Catalan in Barcelona had been their spoken and religious language. But they had also learned to speak and write Castilian, because it was even then the lingua franca of all the Spains. Catalan resembles the Genoese dialect, so that the fugitives had no trouble linguistically in making themselves at home. But they continued as before to learn Castilian as their written, and Catalan as their spoken, language. But the Castilian we have learned is the Castilian we knew when we lived in Spain, one hundred years ago. It is not quite the language of today; perhaps it stamps me as somehow out of place and out of time. Nevertheless it, and not Italian, comes naturally to me. I have never really considered myself Genoese, nor can I feel properly a Spaniard.

I must digress a moment to resolve the question of names. When Juan Italianized his name, he did it completely, so that he became known to his Genoese neighbours as Giovanni. At home, however, he continued with the Spanish form. We have maintained this custom; I, for example, was baptized Christoforo, and known as such outside my home, but to my family, I was never anything but Cristobál. For the sake of consistency, I shall use the Italian forms when talking about our Genoese period - except when reproducing family conversations, when I shall revert to the Spanish.

The Portoria community persisted in distinction, not only of faith and speech, but of occupation as well. They continued their tradition of the woollen trade. Like his father, Giovanni Colombo became a weaver. When he married, it was to a fellow exile.

In 1418, my father, Domenico (Domingo) was born, the second of three children. The eldest, a daughter, eventually married, and passed out of the story. Domenico, and his younger brother Antonio, were in due course apprenticed to their father. Neither turned out to be particularly skilful. Perhaps both would have done better at carding, finishing, or one of the less exalted specialities of the woollen trade. But it had been a dictum among the Colombos that they were to be weavers, the aristocrats of the craft. However poor, they were never to accept the least fall in professional standing; a version of the proverbial Spanish pride, if you like.

But the mould had been broken. After Giovanni died, in 1444, his sons tried to continue the business. Neither, unfortunately, had inherited the modest commercial instincts that had been the old man's saving grace. It seemed as if the Colombos' talents had died with Giovanni. It may be a coincidence, but he was of the last generation to be born in Spain.

Antonio soon left the business to try his luck in other fields. But my father could not bring himself to give up weaving. In 1440, at the age of twenty-two, he had married Susanna de Fontanarossa, another Cathar refugee. The purity of the Colombos' Spanish descent had been kept; to him the preservation of the ancestral trade was therefore a matter of course.

After Antonio had gone, my father moved to a house in the Carrogio dell'Olivella, under the city walls, opposite the Olivella Gate. That is the north-eastern gate through which the main road from Milan enters the city. The Carrogio dell'Olivella is its continuation, and is one of the busiest thoroughfares in Genoa. Tradesmen ought to flourish there, and most in fact did. But not my father.

He hoped to retrieve his fortunes by abandoning the rich fabrics that had hitherto been his ruination, and manufacturing rough cloth for the poor instead. But even the poor looked askance at what he wove. They could buy better and cheaper products imported from Flanders.

My father was soon in difficulties. He could scarcely pay his rent, and was saved from debtors' prison only by being appointed keeper of the Olivella Gate.

Gatekeepers were hard to find, because the work was troublesome, ill paid and, since it meant government service, was considered dangerous, degrading and menial. My father, therefore, had no difficulty in obtaining the post when it mercifully fell vacant. Out of pride, he continued weaving, but it was Pietro Campofregoso, Doge of Genoa, who kept him from starvation, with the princely stipend of thirteen Genoese pounds per annum.

So doth past pretence dissolve and truth begin to emerge. I am not, as I would have posterity believe, the issue of admirals and counts, but of a failed weaver, and a servile gatekeeper. My home was not a mansion in Liguria, but the impoverished household in the Carrogio dell'Olivella. I was born there on the 25th August 1451.

IV

ONCE more I invoke my first conscious memories. I have described how I saw the return of the Genoese fleet from Constantinople, how a wounded figure was borne off one of the ships and laid in a stretcher on the quay, and how my uncle Antonio it was who showed me the happenings and kept them alive.

He was the best person to impress the mind of a child. He was a born storyteller. He could conjure up the places he was describing. He seemed to turn into the person about whom he was talking. He had the gift of inventing conversations which, if they never actually took place, could quite reasonably have done so. As the Genoese saying goes, '*Se non é vero, é ben trovato.*'

After leaving the partnership with my father, Antonio had sought an alternative trade. After various unfortunate experiments, he too ended in government service, eventually being appointed keeper of the Genoa lighthouse so that Genoa was then guarded both from the land and the sea by Colombos. Whatever the consequences to the Republic, it was fortunate for me. I was enabled to avoid my own parents, and spend much time with Antonio and Francesca, his wife. The household in the Carrogio dell'Olivella was not auspicious for a growing boy.

I have broken the Fifth Commandment, but with reason, I contend. If only my father had been an outright failure, I could have forgiven him, for there is a kind of black magnificence in abject defeat. But he floundered in the poisonous degradation of mediocrity, not quite a failed weaver, nor yet good at anything else. My uncle on the other hand kept up no pretences. He knew he had failed and abandoned the cloth trade in token thereof. What is more, he believed that whatever you were called upon to do, you ought to do properly. If he was a bad weaver, at least he could try to be a good lighthouse keeper. But my father constantly lamented over his gatekeeping, perfunctorily carrying out his duties, because he thought them beneath him. And my mother was dull - and she nagged. She nagged her customers, her children, her husband and her few friends. I hate to think what would have become of me without Antonio and Francesca.

Perhaps Antonio took a liking to me because of our resemblance. My red hair and ruddy complexion came from my mother, but my build comes from my father's side, if not directly from my father. He was short, with a broad face, an unfortunate throwback, no doubt; but my height and narrow features are true Colombo, and these I share with Antonio. Perhaps he felt sorry for me living without companionship in the big, dingy house near the city walls; until I was seven years old, when my sister Bianchinetta was born, I was an only child. He often had me to stay with him, and the lighthouse at the end of the breakwater became my second - perhaps I should say my real - home.

Antonio's household was infinitely congenial. To begin with, it was ruled by my aunt Francesca. She was well named; like St Francis, she was the kind of person to whom children and animals are instinctively drawn. Then, the family lived high up, in the lighthouse keeper's quarters. And what better place for a small boy than the top of a tower? I did not have to be content with a make believe castle; I had a real one. I looked on a world spread out below me, like any Doge or knight in his citadel. For battlements, I had a balcony encircling the lighthouse; the eminence from which I saw the return from Constantinople. For fellow-knights - or hostile ones - when I wanted them, I had Antonio's three sons, Giovanni, Matteo and Amighetto; but mostly I played on my own, for I had solitary tastes and, when I felt the need of companionship, preferred to obtain it among my elders.

Now I return to the unfortunate figure on the quay. My uncle, it will be recalled, was talking to a monk and a gentleman in scarlet, bending over the stretcher. The substance of their conversation was this. The monk, who had travelled on the same ship from Constantinople, said that the poor fellow had been horribly wounded, and that it was a miracle that he had survived. Indeed, the gentleman in scarlet, who was in fact a doctor, pronounced him beyond help. Since the only remedies known to our medical practitioners are apparently poultices and purgatives, he was without doubt speaking no more than the truth. He said it would be uncharitable to consign so distressed a person to any of the Genoese hospitals, packed as they were with casualties and camp fever cases from some battle with the French along the coast. So my uncle and aunt took him into their home out of charity - Catharist charity I was about to say. But it was not, as the monk and the doctor assumed, to ease his last hours; it was to try to save him.

In the days before their persecution, the Cathars were celebrated physicians. Some of their lore has been handed down with the old Cathar traditions. It is unorthodox by present ideas. Needless to say, it is not taught in the universities, and is regarded as quackery by the medical profession.

I have already explained that cleanliness, in the Cathar

religion, was a cardinal virtue. In Cathar medicine, it was the foundation of all treatment. Without it, drugs were considered to be worse than useless. Dirt, being of the Kingdom of Evil, induced putrefaction, and destroyed medicines, which were of the Kingdom of Good - but I am venturing into heresy again. Well, I am talking about heretical medicine - which is what Francesca, who had taken upon herself the nursing of the unfortunate stranger, now proceeded to apply.

One of the most important items in the Cathar pharmacopoeia is a certain mould, and it was with this that she elected to treat her patient. Following the ancient instructions, she continually dressed his wounds with fresh mould, and forced down his throat a decoction made from the same substance. The wounds stopped festering, and the fever consuming him started to subside. He was soon on the way to recovery. For my part, I believe it was the medicine that saved his life. So, I suspect, did the doctor who had examined him on the quay. He afterwards visited the invalid, and, according to Francesca, was not entirely pleased at the spectacle before him. She got the impression that he disapproved of a live patient cured unorthodoxly, and would have preferred a dead one orthodoxly killed.

The stranger was a Norwegian, called Jón Scolvessen. He had been in the Varangian Guards, the household regiment of the Byzantine Emperors.

V

Now I move into the world of memory, authentic and untampered. I reach the age from which I have the power of total, or almost total, recall.

Scolvessen remained for more than five years. He helped with the work of the lighthouse, becoming in all but pay the assistant keeper. I found it hard to understand why he chose to do this. Genoa was in the grip of even worse disorder than usual and, to my immature mind, the only sane course was to leave as soon as possible.

'But you mustn't forget,' said my uncle, 'that even if Genoa happens to be, shall we say, somewhat less than peaceful, there is quite a lot to learn here. And that's what Jón was interested in - learning. Even if Genoa has lost most of its colonies and isn't the Power it used to be, it still leads the world in banking and business. Jón used to talk for hours to the men who ran the big trading houses, and the merchant banks, and even the august Bank of St George, to find how they were run. You mustn't forget, where Jón comes from, they don't even know what a cheque is!

'Besides, he wanted to learn languages, and he couldn't do that at home. He learned Greek in Constantinople. He mastered Italian here. And I taught him Castilian. Everybody laughs at me when I say that Spain is a country of the future. Jón didn't. He even took the trouble to learn some Catalan.'

Partly on that account, perhaps, I appointed Scolvessen my tutelary childhood god. He showed me the doors which, since then, I have been trying so persistently to open.

Those early years were oppressed by the doomsday mood brought upon Genoa (and all of Europe I suppose) by the disaster of Constantinople. It had happened so recently; the fall of the city was still on everybody's minds. The outworks of Christendom seemed to have been swept away; the infidel was battering at the gates. One felt that now there was nothing to stop the Turks murdering us in our beds. Children were threatened with them. 'If you don't do such-and-such, the Turk will come and cut off your head,' is a phrase that liberally peppered my childhood.

I wanted to know every last detail about the siege. I pestered Scolvessen to tell me. It was not, I think, a subject on which he was particularly anxious to dwell, but he patiently suffered my curiosity.

'Uncle says you almost saved the Emperor at Constantinople,' I began one of these childhood dialogues. 'He says you're a hero.'

'Your uncle's too kind. No, not a hero.'

I naturally refused to believe him. To me, he was incontrovertibly heroic, if only because he looked the part. He was taller than anyone I had ever seen, tremendously broad in the shoulder, and he had a wide, square face, with blue eyes and a shock of dark hair. I imagined him a raging giant in battle, effortlessly cutting down everything and everyone in his way; the perfect warrior quite without fear.

'But you must have killed lots of Turks,' I said.

'Some, not many.'

'What was it like in the Guards?'

'Boring most of the time. We had to stand to attention at court ceremonies for hours on end.'

'Why were you called the *Varangian* guards?'

'Because it is Russian for corsairs. We all came from Norway and Denmark.'

'Are all Norwegians and Danes corsairs?'

'They used to be. And they still think they are.'

'I think that's wonderful. Lots of Catalans are corsairs. I might be one myself when I grow up. But I don't understand why you had to have a *Russian* name, when you were Norwegians and Danes working for the Greeks.'

'Because it was the Russians who were the first to have the benefit of our company in the East. They gave us the name, and it stuck. In the West, we used to call ourselves Vikings - which means more or less the same thing. The English called us "The wolves of the sea".'

'Aren't Denmark and Norway far from Constantinople?'

'Very.'

'Then why did the Emperor get his guards from there?'

'Because the Emperor couldn't trust his own subjects.'

This was scandal to the grown-ups; but I was too young to worry about slurs on a good cause. To me, it was simply part of a grand tale, told by someone who knew how to talk to a child. It begins six hundred years ago, when Constantinople was still great and rich. To the Scandinavians, it was the navel of the Universe.

'We were great travellers, and we went there in droves,' Scolvessen said. 'Some joined the Byzantine Army; enough in fact for a whole battalion. And that's how the Varangian Guards first began. They soon became a crack regiment - *the* crack regiment I ought to say.

'One of the first guardsmen was an ancestor of mine. Ever since, it has been a family tradition to serve with the Varangians. When my turn came I, too, went out to join the regiment.

'I reached Constantinople on my twentieth birthday, and signed up for the usual twelve years.

'But it was pretty obvious that I wouldn't have to stay the whole time. Constantinople was finished - the Turks were preparing to attack.'

And now the story of the siege poured out; the whole enthralling melancholy pageant, squalor, treachery and all. I heard things the others were never told. But it was the final onslaught on the Byzantine capital that gripped me. I loved above all the last stand of the Varangians:

'The Turks had breached the gates. They were pouring into the city. But we Guards still held out on the walls. By the middle of the afternoon there wasn't much more than a platoon left of the whole regiment. We had to fight it out, because they weren't taking any prisoners. During a breathing space, we were preparing for the next attack, when the Emperor appeared. He was in Varangian uniform instead of his Imperial armour. I guessed what that meant; he had come to meet his end among his soldiers.

'It seemed only yesterday that he had said, as he handed me my commission: "You'll be able to tell your grandchildren that you were an officer of Constantine Paleolagus, the last Emperor of the East."

'And already, his words were about to come horribly true.

'We huddled round Constantine, backs against an angle in the parapet. As we were taking up our positions, some Turks appeared. They wore green plumes in their helmets. They were Janissaries, the Sultan's household troops; his Varangians as it were. I had heard a lot about them: I hoped most of it wasn't true.

'I braced myself for the charge - but no, they walked. Slowly - slowly they crept up. It was far more terrifying than any onslaught. I wanted to break and run: but I was turned to stone. An armoured monster loomed up; in the shadow of a helmet there glinted a pair of eyes. An arm moved; I flinched. The spell was broken, and I it was who struck first. Through the handle of my battleaxe, I felt the grating of steel on bone - and I fainted.

'Stupid, I know, but these things happen in the first taste of battle.

'When I came to, I thought I was in Hell – it was dark, I was suffocating, I was unable to move, and there was a terrible silence. I swooned again; once more I recovered, and began to get my bearings. It was hellish all right, but not yet the underworld. I was lying underneath a pile of bodies, choked by the sickly smell of blood. I waited to make sure that everything was still, and then carefully I crawled out.

'The enemy was out of sight, and my comrades had been slaughtered. I had been saved by the men on top of me – and by fainting so that in the confusion of battle, I seemed beyond the necessity of all further attention. Constantine was dead; the Empire of the East was no more. I was the only survivor. I seemed to have done my duty, and now all that remained was to save myself.

'I ran down the ramparts *away* from the centre of the city, where the Turks were presumably now busy with their butchering, and made for the Sea of Marmora. I left the walls at the first ramp I came to, and crossed the outskirts safely. I went to a secluded little beach where I had hidden a boat in case of a need of this kind. It was still there. I slept under it that night.

'During my stay I had cultivated acquaintances among the Genoese colony – from whom, incidentally, I first learned Italian. The Genoese had a commercial concession at Petra, the suburb across the Golden Horn. I was convinced that once the fighting actually began, they would declare themselves neutral, I proposed to escape with their help.

'Well, I turned out to be right. The Genoese did decide that discretion was the better part of valour, and became neutral. The day after the city fell, their fleet sailed for home, carrying, as it turned out, not only the better off citizens, but the Genoese mercenaries who had cleverly run away when the battle had turned against them.

'From my hiding place on the beach, I saw the ships sail out of the Golden Horn at daybreak, and I rowed out to intercept them in the Sea of Marmora. I believed that the Genoese would take care of a fellow-Christian.

'I ought to have known better. I was not allowed on to the first vessel I approached, nor the next, nor the next. Then I noticed one of my Petra acquaintances watching from the side of a galleass, and appealed to him. It was somebody whom I had helped at court, but the man pretended not to recognize me.

'That was the last straw. I climbed on board without waiting for permission. And as I reached the deck, I was stabbed. Think of it - I had come through the whole siege of Constantinople without so much as a scratch from the enemy, and I was finally wounded by those whom I had every right to consider my friends.

'A Franciscan friar among the passengers stopped the crew from throwing me overboard. By now I was a bleeding wreck; but he shamed them into letting me stay. And that's how I came to be on the quayside at Genoa in such an unfortunate condition.

'The ship's captain did have the grace to apologize - I'll give him credit for that. "But you see, Petra was neutral," he said, "and if we'd been stopped by the Turks and they'd found an enemy soldier on board, there's no knowing what would have happened to us. We couldn't take the risk."'

VI

THUS Scolvessen brought Armageddon on the Bosphorus into my home. I was imbued with an ineradicable contempt for Genoa and the Genoese, because of their pusillanimous behaviour at the siege. But in the end, it was something entirely different that possessed me.

Scolvessen had acquired a small boat in which he used to go fishing. But he also had the peculiar desire of wanting to go sailing *for its own sake*. I have never met anyone else like him, at least in Spain or Genoa. When I was old enough, he took me with him, first in the harbour, and then in the open sea beyond the mole. For some reason or other, my cousins were not often included, and I became his solitary companion. He told me how he had learned to handle boats in the skerries of the coast where he was born; how he fished and caught whales and hunted for seal. He talked about the midnight sun and midday darkness of the high latitudes about Greenland, and storms, and rogue waves, and seas boiling with fish. He taught me how to manage a boat, he showed me how to sail by the stars. He planted the Ocean within me.

When I was about six, we were once becalmed. It often happens in that part of the coast, but it doesn't last very long. We knew that the wind would return as suddenly as it had disappeared, although in the opposite quarter. We were only about a mile offshore, and there was no particular danger. We settled down to wait. After a while Jón pointed to the scene before us. It rises now vividly, before me, making nonsense of the years; the lighthouse growing out of a forest of masts and rigging and, behind, Genoa rising up into the hills.

'It reminds me of home,' he said. 'Perhaps it's time to think of going back.'

I knew he came from Bergen, the seaport on the west of Norway. But he rarely talked about it, at least before me.

'Is it as big as Genoa?' I asked.

'Hardly. But you could call it the Genoa of the North. There's plenty of brawling in the streets. It lies between the mountains and the sea. It has a busy harbour. I was brought up among ships and seamen.'

'Then why did you become a soldier? Why didn't you become a sailor?'

'Young man, you ask too many sensible questions. Why not indeed? Well, in fact, I did start off by being a sailor.

'I've told you how in my family the eldest son was expected to put in some years with the Varangians. "Join the Guards and see the world", as they used to say.

'But when my turn came, I wasn't too keen. I thought there were better ways to see the world. I wanted to go to sea instead. Now my father was a shipowner, and he let me have my way. So when I was seventeen, I went with an uncle to Nyfundrland.

'That is Norwegian for the New Found Land or (which I like best), in Latin, Terra Nova. You won't find it in any of the geography books. It's a secret country discovered by the Norwegians. It lies on the other side of the Ocean, far beyond Iceland.'

So began the tale that will never leave me. I sat transfixed in the thwarts of that little boat gently rocking beyond the breakwater, listening to Scolvessen talk.

'You're probably wondering how I could have taken a crossing of the whole Ocean as easily as if it had been the run between Genoa and Pisa. Well, in the first place, it wasn't really tempting the unknown deep. Our people have been sailing there for centuries. And it's all in the family. The first man to settle in Terra Nova was another ancestor of mine.

'And then, Norwegians have always known how to sail and build ships. The ship in which I went to Terra Nova would make any sailor green with envy. She wasn't very big, and she was narrow and low. But how she sailed! She didn't bob and creak and yaw like the galleons and cogs and galleasses and caravels and galleys and the rest of the weird assortment you see in Genoa. She answered to a touch of the helm. She flew over the long ocean swell like a seagull beating up the spray with its wings. There isn't another ship outside Norway that could hold a candle to her. She was called *Leidarstjernen*, which means The Star of the North.

'We left Bergen early in the summer eleven years ago. We had north-easterly gales all the way, and reached Terra Nova after a month out of sight of land.

'We sailed along a wild coast where forest ran down to the sea. There wasn't a sign of life until we rounded a headland and saw a watchtower on a low hill. In a clearing on the shore, there were houses surrounded by a stockade. That was our destination. It was called Straumsvik. It was our trading post in Terra Nova.

'We tied up at a wooden jetty full of people waving and shouting. They were glad to see us, because ours was the first ship that year. And I was glad to have arrived, because I wanted to feel solid earth under my feet again.

'Outside the stockade, I found a small encampment of natives. They were very dark, and they had painted their faces with fantastic red patterns. I was told that they were thus decorated all over, and made a horrid sight when the weather was warm and they went about naked. We called them Redskins, although in their own language they called themselves Beothuk. I must say, they weren't exactly beautiful. They had flat noses, coarse hair and eyes too far apart.

'But they were marvellous hunters. They would come out of the forests to sell furs to the Norwegian traders.

'They could also be quite unpleasant when they wanted. And I was told of other tribesmen who were even worse. The settlers called them The Savages. That's what they were, it seems. They killed the Redskins when they could, and they had even attacked Straumsvik. So I could see the point of the stockade.

'I wanted to look at The Savages, and go seal hunting, and explore up-country. But I didn't have the time. The captain of the *Leidarstjernen* had come out with strict instructions to return as soon as possible. My father wanted his furs, you see. So, about three weeks after arriving, we sailed for home.

'The next year I sailed to Terra Nova in the *Leidarstjernen* again. That voyage was nearly the end of me; we ran into a frightful storm, and the ship just about foundered in the middle of the North Atlantic. And for good measure we hit an iceberg as we were making land. But the ship survived - just - and we limped into port, all hands bailing like mad.

'We had to wait for repairs, and got away a little later than the previous year. This time, we loaded up with ivory, which came from the coast to the north. Most of the ivory you see comes from narwhales and walrus in the West, and not from elephants in the East, whatever the shopkeepers say. And a lot of the furs on your rich Genoese have come across the Ocean from Terra Nova - although of course they wouldn't understand what you were talking about if you told them.

'The next year, I went out again. And then, I thought that this was too much of a good thing. It was to and fro across the Atlantic with the same old routine at each end. I wanted to see something new and start learning about the world. I told my father that, after all, I'd like to go into the Varangians, and he said he thought I'd say that sooner or later. So he gave me money and his blessing and I went to Constantinople. There, of course, I was just in time for the siege - but we've talked about that before, haven't we? All things considered, I think I prefer the Terra Nova run.'

VII

Jón left Genoa soon after the conversation in the boat. But he had become too much a part of our lives ever to be forgotten. We continued to talk about him for years after he had gone Constantinople was the theme; but for me Constantinople was now of rather less than passionate concern. I had fallen in love with Terra Nova.

Now *there* was something for a boy to think about. It became as real to me as Genoa. I had been told it as a secret. But with Jón gone, I had nobody with whom to share it. I confided in Aunt Francesca. When I grew up, I said, I was going to be an admiral and the Governor of Terra Nova. She told Antonio; and as it was perfectly clear that neither understood what I was talking about, I had to explain what I meant.

'I hope,' was Antonio's reply, 'that you don't believe all that. Jón, you know, is a bit of a romancer. He admitted it himself. Didn't he keep on saying that he came from a family of soldiers, sailors and poets, and that to be a poet was the best of all? If you're not inventing it all, he claims that he has sailed out into the open sea for weeks on end, out of sight of land. Well, nobody could do that and find his way back again. Even the Portuguese keep near the coast when they explore Africa. No, you can take it from me; Terra Nova doesn't exist. Our friend was making it up.'

But I thought of the houses on a forest-covered shore and the ship that flew like a seagull beating up the spray with its wings. It seemed real enough to me.

I invented a game which I called Crossing the Ocean Sea. Forewarned by my uncle of the world's disbelief, I prudently played it alone, and I made it a secret.

The quay near the lighthouse was Genoa - not Bergen - because this was my own enterprise, not a copy - and the new mole on the other side of the harbour, Terra Nova. The water in between was the Ocean, to be crossed in a rowing boat I called, naturally, *Star of the North* or, more precisely, *Tramuntana*, in the Catalan I spoke. *Tramuntana* had been a present from Jón when he departed. She was small, old and ugly, but she floated, and she was mine, my very first command. I lettered the name prominently along the bows and across the stern, but it made a ragged show: my handwriting has been unlovely from the start. I would row across the harbour in *Tramuntana*, zig-zagging, back-tracking, resting, avoiding ships that happened to be leaving or entering port: playing at storms, calms, pirate attacks, and all the hazards that could conceivably delay a voyage in reality. Reaching 'Terra Nova', I would jump ashore and take possession of the country. It was always in the name of a queen; although Genoa was a republic, I had been brought up in the Spanish tradition as a staunch Royalist. I identified that queen with a certain Madonna in the Church of St Stephen. She was in a small painting I saw every time I was taken to Mass. I genuinely worshipped that Lady of the picture. She was placid, regal, stately, kind and aloof; all in fact, that my mother was not. When I landed in 'Terra Nova', I planted a rag on a stick, which did for a flag, said three Paternosters and three Salve Reginas (I have always had a horror of even numbers), and held a speech in honour of the Queen, ending with an announcement that I had fulfilled my side of a bargain struck with Her Majesty, and that therefore hers was deemed to take effect forthwith. I had promised her new possessions in return for which she had agreed to ennoble me. When I landed, I was therefore no longer plain Christoforo Colombo, but Lord Christóbal Colóm, Admiral of the Ocean Sea, titles of my own device, already Spanish-sounding. I hurried through the ritual, and returned over 'The Ocean Sea' as quickly as I could, in order to embark on another voyage of exploration. It was in the journey, not the goal, that my pleasure lay. The moment of discovery and landing, while it was the climax, was also the end of the game. It had to be postponed as long as possible. I had learned that it is better to travel than to arrive.

VIII

I COME now to an incident which may seem trivial to the outsider, but which has indelibly left its mark on me.

One afternoon, I went to the harbour as usual for my solitary game, to find *Tramuntana* gone. At first, I thought that she had simply been moved. But I was unable to find her anywhere. Antonio had by now left the lighthouse, so that there was nobody to whom I could turn for help. There was nothing left but to trudge dejectedly home.

As I came in through the doorway, my mother said: 'I suppose you've been looking for your precious boat?'

She then proceeded to inform me, that she had got someone to sink it. At first, I could not believe my ears; then I thought she was joking. It took some time for me to understand that she was in earnest. She told me that I was wasting too much time at the harbour; that I was not going to be a sailor, and that I had no business playing with boats. It was about time that I took my lessons seriously and started learning about looms. My boat was on the sea bottom; I had better forget all about it.

I have never forgiven my mother for that act of wanton callousness. To this day, I bear her a grudge for the anguish that she caused me. My bitterness has not mellowed with the years. That boat was everything to me; without it, I seemed shut out from the world that Scolvessen had shown me. My mother had cleverly destroyed my one refuge.

My father was sorry for me, but I despised him for letting my mother act as she did. It was then that I began to understand that he was a weakling and a failure. It was then that the seeds were sown of the dread of contamination by his deficiencies that have since coloured my actions. And then also I received the first glimmerings of the great guiding lesson I have learned. What I really think and feel is for myself alone. To give anything of myself is to give a hostage to Fortune. I must never bare my spirit, because that way lies mockery and betrayal. On this earth, I trust myself alone.

IX

As my mother had so unpleasantly reminded me, I may have been interested in exploration but, as I came from a clothmaking family, I was naturally to go into the clothmaking trade. As far as my schooling was concerned, I am bound to admit that nothing could have been more fortunate.

Although nobody was illiterate in the Genoa of my youth (and of how many Spanish towns can that be said today?) it took some care to obtain a good education. There were free schools run by the Church, but they were unsuitable for anyone outside the menial occupations. The guilds, therefore, maintained their own schools, and the best were acknowledged to be those of the clothmakers.

I was sent to St Germanus', a school belonging to the Greater, or Merchants' Wool Guild. Since the Colombos were artisans, and therefore of the Lesser Guild, this was strictly speaking against the rules. But in practice, the ability to pay was the only qualification. And, inheriting from his Cathar background an almost superstitious awe of learning, my father was bent on giving me a good education, whatever the cost. Of a total income of about thirty Genoese pounds annually, he somehow managed to find six pounds ten *soldi* for school fees.

I began at St Germanus' when I was about six years old, not long before Scolvessen left Genoa. I enjoyed my schooldays. St Germanus' was run by Franciscans, who believed in persuasion rather than force. I was saved the misery of most of my contemporaries, to whom school was a succession of arbitrary thrashings.

As behoved one of the best schools in Genoa, St Germanus' was unusually well housed. It lay in a rather patrician building with an elaborate doorway, in the Piazza dell'Olivella, at the corner of the street where I lived. It had originally belonged to some merchant who went bankrupt speculating in Black Sea shipping at a time when Venice, not Genoa, ruled the waves. He built better than he knew; he provided generations of schoolboys with a comfort of which most of their fellows were decidedly envious.

In the conventional grounding in reading, writing and Latin, there was little to distinguish St Germanus'. It was in the practical subjects that the difference lay. The other Guild schools were sadly out of date. In arithmetic, for example, they still stuck to the old fashioned methods, with Roman numerals and the abacus. St Germanus', on the other hand, had already started teaching the modern system with Arabic numerals. The curriculum also included double entry bookkeeping (then being introduced from Florence, and usually taught only to apprentices in the big merchant houses) the elements of geometry and, rarest of all, geography. It was probably the best education to be had in Genoa at the time. Italian was the one weakness, which led to a most important oddity in my upbringing.

I continued to speak Catalan at home. My father taught me to read and write Castilian. Such acquaintances as I had, came from other Cathar children of whom there were one or two at my school, and we also spoke Catalan exclusively among ourselves. Spanish consequently got the upper hand. Although I spoke Italian fluently, I could never learn to write it perfectly: Spanish mistakes kept on creeping in. And that explains the peculiarity which has so troubled my interrogators: that although I am supposed to be Genoese, a kind of Spanish is clearly my mother tongue.

After Scolvessen's tale, my game of Terra Nova in the port, and the loss of *Tramuntana*, the next great landmark of my life was my first geography lesson. I know this sounds too plausible by half, but it happens to be true.

It happened when I was about ten years old. A cowled figure stood impressively on the daïs at the end of the classroom. In one hand he held a brass sphere, in the other, a tiny toy boat, complete with sails.

'The world is round,' he began. 'Once you have grasped that, you have grasped everything. You will sometimes hear people say that the world is flat, but that's a lot of nonsense.

'You can have the proof next time you go down to the docks and watch a ship disappear below the horizon.' And he demonstrated the point by moving the boat over the sphere, so that it gradually was lost to view over the rim; first hull, and finally the sails, exactly as I had seen in reality so many times before.

The teacher who thus began my true education was a Franciscan monk called Niccolò Carducci. He was a Genoese of good family, who had been a soldier of fortune, and gone into the Order late in life. Gossip ascribed to him a scabrous past. A fearful scar marked in a diagonal rift his forehead, left cheekbone and neck, as if he had been ineptly slashed with a sword. He had the placid manner of an old soldier who has been sated with action.

Brother Niccolò was more than a teacher; he was an inspired storyteller, and he knew how to talk to schoolboys. Before taking his vows, he had served with the Portuguese in Africa. He had been on the expedition under Ca'Da Mosto that discovered the Cape Verde Islands. When, as frequently happened, he did not feel like teaching, he talked about his experiences. There are worse ways of learning.

In one of his more formal moments he touched on the other shore of the Atlantic. 'Nobody knows what lies there,' he said, 'but it's probably the fleshpots of Asia.'

I stayed behind after the lesson to administer the necessary correction. *I* knew! I treated him to Scolvessen's tale of Terra Nova; of its forests and Redskins, its waters boiling with fish, and how it ran south so far, that no one had ever reached the end of it.

It must have been an extraordinary sight. There was I, a presumptuous urchin, expounding geographical truth to my learned teacher. But Brother Niccolò did not take umbrage, as most others in his place would have done. Instead, he asked me civilly how I knew. I explained about Scolvessen. I mentioned Antonio's disbelief.

'But Jón was telling the truth,' I finished by saying. 'He always did.'

It was the first time I had unburdened myself since talking to Antonio. I desperately wanted Brother Niccolò to believe what I had told him. To have my secret laughed away would have been a wound almost too deep to bear.

'*You* believe in Terra Nova, don't you?' I asked.

'Sometimes,' he answered, 'I don't know what to believe. I

have heard odd tales about new land in the West. I have not been so fortunate as to meet somebody who actually says he has been there. My own experience is that there is rarely smoke without fire.'

Brother Niccolò then took me under his wing, and taught me what he knew about geography. In that subject (but in no others), I was soon far ahead of my school-fellows. But the shade of my father's occupation was closing around me, and for some time outside events were of more importance than Atlantic islands.

Life in Genoa as I have explained, was lived against a background of disorder. Doges came and went. Their various supporters bickered and fought. Violence in the streets was considered a normal ingredient of existence. One locked and barred one's house before dusk.

At first a certain rough good humour usually tempered the political brawls to which the Genoese were now continuously entertained. But eventually a change came. For my part, it was a certain Friday in January, 1458. I remember the date very well. It was shortly after Scolvessen had left. A man was found stabbed to death in the street almost opposite our house. A note was pinned to him, saying: 'This man knew too much.' My father said that the murder had been ordered by the Doge as a warning to his enemies.

One morning, not long afterwards, I woke early to the clatter of hooves on the cobblestones. It was not the usual leisurely, punctuated ambling of carriers on their way to market, but massed, unbroken and insistent. I looked out of the window, to see the Carrogio dell'Olivella choked with cavalry. A few public-spirited citizens were waving from windows opposite.

I went downstairs, to find the street door barricaded, my father gloomily looking through the grille.

'It's the French,' he said. 'I got orders from the Doge at an ungodly hour to open the gate and let them in. I suppose I was right to obey. I hope nothing happens.'

I understood what he meant. Genoese politics impregnated everything, even the children's world. At a very tender age I had grasped the principle behind the sometimes complicated alternation of our Doges. Some belonged to the Adorno family and wanted Naples to take over Genoa; others, surnamed Campofregoso, preferred France. It was unwise to take sides too openly. Uncle Antonio had been so rash as to come out loudly in favour of the Adornos (chiefly because Alfonso, the King of Naples, was a Spaniard) when the French party appeared to be on the wane. He was dismissed from the lighthouse in a subsequent purge of Adorno sympathisers. The Doge was now a Campofregoso, and the French therefore had the upper hand, but no one knew when the wind would change again.

A few weeks after the arrival of the occupation troops, another mounted procession clattered down the Carrogio dell'Olivella. This time it was the entry of the French governor, Jean d'Anjou. My Spanish prejudices were gratified by his appearance, a squat, dark and ugly man who most decidedly did not sit a horse well.

With undiminished vigour, the political brawls continued in the Carrogio dell'Olivella. One day, a French patrol rode up during a particularly nasty scuffle. They separated the contestants, selected an Adorno and a Campofregoso supporter, and impartially hanged them from the Olivella gate. 'That,' said my father when we passed the dangling figures the following day, 'is what happens when you wear your opinions on your sleeve. Whichever side you're on.'

Now the streets became comparatively safe again, and I returned to school. St Germanus' had prudently closed during the worst of the disorder.

X

'YOU'VE got to admit,' said old Paolo Bavarello, our next door neighbour, 'that at least there's law and order now.'

'Even if foreigners had to bring it,' remarked my father, rather incautiously for him.

Bavarello was sitting over a jug of wine in our house, something he had not done for a long time. People had preferred to barricade themselves into their own homes, and the police frowned on all gatherings however small, as potential conspiracies. There was now a law prohibiting more than six people congregating. But it was no longer too literally applied. Things were on the mend, and once more we were able to dispense our usual hospitality.

The Colombos' house was larger than their standing strictly justified. Like my school it had once belonged to a bankrupt merchant. My father had got the place for a tiny quit-rent because tenants were hard to find. Built at the corner of the street, overlooking the Olivella Gate, it was exposed to all the noise around the entrance to the city.

The house was one of the few stone structures among the brick and plaster façades of the Carrogio dell'Olivella. A doorway, large enough for a horse to pass through, led into a small courtyard, from which the rooms opened. Galleries running round the walls gave access to the three upper storeys. An ironbound oaken door, thick as a man's palm, securely shut the house off from the street. A well in the courtyard gave us a private water supply. Whatever else our troubles, we could barricade ourselves inside with comfort.

Leading off to the left from the street entrance was what had once been the counting house, and was now a shop. Although a craftsman, and therefore barred by the rules of the guilds from the retail trade, my father had obtained permission to sell cloth as well as weave it. It was a fairly common dispensation in Genoa at the time, because merchants were reluctant to risk their business in the prevalent disorder. My father overcame lack of capital by selling on commission, and paying the dyers and finishers in kind, with the cloth that he wove.

Occasionally one of the tailors in the Via Pagani would come across for a length of cheap cloth, or a housewife would look for a remnant. If ever the place came to life, it was when the neighbours were there and jugs of wine appeared. It was not so much a place of trade as of gossip. It had always been the natural meeting place for those living around the Olivella Gate.

It became so again; but things were not quite as before. I now had a sister, Bianchinetta, born on the 8th May 1458, a few days after the entry of the French. And we had a French officer billeted with us. He was a captain of infantry from Orléans with the grand-sounding name of Roger de Villhardon. He turned out to be a sympathetic person, although his presence naturally caused restraint. No politics were now discussed in our house.

My father now had orders only to open the gate for a few hours each day. He was swamped with soldiers and customs officers who scrutinized every single traveller. He had little time for his own business.

Now a Neapolitan fleet attacked Genoa. I went down to the lighthouse and persuaded the new keeper to allow me on to the so familiar balcony. I saw the ships mustered in a neat crescent out in the roadstead. I thought of the Siege of Constantinople as Jón had described it.

I was lucky enough to see some shooting; my first sight of a naval bombardment. At leisurely intervals a puff of grey smoke issued from some ship, followed by a futile splash as the projectile fell far short of the land. I could not understand how a fleet so signally ineffective could hope to take Genoa, and inwardly I grieved for Naples because of Alfonso, its Spanish sovereign.

There were few to share my feelings. Although we knew that Raphael Adorno, the aspiring Doge, was with the fleet, even his supporters had rallied round Campofregoso and the French. Genoese, whatever their party, were badly frightened of the Catalans, who manned Alfonso's fleet. Those versatile corsairs had a terrible reputation, and nobody wanted them within the city walls.

Genoa was now in a state of semi-siege. Food became scarce and expensive. The discussions in the shop took a bleak turn.

And then, one morning, the fleet was no longer there. Alfonso had died, and his campaign had collapsed. Unlike our neighbours, my father was not entirely pleased.

'War is better than rioting,' was all he would say.

The next thing that happened was that Campofregoso sneaked out of the city in disguise. My father had unwittingly let him through the gate. Villhardon, who had grown extraordinarily friendly over the year he had been billeted on us, told him not to worry.

'Good riddance to bad rubbish,' he said. 'The Doge had

started to intrigue with the Milanese against us. That old fox only called us in to help him against the Adornos, and now they seem to be out of the way, he wants to get rid of us.'

Then we heard that Campofregoso was back in Genoa. The rumours came and went. He was in a dungeon; he was Doge again; he was deposed. My father told my mother to lay in stocks of food and once more prepare for a siege. His prudence was duly justified. One morning, the alarm was raised. Suddenly the Carrogio dell'Olivella was deserted. We locked and barred our door, and waited in resignation for whatever disaster was on the way. It was like the days before French rule again.

Soon we heard a distant shouting, which grew steadily closer. I ran upstairs, to have a better view. What I then saw, has ever since been Genoa for me.

A small detachment of French cavalry was driving a crowd down the Carrogio dell'Olivella like a herd of cattle. As the fugitives reached our house, I saw that poor Campofregoso was among them. I say 'poor' because the erstwhile Doge was in a parlous state: dirty, bleeding and obviously terror-stricken. And the Olivella Gate was locked; he was trapped. He screamed for help; but there was no answer: the faces which, like mine, must have been watching from every window, kept discreetly hidden, and mute. I heard the muffled meeting of steel and flesh. There was a surge among the soldiers, and when it receded, another body was strung up on the Olivella Gate. This time it was Pietro Campofregoso, sometime lord of Genoa.

In the afternoon a mob appeared, and now the soldiers were the hunted. Later we heard that two thousand Frenchmen had been killed, and thousands of Genoese massacred. Villhardon had disappeared, and we never saw him again.

Now the Carrogio dell'Olivella became a military playground. First it was the Milanese marching in to attack the French, and marching out again, repulsed; then it was the Genoese levies, drab and unruly, shambling out to oppose an advancing French army; then the Milanese coming in again led by a splendid looking *condottiere* called Marc Pie de Carpi. A week later it was the survivors of the French garrison trailing out, having surrendered after the Milanese had defeated a French army at Savona.

Things now went from bad to worse. The following year –

1462 - the Doge changed three times. My younger brother, Bartolomé, was born three days after the Battle of Savona, on the 20th May, 1461. My father lost his gatekeeping job in June, 1462.

Genoa had become an appalling place in which to live. The only law was that of the gangs roaming the streets. The Carrogio dell'Olivella was now completely unsafe. The last straw came when Bavarello's eldest son was murdered in broad daylight on his own doorstep.

We fled to Savona. We were not alone; we joined a long caravan in quest of safety.

Savona was quiet. We stayed with Uncle Antonio, who had moved some time before. He was now back in the cloth trade, as some kind of clerk in the local branch of di Marto, the Florentine export house. I remember his once showing me a ledger with 'For God and Profit' inscribed on the first page.

The news from Genoa was the same depressing old tale of violence and misrule. But suddenly, there were changes. The Genoese threw their Doges out, and the Milanese took over the Republic, sending as Governor - of all things - a Catalan called Gaspar Vinecarte. The time had come, my father announced, to return home.

We arrived back in Genoa during the summer of 1464, having been away a little over a year. My father was right. The worst of the troubles were over.

I was now thirteen, the age at which it had been decided to apprentice me. But my parents decided to let me stay on at school in order to make up for the years lost in the various upheavals. I was finally apprenticed in 1466 on my fifteenth birthday. It was a late start that has bedevilled me all my life.

XI

WHO cared for Colón then, gawky, red-haired and freckled? I was apprenticed to my father, because we could not afford the indentures elsewhere. I remember that when he and I returned from signing the papers at the public notary, my mother remarked that, since he had not been noticeably successful in his trade, he was scarcely qualified to teach it to anyone else. My father, uncharacteristically for him, made no answer. Even I could see that he was hurt, but I made no attempt to comfort him. On the contrary, keenly feeling the disgrace of being too poor for a proper apprenticeship, I added my reproaches to my Mother's jeers.

My father very reasonably pointed out that a man had to have something to cover his back, so that, whatever one's training, to be a weaver was to be certain of reasonable wealth. The fact that he was a walking contradiction of that creed did not, to my immature mind, detract from its basic soundness. I had grasped that it was perfectly natural to combine good precepts with a bad example. 'Do as I say, not as I do,' as my father declaimed in his moments of tragi-comic despair.

So I grew into the weaver's trade. I learned to submit to the monotony of the loom. The dark workshop, the feel of the shuttle, the slow progression of the cloth upon the reel became the substance of my days. For company, I had my father and a single fellow apprentice. He was a poor relation of my mother, called Alonso Bacorio, whom my father had accepted for nothing. I had found it difficult to imagine anyone poorer than the Colombos, but Alonso was apparently so. He too belonged to what I suppose I must now call the pseudo-Catharist community, and we talked our archaic version of Catalan in the workshop.

One Sunday I happened to hear Mass at St Mary's Cathedral. I am fond of music and went to St Mary's from time to time because the singing of the choir there was rather more enjoyable than anything offered by the Annunciation in the Portoria, our parish church. On this particular Sunday, as I left the cathedral, I heard my name called out. It was a voice from the past. It belonged to Brother Niccolò.

I had last seen him seven years previously, before the flight to Savona. I felt, not as one usually does in such circumstances, again a gawky schoolchild, but immeasurably old. I had now been apprenticed for three years. I was almost eighteen. And Brother Niccolò, far from playing the former teacher, traded reminiscences as like to like.

'I've never forgotten the geography lesson you gave me,' he said. 'It may possibly have had some effect on my subsequent career. Since we last met, I've left schoolmastering, and become the Master of a chapter of Franciscan Tertiaries. The change is refreshing. Between ourselves I never found teaching particularly congenial.'

Before we parted, Brother Niccolò invited me to visit the Chapter. He hinted crudely that he knew all about the Colombos' 'religious peculiarities', and that, as far as he was concerned, it was no impediment at all. 'I've usually found heretics much the most interesting people to talk to,' he said. 'Do come along. I think you might find our little meetings quite enjoyable.'

It was an invitation I had every reason to accept. I yearned for sympathetic companionship. The Franciscans, despite their notorious defects, had begun to attract me and, whatever Brother Niccolò was, he was not the usual obese monastic fraud. I went to a meeting of his chapter soon after the encounter outside the Cathedral.

It was on a Sunday in January, 1470 that I went. I remember the occasion very well. The Church of St Stephens had just had its chiming clock installed, and the novelty had not yet worn off. Instead of running upstairs to look at the dial whenever we wanted to know the time (the building opposite obscured the church tower) we now had the time brought to our attention every half an hour, day and night. As the clock struck half past seven in the morning, I turned out into the Carrogio dell'Olivella, and made my way through the yet deserted streets to the Church of St Ambrose, or rather a Franciscan House nearby. A porter, lurking in a small lodge inside the entrance, darted out as I came in. Who was I? Didn't I know this was a Franciscan House, not a public house? What did I want? I explained about Brother Niccolò's invitation. At first, he was not impressed, advising me to return where I belonged, swiftly. I was about to comply - I have always been sensitive to unpleasantness - when, muttering that I was to wait where I was, he disappeared to 'find out about all this.' He soon returned with Brother Niccolò.

Brother Niccolò greeted me quite effusively. '*So* glad you could come along - we're just going in to Mass. You found the good Mario a trifle aggressive? I'm sorry, 1 forgot to prepare him for your arrival. You mustn't take his gruffness to heart. He's a faithful old watchdog. You'll find him full of unsuspected virtues when you grow to know him better.'

The implication was not lost on me. To Brother Niccolò, I was a prospective Tertiary. But I made no comment. I was too engrossed in watching the arrivals. As each entered, he turned into a doorway leading off the entrance. He went in wearing everyday clothes, and reappeared in a habit, differing from the Regulars' only in that it lacked a hood. The cord and sandals were worn and, at a distance, the Tertiary so garbed would be confused with a full Franciscan. Not for the first time, I reflected how becoming was a monastic habit, and how it gave a quiet distinction to the most humdrum of men. It was a garb which I would not have required too much persuasion to assume.

After changing, the Tertiaries left the building. When all had gone, Brother Niccolò followed, taking me with him. We went into the Church of St Ambrose next door to hear Mass. About a third of the worshippers appeared to be Franciscans; Regulars on one side, Tertiaries on the other. Brother Niccolò motioned me to the latter, and then went to another part of the church.

I had never been to St Ambrose before; it was neither known for its liturgy, nor was it associated with any of the guilds. Devoted to things of the sea, it resembled nothing so much as a seaman's shrine. There was a chapel dedicated to Our Lady, filled with votive offerings for mariners saved from shipwreck. The office began with everybody singing the 'Salve Regina', as if it had been the deck of a ship at sea. The sermon was delivered by a robust Franciscan who appeared to have an intimate acquaintance with the workings of a ship and the processes of navigation. It was hard to tell whether he was giving a lecture on seamanship or an exhortation to the Christian life. Either way, it seemed to me at the time, he succeeded.

After the Mass, I followed the Tertiaries out of the church, and Brother Niccolò joined me.

'We will now return to the House,' he said 'and have an early lunch.'

I was ushered into a refectory, in which about fifty Franciscans, regulars and Tertiaries, were seated around two tables.

At the head of my table, in the place of honour next to the Father Superior, there sat a most distinguished looking Tertiary, a man with finely drawn features and fastidiously groomed hair and beard. After Grace he produced out of the folds of his scapular a narrow case from which he extracted an implement, like a trident with the middle prong missing, fitted with an ivory handle. This, he carefully placed before him, next to the knife, spoon and wooden bowl with which each place was set. He proceeded to eat by cutting off a suitable morsel, which he then speared with this device, and transferred to his mouth perched at the end. At the time it seemed to me an undisguisedly affected way of eating. It was the first fork I had seen.

'You find our guest's table manners a little odd?' enquired Brother Niccolò, who was sitting next to me. 'He is, as you have no doubt divined, a Venetian. And Venetians have such *peculiar* habits. But this particular one ought to be forgiven. He is my old commander, Alvise Ca'Da Mosto, the man under whom I sailed to Africa. You remember, I used to talk about him at school in our classes. After luncheon he will address us. That is our routine; first Mass, then a good meal, and finally an interesting lecture; the care of the soul, the belly and the mind, in that order.'

I am no sybarite, but I remember that meal with singular enjoyment, because it was a stark contrast to the stodgy fare in the Carrogio dell'Olivella. There was only one course - but it was Boui-abasso, one of the great Ligurian dishes. It consists of at least a dozen different kinds of fish boiled in a rich broth flavoured with onions, leek, garlic, thyme, real pepper and saffron. It is served in the broth, with slices of Parma cheese and eaten with a bitter sauce.

'I have often thought,' said a Tertiary sitting opposite me, 'that one of those Florentine artists ought to paint the Boui-abasso. That saffron yellow's such a beautiful colour. If I had the money, I'd commission a picture, and hang it in my bedroom, then, when I felt hungry I'd look at it, and remember the glorious taste, and enjoy the sensation of a meal without the distressing physical consequences - alas, I suffer from gallstone.'

'Our friend,' Brother Niccolò chimed in, 'is a voluptuary and a glutton but Franciscan influences, as you will have observed, have inclined him to something approaching spiritual thoughts. Allow me to introduce you: Messer Bartolomeo Pareto, the cartographer. His charts are famous wherever Genoese ships sail the seas - so are his prices.'

'Still his belly's in the right place. I hope you like our Bouiabasso. It is, so to speak, a speciality of the House, and here comes the cook for his praise.'

There entered a Regular, wearing a food-spattered apron over his habit. A cheer went up, and someone ran over to a lectern upon which rested what turned out to be *The Little Flowers of St Francis*. Leafing rapidly through the volume, he proceeded to read aloud the incident of Brother Juniper who, out of charity, cooked a meal for the brethren, 'but there was never hog in the Campagna of Rome so hungry he could have eaten it.'

'You must allow us our little jokes,' said Brother Niccolò. 'Although you may not, perhaps, find them very funny.'

'The man's not a cook, he's an artist; a real artist. And how he's wasted here. Talk about casting pearls . . .'

Thus Pareto, after the cook had gone, in between expelling with accomplished care a mouthful of bones.

'Please,' said Brother Niccolò,' remember we have a new guest here. You might give him the wrong impression of our little society. And that would be a pity. This is the young man I told you about. The one who knows all about the other side of the Atlantic, and who told me so in no uncertain terms when he was a scraggy schoolboy.'

Brother Niccolò now induced me to recount what I had said to him. It was not difficult. Our encounter had instantly retrieved Scolvessen's tale from the half-forgotten recesses of my mind. I spoke with the urgent sense of memory flowing.

My listeners betrayed not the slightest inclination (as I had at first feared they would), to laugh me out of court. They heard me through to the end.

The first to speak was a pock-marked Regular sitting near me. 'What you have told us,' he said, 'is not at first sight compatible with accepted geographical theory, but I would say that a reconciliation between the two points of view is not inherently excluded.'

'Dear Brother Luigi,' said Brother Niccolò to me in a loud, mock-confidential tone, 'always the academic. He never can forget that he was once a lecturer - even if it was at some obscure institution called the University of Pavia.' Brother Niccolò, I knew, had been at Bologna before going to the wars.

But Pareto did not join in the banter.

'Odd - very odd,' he said, slowly and deliberately as if arranging his thoughts - 'Terra Nova - Terra Nova: you're sure that's what the country was called?'

'It's what Scolvessen called it. It wasn't my invention.'

'No, I didn't suppose it was. But it's very odd, all the same. Let me tell you something that once happened to me.

'Years ago, I was commissioned to draw a map of the Atlantic, with all its islands. My client was a rich Genoese, and he wanted "the best map in the world", regardless of cost. It had to be absolutely up to date. So, to find out all I could about the latest discoveries I went at his expense to Venice, since it has the reputation of being the centre of cartography at present. I must say that in my view it is a grossly exaggerated reputation. I learned next to nothing there. In the end, I had to make do with the old hackneyed material: you know, the real islands - the Canaries, the Azores, the Brissagos, the Cape Verdes and Madeira - and the familiar theoretical ones like Antillia and Satanaxes. I might just as well have stayed at home, for all the benefit I got out of the journey.

'But that's by the way. What I was going to say was this. In Venice, I called on Grazioso Benincasa, an old, very respected cartographer - and a Genoese by origin, incidentally. He told me that in Basle he once saw a world map which showed out in the Atlantic at about the latitude of England, a large island labelled Vineland or Wineland.

'Benincasa wasn't inclined to take it seriously, because the mysterious island was too neatly constructed, as if it were the product of wishful thinking. It didn't seem worthwhile pursuing the matter, so I let it drop. And yet, this mysterious map and your friend seem both to point to the same place in approximately the same position, but with different names. It's decidedly odd.'

'Islands, islands, islands,' chanted the pock-marked pedant whom Brother Niccolò had addressed as Brother Luigi. 'Why is everybody obsessed with islands? Every new world map is mottled more than its predecessors with a rash of islands. The Atlantic is beginning to look like my poor face.'

At that point the conversation was interrupted by the ringing of a bell. There was a rapid swallowing; a flurried scooping of yet unemptied bowls before the Benediction was said. The remains of the meal were cleared away, but more wine was brought in. It was the first time that I had tasted Chianti - hitherto I had only known the Ligurian wines. This, Brother Niccolò assured me, came from the very best Florentine vineyards, and had been specially imported for the Brethren by a sympathetic and knowledgeable firm. It was 'the best wine in Genoa'. I took his word for it. The subtleties of the vineyard have always been lost on me.

'We are gathered here,' said the Father Superior after we had settled down, and the servitors had done their work, 'to hear a talk by our distinguished Brother Alvise Ca'Da Mosto. He's a very brave man - one Venetian among all these Genoese' - we all laughed rather more than this antediluvian joke warranted, but the wine, as everybody said, *was* good.

'Now the most distinguished explorer of our day scarcely needs my introduction, I would however like to remind you of his achievements. He discovered the Cape Verde Islands. He has explored hundreds of miles of the African coast. He was the first European, the first Christian, to penetrate the hinterland south of Cape Verde. He has contributed more than any man before or since to our knowledge of the Atlantic seaboard of Africa.

'I think it must be a matter of some pride to us that it is an Italian who has done all this. Oh, I know, here we are Genoese or Venetians or Florentines or Pisans, and always at each others' throats, but in matters such as these, surely it is beginning to dawn on us we are all Italians. My only regret is that Brother Alvise has had to sail under a foreign flag.

'But it seems that today there is no one in Italy with the imagination to finance exploration. Only the Portuguese are interested. So Brother Alvise really had no alternative.

'But remember - when the late Lord Infante of Portugal was dubbed Prince Henry the Navigator it was partly because of what Brother Alvise did. When the sea route to the East is discovered – as indeed it must be one day – the name of Ca'Da Mosto will be an honoured one in its annals.

'And now – to business. I am sure we are all very grateful to Brother Alvise for finding the time to address us. He is a busy man, and he is only in Genoa for a few days on his way from Lisbon to Venice.'

Ca'Da Mosto then mounted a daïs positioned at the end of the room next to a large slate mounted on the wall. Before uttering a word, he had already commanded the attention of that company, well informed, experienced and hard to please as they were. There was something about him; that I later came to recognize as the aura of the man of action. It was like a return to that day in the harbour when Scolvessen told his tale. I found the excitement of my childhood – so long forgotten – unexpectedly invoked.

'I promised Brother Niccolò,' said Ca'Da Mosto, after the formalities had been disposed of, 'that I would tell you something of my own experiences. However, in order to put my own work into perspective, I must begin by reminding you of the latest state of African exploration.

'As you may perhaps know, I sailed on my voyages in 1455 and 1456. I then explored the territory as far as the Rio Grande – which some call the River Gambia – the limit of the known coast at the time. But since then, others have done more. About eight years ago – in fourteen sixty-one and fourteen sixty-two, to be precise – a Portuguese friend of mine, Pedro de Cintra, sailed almost five hundred miles farther than I. He discovered Sierra Leone, and reached Cape Mesurado, six degrees north of the Equator.'

Ca'Da Mosto then proceeded to draw on the slate the outline of Africa, filling in the principal landmarks. There was the familiar westwards bulge past the Canaries and Cape Bojador to Cape Verde, before the coast turned south-east to end at Cape Mesurado and St Mary's Wood. How things have changed in twenty years! Today we have rounded the Cape of Good Hope and know the full extent of Africa. But on that afternoon in Genoa, the firm chalk line stopped dead at St Mary's Wood, before the opening of the Bight of Benin, not half way to the River Congo, and beyond was black emptiness broken only by Brother Alvise's label: 'Terra Incognita.'

'What I am going to tell you,' continued Ca'Da Mosto, 'is therefore not about how I reached the farthest south. I can only talk about explorations in tolerably familiar latitudes along coasts already known.'

But he had enough to tell. He had been among the Moors and the Negroes. He had visited parts of the African hinterland never explored before. He had sailed along rivers and seen animals unknown to Christendom. He told of hostile Negroes and battles on a river; of grand Kings of Senegal, of treacherous Arabs called Tuaregs, of blacks whose lips hung down to their chins.

'... most interesting lecture ...' I heard the Superior say above the applause and chatter that erupted when the lecture was over '... grateful for opportunity ... delighted to welcome another time ... now answer any questions you would like to put.'

Ca'Da Mosto was immediately subjected to a spate of elaborate questioning mostly, it seemed, designed to display the erudition of the questioner, rather than to hear an answer. Somebody asked what he had hoped to gain from his voyages.

'Spices, fame, gold and slaves – in that order,' was the answer; unhesitatingly, and absolutely matter of fact.

The company was apparently stunned by unaccustomed frankness.

'Were you successful?' called Pareto, muttering under his breath something about 'insufferable Venetian self-importance.'

'Moderately, I would say, moderately.'

Then followed a spate of technical questions mostly about the difficulties of navigation along the coast of Africa, from which I learned that the worst hazard was sandbanks.

As the discussion proceeded, I decided that I too wanted to put a question, but could not for the life of me bring myself to do so publicly.

When the session was declared closed, I told Brother Niccolò.

'No problem,' he said. 'Let's go and talk to him.' We went up to Ca'Da Mosto, and Brother Niccolò drew him aside. After the necessary introductions, I was allowed to tell Scolvessen's tale again. Faced now with a real explorer instead of a mere mapmaker, I felt somewhat diffident. I need not have done so.

Ca'Da Mosto listened to me with the greatest of attention and courtesy.

I finished by putting the question I had been wanting to ask: had he ever seen anything which might confirm the existence of Terra Nova?

'I was going to say,' came the answer, 'that when I was returning from my second African voyage, I picked up a curious object out of the sea off Madeira. It was a small log decorated with strange patterns. The wood was dark and heavy, and I didn't recognize it. What is more, it had been worked with some tool that was not made of metal. I'm almost certain it didn't come from Africa - the currents alone made it most unlikely. And one of the seamen said it was quite common in those waters to see pieces of carved driftwood after the wind had stood from the west for some time.'

'You see,' said Brother Niccolò. 'Your Terra Nova is sending out signals of its existence all the time.'

Ca'Da Mosto left me with an odd, restless state of mind in which Africa and Atlantic islands gradually became illuminated with the blaze of reality, and the Carrogio dell'Olivella receded into the limbo of dead thoughts. A cloud of dissatisfaction had begun to settle on me. Diego, my youngest brother and the last living child to be born into our family, had arrived, and now was a squalling infant of one year. As the eldest of the brood I was clearly expected to be the saviour of the household and lift the family out of its penury. It was a rôle I found myself less and less inclined to play. Why should I sacrifice myself to them? The meeting of the Tertiaries had resurrected the vision of discovery that seemed to have passed away with my own childhood. Surely Mali, Senegal and Terra Nova ought to be the goal of my ambitions, and not Colombo and Son, wool workers?

It seemed to me that Brother Niccolò might be the agent of escape. I sought him out. He naturally asked me how I had liked the meeting. I told him that I had enjoyed it tremendously, and that I had found the company most congenial.

'They were all connected with navigation, one way or another.'

I said that it had not escaped my attention.

We met regularly thereafter for a few weeks: Brother

Niccolò probed my mind and we discussed my future. Finally, he invited me to join the Chapter.

'The Franciscan Tertiaries,' he said, 'are the discoverers' guild. Our Chapter contains all that is worthwhile in Genoese knowledge and experience. We have at our disposal a remarkably good library. We are, if I may say so, the leading college of navigation. I cannot guarantee to make you a discoverer, but I can promise you the very finest grounding in cosmography.'

And so, in the early spring of 1470, I was inducted into the Genoese Chapter of the Tertiary, or Third Order, Secular, of the Holy Order of St Francis of Assisi. In the House next to St Ambrose's, an elderly, somewhat abstracted Provincial handed over to me a full habit, a short scapular and a medal with the image of St Francis on the obverse and of Our Lady on the reverse. I promised to lead the Christian life, and to wear the scapular and medal under my everyday clothes. He hoped that my membership would be of mutual benefit to the Order and myself, and hurried off, as if he had other things on his mind.

'You won't find your religious duties too demanding,' said Brother Niccolò, who had been the sole witness. 'I know you've just promised always to wear scapular and medal, but in practice, the medal will usually do by itself. You may confine the scapular to Lent, Easter, and odd moments when you feel a pressing need for atonement. It is not the most comfortable of undergarments, and, in summer might almost be classified as an unnaturally harsh penance. Once a month, you will be expected to hear Mass together with the Chapter. And that's about all. The full habit is only for meetings and formal occasions. It is kept here.'

Brother Niccolò showed me into the vestiary. It was a long, narrow room, furnished only with a rough bench running round the walls, and crowded with Tertiary habits suspended from wooden pegs. We found a vacant peg, and I hung up my own habit, painfully new by the side of its venerable neighbours. I was now a member of 'The discoverers' guild'.

I had looked forward to an elaborate ceremony and a momentous experience. Instead, the whole procedure had taken a few minutes and been remarkably prosaic. Brother Niccolò's comments completed the process of disenchantment. I returned to the Carrogio dell'Olivella depressed by the taste of anti-climax.

XII

I KEPT secret my Franciscan connection. This was not because I was ashamed of what I had done, but because I thought it was important. I wanted to protect it from destructive influences. Above all, I had to hide it from my parents. To have exposed it to their scrutiny would have been to expose it to the contagion of failure that enveloped them.

Concealment was not difficult: I had learned to hide my thoughts. I continued my apprenticeship, of which I had by now completed four of the customary five years. I persevered with the family's Catharist observances.

I admit that this suggests betrayal of my Franciscan promise to uphold the Faith. But the lapse, if lapse it be, was part of the search for religious experience which also is surely part of the Franciscan ideal.

And was my misdemeanour so obnoxious? Let me describe it. Every Sunday after Mass - which we religiously attended - I and my family would go to a certain vault under our house. It was plain, whitewashed, undecorated and unfurnished except for a few chairs, and lit by a single grating. Whoever was officiating would go to a rough lectern, supporting a bible in the Catalan language. He would begin by saying the Lord's prayer, which we others would repeat, verse by verse. Afterwards he would read a portion of both the Old and the New Testament for not less than an hour. We finished by reciting the Lord's prayer again. It was nothing more terrible than that.

Both my father and mother officiated. When I turned fourteen, the traditional Catharist coming of age, I was allowed to read part of the text. At fifteen I carried out the whole ceremony. There were no longer priests among the Cathars; anyone could conduct a service; man or woman. But the bible reading was the heart of the matter.

I was now working harder than ever. Besides my watches at the loom, I had lately started keeping my parents' accounts, and was now also helping with their auxiliary occupation.

Unable to live by the textile trade alone, they had turned to inn-keeping as well.

The upper rooms were now let. My mother cooked. Bartolomé and Bianchinetta helped with the housework and ran errands. I acted ostler and porter. We served good, plain food, charged reasonable prices and kept a clean house. We had, indeed, preserved that part of the Catharist tradition that made cleanliness an article of faith. We changed our linen once a week, where our neighbours scarcely did so from one month's end to the other. The Colombos' house was always distinguished by the laundry hung out to dry on the roof, and the bedclothes airing from the windows. We soon became known as one of the few hostelries without fleas and bedbugs, and without the usual publican's rapacity.

The situation that had made our house so undesirable as an ordinary residence became of enormous advantage as an inn. Lying opposite one of the principal gates, at the corner of an important thoroughfare, the house was undeniably noisy. But it was also seen by travellers as soon as they had arrived within the city walls.

I must now turn to a particular customer who arrived about six months after my entry into the Tertiaries. He spoke with a harsh accent I recognized as German. He had heard about us from somebody in Milan. Did we have a room free?

His air of supplication was appropriate. We did not keep an ordinary hotel, we took in paying guests, preferably on personal recommendation. I think I detected the faintest trace of irony when, as I led in the three horses with which he was travelling, he indicated their panniers, saying: 'As you see, I am only a pedlar, albeit a *Hanseatic* pedlar.'

It was January, the dead season of the year, and Pleskow was the only guest that night. After dinner, the rest of the family having other things to do, I found myself alone with him, and under the necessity of playing the host. I started the usual desultory kind of conversation, and anticipating a common request, I mentioned the brothels of the Carrogio di Ripalta. Pleskow almost blanched.

'Thanks for telling me,' he said. 'But I want a quiet evening for a change. I've had enough of that sort of thing all the way across Europe, and what happened in Milan will do for some time. The way I feel now, I don't want to see a woman for a month.

'You think I'm mad? Well, the way Hanseatic merchants are brought up is hardly sane. You spend eight years as an apprentice cloistered in residential offices from which women are excluded. You are sworn to celibacy. Of course, the rule is broken, but not too often, and always with the greatest care. If you're discovered, you're expelled forever from the Hansa organization. When you finally pass out as a full merchant - *meister* we call it - you are graciously allowed to follow your urges. Most celebrate with a vengeance. I have been no exception. I qualified three months ago. This is my first job as a *meister*. It is supposed to test my commercial abilities. It's tested other abilities as well. I'm exhausted.'

I sympathized politely. The atmosphere was growing a little uncomfortable. Pleskow was clearly becoming drunk, with a heavy jocosity and familiarity that I have never liked. To divert the conversation, I remarked that I had always believed that the Hanseatic League was a seafaring organization, but that he seemed to have travelled overland.

'You're a sharp lad' - he could scarcely have been five years older than I - 'As you say, we do most of our business by sea. But we've a lot to do inland as well. I was sent across Europe as a test in salesmanship. I was given a load of fur and ivory and told to get rid of it. I haven't sold half. Trade isn't good. There's too much politics and war about. People are afraid to buy.'

Pleskow now tried to interest me in his ivory - half desperate, no doubt, to sell a few pieces, even at a cut rate to an indigent hotelier. He went out of the room - steadily enough, considering the amount of wine he had poured into himself - to fetch samples, and returned with a selection of raw tusks.

'I daresay,' I said, to make conversation, and disguise my lack of interest, 'that you've got good agents in Constantinople.'

'Constantinople? Young man, don't display your ignorance. Constantinople is the hunting ground of you Genoese. No, no, *my* ivory comes from the Arctic. Indian ivory is just about impossible to get hold of. But what can you expect, with the Turks controlling the caravan routes, and war in the East?

Anyway if I may say so, my ivory's every bit as good as your Eastern stuff.

'Now this,' he said, showing a slender tusk about two feet long, 'comes from a walrus. And this,' holding up a cone about the size of a man's thumb, 'is the tooth of a killer whale.'

Memory clawed at me. Scolvessen had talked about animals like that.

'Where exactly do they come from?' I asked.

'It's hard to say. I brought this from Lübeck, but it really comes from Bergen.'

'I know,' I broke in, 'it's in Norway; on the Atlantic. Someone I knew called it the Genoa of the North . . .'

'Exactly. Well, Bergen is one of our depots - "staples" in Hansa jargon. In fact, it's the terminal for the whole Arctic trade. You get hides and furs there and ivory, and a certain tough kind of cloth which you can't find anywhere else, and which is used for storm sails. It's quite an important place.

'I once spent a summer there, helping to invoice cargoes - as part of my journeyman's examination. Awful place - it's always raining. I was glad to leave, I can tell you. And as for the people we have to deal with' - and he made a gesture of distaste.

'Our goods were delivered by some rough and ready Norwegians. They would get fighting drunk whenever they could. It was not a nice sight - they were worse than our own people, and that's saying a great deal.

'They're supposed to get their stuff in Russia, round the White Sea. But everybody knows they don't like going there, because the coast is dangerous, and they're having trouble with the natives. Also, the beasts have started to leave, and the hunting's bad. It's an open secret that what they're really doing is dealing with Greenland.

'But there's something odd about that as well. You probably know that Greenland is a big island in the Arctic. But the best ivory is supposed to come from another country much farther to the west. They also tell me that you get good timber there, and first class sable as well.'

Scolvessen's tale again - and Ca'Da Mosto's. A barbarian adventurer could, as my family insisted tell lies. So, conceivably could a Venetian. But surely not a hard-headed Geman merchant. And if they all did, why the same ones?

I asked Pleskow the name of the other country.

'I can't say. It's all so mysterious. Nobody talks very much – and I can understand that. If they've really got hold of new hunting grounds, they don't want everybody to know about it. But I do know this much, that occasionally English or Flemish or French sailors get wind of what's supposed to be happening, and they try to go there themselves. *They never come back.*'

Did he know Scolvessen? I explained briefly.

'Well, that goes to show that there's something in the gossip after all,' said Pleskow. 'As far as the name goes, I do know that it belongs to a Bergen family. But more I can't say.'

It would be too dramatic to say that Pleskow's visit changed my life. But it was a kind of turning point. It removed something from my private fantasy into the world of reality. It was not entirely a pleasant sensation. In the first case, I could persevere in the quiet delights of contemplation; now something was nagging me into action.

After Pleskow's departure, there gradually formed in my mind two separate resolutions. I would go and look for Terra Nova, and I would make myself fit to do so. The first could look after itself: now I must persevere with the second.

XIII

SEAMANSHIP, Ca'Da Mosto had maintained, was the least part of exploration. Knowing what to look for and where, was far more important.

'Sailors,' he had declared on that memorable Sunday afternoon, 'are obsessed with the mechanical details of managing the new ocean going rigs, and can't see beyond their own decks. The explorer has to provide the goal and direct the enterprise. He is the master; the seaman, even if an officer, is merely the servant of his will.'

This stood on its head the accepted idea of the professional mariner as the supreme arbiter of exploration. I liked Ca'Da

Mosto's point of view, and decided to model myself on him when he said that 'the art of the explorer is best learned ashore'. I had no intention of beginning by going to sea, since that only led to the menial trade of the mariner.

I did not, however, propose to copy Ca'Da Mosto slavishly. He was a businessman, with a businessman's limitations. His geographical ideas according to Brother Niccolò were hazy. I was no businessman, but I could master the principles of geography. I could learn all there was to learn about astronomy. I would go one better than Ca'Da Mosto and bring cosmography to exploration. I would be a new kind of discoverer.

I went to Brother Niccolò, and asked him where to begin. I did not tell him my ambitions to the full; I explained in guarded terms that I now had a serious interest in cosmography. Maps, he said, that was where one ought to start. Learn to draw them. He sent me to Pareto.

Pareto received me with elaborate mockery.

'As one Tertiary to another,' he said, 'are you not demeaning yourself by moving from the wool-workers' to the cartographer's trade? Map-making is hack work. Well paid, I admit, but still hack work. I'd better show you what you're letting yourself in for.' And he led me to the top of the building.

Being thin, myself, I have always despised fat people. I expected - no, I wanted - Pareto to struggle upstairs pausing frequently for breath. But he negotiated the four flights without observable discomfort. I did not find it easy to keep up with him.

We emerged into a large room flooded with light from big glazed windows.

'Cost me a fortune,' said Pareto, 'you've no idea how expensive clear glass is. I had to import all this from Venice. But, open windows were even more expensive. People couldn't - or wouldn't - work in bad weather. The windows in the ceiling are my own idea. I had quite a struggle to have them put in. Never been done before, said the workman, and couldn't be done. Nobody as pig-headed as a workman. However, we haven't come here to discuss my troubles; we are going to talk about *yours*. Now look at those poor devils,' and he indicated the silent figures bent industriously over long tables that filled the room. There were about a score of men, some with grey hair.

We looked over the shoulder of somebody deftly colouring a small map.

'Disappointed artists,' said Pareto, without trying to conceal what he was saying. 'This is the last resort of a failure. I pick up my draughtsmen from painters' studios. Men who've learned to copy a line and apply colours, but who can't draw or paint. Their employers are only too pleased to get rid of them, and they, I flatter myself, are only too pleased to be taken on by me. They may be bored, but they're no longer heartbroken. Some of them have been doing the same thing for twenty years. Is that your ambition?'

I explained the true state of the case. Pareto called over to a man sitting at a high desk; plainly an overseer of some kind. He had a massive, bald head, and an expression on his face that did not suggest unrelieved kindness. 'Give this gentleman a test,' said Pareto - I noticed the categorization of myself - 'and send him downstairs when he's finished.' He started to leave, but turned back to say, 'For Heaven's sake don't forget to use paper.'

'Very economical, Signor Pareto is,' commented the overseer, 'but he does keep on at you. Of course I know I've got to use paper. Parchment's only for special jobs now. I don't really hold with it; it's skimping, that's what I say. Still, you've got to keep up with the times. And paper's cheap: it's the coming thing, isn't it?'

I was given my sheet of paper, a piece of crayon, put at the end of one of the tables, and told to copy a sketch of the coast-line between Bordighera and Livorno.

'You haven't the ability to become a professional cartographer,' said Pareto, upon examining my effort, 'but you will probably be able to learn enough for your purposes. At any rate, you'll be able to draw passable maps for your own pleasure, and you'll appreciate good work when you see it.' I asked how long my training would take. There was no simple answer. We decided that a formal apprenticeship would be unsuitable and settled instead for a loose agreement. I would attend the studio four afternoons a week. I would continue as long as it seemed necessary. I estimated that eighteen months would suffice. The sight of the massed industry among the mapmakers had suggested that eighteen months was all I would be able to bear.

My father complained that the arrangement would deprive him of help that he badly needed. I coldly replied that he ought to be grateful that I was available at all. I had now completed my apprenticeship, and was beholden to no man. He was clearly hurt, but his feelings did not concern me: and he meekly submitted. My mother objected more strongly, but the only effect was to provoke me to anger and a bitter rebuff.

The Carrogio dell'Olivella now seemed a Purgatory; I had glimpsed a means of escape, and neither mother nor father nor any other human agency was going to stand in my way.

The next step was to learn cosmographical theory. Again I went to Brother Niccolò. He seemed impressed or amused, I could not tell which, at my earnestness. But he took me seriously enough to propose a course of reading. I was to begin with Sacrobosco's *On the Celestial Spheres*, that evergreen primer of astronomy.

The Tertiaries had a specialized library on everything connected with geography, astronomy and navigation. It was said to stand comparison with anything at Florence and Venice. I was prepared to spend all my spare time there, since I could afford none of the works prescribed. Sacrobosco, the cheapest, would have cost more than a month of the Colombos' income from all sources.

I was, therefore, overwhelmed with gratitude when Brother Niccolò presented me with a copy. 'It's a duplicate,' he said, 'and the library doesn't need it. It's not in very good condition, and I'm afraid that the copyist who made it was not at the top of his profession. But it's all on vellum - no shoddy paper - and it's an accurate text.

'It will save you from having to work in the library, at least to start with. I've always hated libraries. All those books and studious readers produce an overpowering desire to sleep. You'll do better in the privacy of your own room at home.' Together with the volume, Brother Niccolò presented me with some candles. It was an understanding gesture. Candles were abominably expensive, and I doubt whether my father would have allowed me to light my room far into the night at his expense.

After being away from school for five years, I expected difficulty in learning. But, somewhat to my own surprise,

Spheres turned out to be easy to absorb. Some kind of inner force removed conscious effort. Of course knowing why one wants to learn, makes understanding easy. But I was also fascinated by the subject itself.

There was in the system of concentric spheres spinning about the earth a pattern and an order that appealed to something in me perhaps, who knows, because of having learned to weave? It also had the power of numbers. Consider: *seven* planetary spheres, for the Moon, Mercury, Venus, the Sun, Mars, Jupiter and Saturn which, together with the spheres of the fixed stars and the Prime Mover make *nine*. And in the behaviour of the planets I saw the action of the loom: the rotation of the spheres once every twenty-four hours and the oscillation of each planet on its appointed sphere were to me like the unvarying pendulation of the warp and the rhythmic alterations of the woof in weaving patterned cloth. Now I understood the movement of the sun through the signs of the Zodiac and its depression and elevation with the seasons. One concept only defeated me - that the speed of the Prime Mover cannot be measured since, from this sphere, the others acquire their movement, and time and space take their measurement. Brother Niccolò advised me to leave it to the philosophers. But I continued to think about the subject and, sporadically, have worried at it ever since. The question still eludes me - as, I have a suspicion, it eludes the philosophers.

After Sacrobosco, and the movements of the stars, I turned, at the direction of Brother Niccolò, to the construction of the Earth, and Ptolemy's *Geography*. I could not take that august work home, and so I was now compelled to work in the Tertiaries' library.

I was frequently told that the rediscovery of the *Geography* was a momentous event because it brought Ptolemy's invention of latitude and longitude to the West. I was prepared to believe it, but the subject was dry as dust. I found myself falling asleep over Ptolemy. I now understood Brother Niccolò's objection to working in a library.

Before reading the *Geography*, I had scarcely heard of latitude and longitude. The maps Pareto was teaching me to draw were old fashioned portolanos, with positions fixed by wind roses. The new-fangled system of rectilinear co-ordinates based on arbitrary lines drawn on the globe seemed academic, with no practical use whatsoever. But Brother Niccolò insisted on my mastering it. It was, he said, the only logical system and the cartography of the future. Of course he was right, and I am glad I listened to him, although it was hard at the time.

The months now drifted by, while I continued to grapple with geography. I fell into a routine of study and work. I became a creature of habit, and the experience was not entirely unpleasant.

One day, Brother Niccolò waylaid me as I was about to enter the library, and took me to his study, where without a word, he placed a document in my hands. It was the text of a dispatch from a Franciscan House in Lisbon.

'You will be pleased to hear,' it ran, 'that the Equator has been crossed for the first time. It happened on the voyage of a Portuguese ship along the coast of Africa. The captain was Lopo Gonçalves, who comes from Rastelo, down the river from Lisbon.

'The news was concealed as long as humanly - or inhumanly - possible, but I managed to see one of Gonçalves' officers the other day, and he confirmed the rumours, which have been circulating for some time. He informs me that the ship sailed across the Line on the 24th June, 1471. When Gonçalves realized what he had done, he said to his companions: "God be praised! A little step for us, a great step for Christendom." Obviously a man with a sense of occasion. We live in stirring times, my friend.

'You may say that I am making a fuss about nothing; that after all, it is only an imaginary line that has been crossed; that nothing has been changed. I disagree. It is a real divide that has been overcome, and nothing will ever be quite the same as before. For the first time, a man has crossed over into the other half of the globe, and has proved that the horrors supposed to exist there are in fact illusory. The fears burdening our explorers have been shown to be the machinations of the Devil, rather than the Light of God. It is truly a tremendous achievement. Gonçalves has done something to change men's minds.

'Since divulging navigational secrets is a capital offence here, I am adopting the double precaution of sending this in code and by sea. I realize that it will not entirely obviate the possibility of interception by our authorities, but I feel that what I have to tell is so important that I must take the risk of writing.

'I despise the secretiveness and selfishness of my fellow-countrymen who, out of a desire to keep the benefits of their exploration for themselves, are prepared to deprive Christendom of worthwhile knowledge. God be with you - and me.'

The dispatch was dated 9th July, 1472, about two months previously. It was signed Fr João Carvalho.

When I had finished reading, Brother Niccolò proceeded to expatiate on the significance of what had been done. The consequences were reviewed in a spirit of grotesque optimism.

It is hard, looking back, to recall the turbulent emotions aroused by the news from Lisbon. So much has changed in twenty years. Today, we sail round Africa, and cross from one hemisphere to the other without a second thought. But then - nobody knew where Africa would end; every mile was a notable victory. The Equator loomed like some fabulous impenetrable barrier. Brother Carvalho was quite right when he said that 'a real divide has been overcome, and everything has been changed.'

I understood Brother Niccolò's facile enthusiasm, but I could not share it. I, instead, was afflicted by a black tide of discontent. It welled up within me so that I felt as if I were almost physically sick.

Gonçalves had undoubtedly been right when he said that crossing the Equator was 'a great step for Christendom.' But to me, it was a brutal reminder that time was rushing by. Others were out and realizing their ambitions, while I sat passively at home, shackled by some monstrous, invisible chain. My birthright seemed to be slipping from me. Gonçalves had crossed the Equator - somebody else would soon discover Terra Nova. I was late, too late!

I had committed the terrible sin of self-deception. There was I, solemnly reading tome upon tome of cosmographical theory, in the smug belief that I would thus become a discoverer. I had seen myself growing profoundly learned, but now I swung to the other extreme and accused myself - with a grain of truth - of only half understanding what I read. I read, not to learn, but to boast of having devoured so and so many volumes. Such was the depth of self-reproach to which I had been plunged by a distant stranger; a man of whom I had never heard before, and whom I was unlikely to meet.

Gradually my panic subsided. I was able to look a little more calmly on what had happened, and extract a lesson. I had concentrated unhealthily on theory. I knew all - or nearly all - about the movements of the heavenly bodies, but next to nothing about how to navigate by them. The compass was as yet a half-understood mystery. If I was ever to make discoveries of my own, and not be the drudge to record other men's achievements, I would have to mend my ways.

I have never been given to half measures: I abruptly changed direction and now devoted myself exclusively to manuals of practical navigation.

Again, how much has changed in less than twenty years! Today every navigator worth the name knows how to fix his latitude by the sun. But then, the only method available was by the Pole Star. Longitude, I need hardly say, was just as much a matter of guesswork as it is now. I have heard it said that accurate measurement will only be possible when a clock able to run perfectly at sea is constructed. That will take centuries yet.

I mastered the principles of astronomical navigation on my own. Pareto lent me an astrolabe to practise taking star sights. Night after night, on the roof of our house, I squinted at the sky through the instrument until my head swam and my neck ached. My parents, predictably I suppose, jeered at me, saying that I was a baby playing with a toy. They made me the laughing stock of our street. I retaliated with one or two outbursts of temper, but then turned to surliness for a weapon.

Time plodded on. I became adept at taking observations - at least on dry land. And against Pareto's predictions, I became a passable cartographical draughtsman.

XIV

ONE afternoon, towards the end of May, 1475, I was working as usual in the cartographic studio, when Pareto sent for me. I found him alone in his private office.

'You've been here three years,' he began with his customary abruptness, 'I should have thought it was time for a change.'

I had, in fact, been thinking along the same lines. I had, after all, roundly exceeded the eighteen months originally proposed. But this sounded as if I were about to be dismissed, which was not quite the way in which I wanted to depart.

'You know, we have once or twice discussed a map of new Atlantic islands, in Basle,' Pareto then surprised me by saying. 'I am now convinced that the matter is worth investigating. I want you to go there and obtain either the original or a reliable copy.

'I had considered making the effort myself but I'm too well known. People would be suspicious if they knew what I was after. I shall have to send somebody less celebrated. He must have enough cartographical training to be able to judge maps and make copies. He must know enough about cosmography to carry on a convincing conversation and glean information. He must be able to conceal his thoughts and worm his way into the confidence of strangers. In other words, I want an educated spy. And you, my dear Cristoforo, fill the bill.

'You must be prepared for *innumerable* difficulties. On the other hand, you will enjoy certain advantages. As a Tertiary, you can depend on the local Franciscans for help. And I will finance a reasonable amount of bribery and corruption.

'Needless to say, all your expenses will be paid. I think we may regard this venture as the examination task for your apprenticeship. I confidently predict that it will be the first step to bigger and better things.

'You'd better start making your arrangements immediately.'

It was characteristic of the man that he did not trouble to wait for an answer, blithely taking obedience as a matter of course.

In fact, his proposal suited me perfectly, but I had to settle certain matters first. I opened my mouth to speak, and was unceremoniously interrupted in the middle of a sentence.

'Are you stipulating conditions?' said Pareto in the quiet tones, accompanied by the slow contraction of his great face, which I had learned to recognize as the onset of his anger.

I hastened to assure him that nothing was farther from my mind. It was chiefly a question of family finances. I still helped my parents with their business and as I would probably be absent for at least three months, I wanted to pay for a replacement or at least compensate for their loss of income.

'How much will you need?' The anger had been staunched - thank God. Like so many jocose people, Pareto's temper was not to be trifled with.

Diffidently, I suggested £50. Had I overstepped the limit? Evidently not. He nodded, scribbled something on a piece of paper, and said:

'You'll want £100 for travelling expenses, £250 for obtaining the map, and £50 reserve. You'll also need another £100 in Genoese money; £50 for your parents, and £50 as an advance on the fee for your trouble. I make that £600 in all. I think it covers everything.'

Six hundred Genoese pounds! My father's total income was seventy-five pounds per year, the salary which Pareto had started to pay me in recognition of my efforts was ten pounds annually. All my savings amounted to exactly seven pounds eight soldi and five dinari. Six hundred pounds! it beggared the imagination.

Now I plunged into the unwonted round of travel preparations. I looked at horses and saddlery. I applied for a safe-conduct. I was introduced to the intricacies of foreign exchange.

Pareto being a man of substance, my path was smoothed. In the very precincts of the great Bank of St George, his patronage secured preferential treatment. I was not required to jostle at the counters of the public hall; I was invited to transact my business in a private office upstairs. There, a director of the bank, magnificent in red velvet, enthroned in surroundings of impeccable opulence, issued with his own hands my bill of exchange.

It was the first time that I had experienced the consideration due to men of means or, at least, of significance. I felt like one of the lords of Creation. I will not say that I did not enjoy the sensation. And when I read the bill, I felt, also, for the first time the reality of what was going to happen; until then the enterprise seemed still in the region of make-believe.

The bill was drawn on Pestalozzi and Co. of Basle for 480 guilders, being the equivalent of £575 Genoese. The director, whose name was Carmogli, explained that the Basle bankers were quite reasonable, rarely taking more than 10 per cent for changing a bill, so that I had £500 clear.

We discussed my mission; I saw no reason to hedge before a director of the Bank of St George.

'You'll find Pestalozzi very helpful,' said Carmogli. 'They know a lot of people. They're Italian of course, so you won't have any difficulty in making yourself understood.

'By the way,' he said, as he saw me to the door, 'if that map comes to anything, why don't you come and see me again? I might be able to help. I know the Bank is only interested in the Mediterranean at present, but I'm looking ahead. I think we ought to extend our activities, and it is not impossible that some time in the future we might look at other regions as well.'

I walked down the steps into the street with the unwonted feeling of one who has good, solid gold in his pouch and a friend in the Bank of St George. But I also had a sense of uneasiness. An attempt had been made to suborn me. How could this be explained, unless Atlantic islands were to be taken seriously, and others were on their track?

And Pareto was so obviously in a hurry to see me go. Why? Was I perhaps being used as a tool? The visit to the Bank had opened the floodgates of my native suspicion.

I was scarcely reassured by Brother Niccolò.

'Pareto,' he said in a farewell conversation, 'is living proof of my contention that the joint stock company is the greatest invention of our times. It makes money work, and it exploits talent that would otherwise go to waste. Now like a good Genoese, Pareto's passionately interested in shares. He's got substantial shipping holdings, as you know. And he's done very well. He seems to have an instinct for investment - or perhaps he is just particularly well informed. The captains and indent clerks with whom he deals ought to see to that - not to mention the Tertiaries of course!'

'Perhaps,' I said, 'that explains his real interest in the map. He might want to finance an Atlantic expedition on his own.'

'Not at all improbable. Discovery's in the air today. I suspect, by the way, that Pareto has already made some enquiries on his own, and drawn blank.'

Perplexities crowded in upon me. But I kept them to myself. They were in any case overshadowed by the coming separation from my family. I regarded this as my act of manumission, and I wanted it accomplished in proper style.

I therefore concealed my plans from my parents until the Sunday before I left, allowing them three days for the inevitable lamentations. More than that, I assuredly could not bear.

I broke the news immediately after the customary bible reading. I had taken care to officiate on that particular Sunday, because I wanted to be in control of the situation. I chose the story of Tobias and the Angel from the Book of Tobit.

I had been led to it by Brother Niccolò, who had acquired an abiding interest in the Apocrypha from, I think, a Cabbalistic circle in Genoa to which he had recently been introduced. He may have been dabbling in the occult, but I was no ecclesiastical policeman. I was solely interested in having discovered an appropriate text. Moved by the occasion, I read with unaccustomed verve:

> 'But Anna his mother wept, and said to Tobit, Why hast thou sent away our son? is he not the staff of our hand, in going in and out before us?
>
> Be not greedy to add money to money: but let it be as refuse in respect of our child.
>
> For that which the Lord hath given us to live with doth suffice us.
>
> Then said Tobit to her, Take no care, my sister; he shall return safely, and thine eyes shall see him.
>
> For the good angel will keep him company, and his journey shall be prosperous, and he shall return safe.
>
> Then she made an end of weeping.'

I stopped short, as I had rehearsed beforehand. With the words of the biblical chronicler still hanging in the air, I delivered my message. It was almost as if what I had to say was an extension of what I had been reading.

The effect was all I had hoped for. Before me was an almost grotesque pageant of surprise, shock, silence. My mother, short; greying, fixed me with her saucer-like eyes that always seemed to be brimming over with tears of self-pity or reproach. Then my father, he too, short; balding, uncertain as usual whether to be gentle or carping. My sister Bianchinetta; sixteen years old, surly, stupid, already a woman in a gross and unhandsome way. Next, Bartolomé, my elder brother, a sagacious thirteen year old, and clearly enjoying the situation; finally Diego, the youngest; he, six years old, and my favourite; not quite knowing what to make of it all. *Sancta Familia*, indeed.

My mother, as I had expected, was the first to break the silence. She poured out a torrent of complaint, which was really no more than a wordy paraphrase of the verse of Tobit concerning what Anna said about her son. My reply was ready. I was of age, owed nothing to anyone, and was within my full legal rights to do as I pleased.

'What has the law got to do with it?' demanded my mother. 'It's your duty to stay and look after your parents. Honour your father and mother - have you forgotten the Ten Commandments?'

'At any rate, I haven't forgotten St Paul; he said: "Provoke not your children to wrath." '

This certainly provoked a parent once more to wrath. I had hoped to exhaust my mother by a long burst of temper, so that the rest of the time would pass in relative calm. I succeeded reasonably well. She hurled a few sporadic reproaches at me during the following days, but that was all. And I scarcely noticed what she said. The final preparations were claiming all my attention. Clothes were being got in order. I took delivery of my horse. The sight of my very own beast tethered in our yard was the first tangible evidence of my advance in the world. It brought the respect, and what was more important, the silence of my mother and sister.

The evening before my departure, my father gave me five florins for the journey. I looked down at the gold coins in my palm, the fleur-de-lys on the topmost one glinting like a flower of paradise in the candlelight. How he had managed to scrape together such a sum, passed my comprehension. I was touched - but I returned the money. I saw that he was hurt, and I tried to save his feelings with some spurious excuse. I could not explain that the real reason was that I wanted to avoid taking anything from our house because of a profound fear of bad luck.

I did not sleep well that night; I rose early, heard Matins and saddled my horse. The family gathered in the courtyard to watch me leave - even Bianchinetta. My parents, I think, were crying a little. A lump rose in my throat as I started: the clink of hooves on the paving, which for so long had heralded others' travels, now echoed for my own.

XV

I FOLLOWED the usual route to Basle, via Milan and the St Gotthard Pass. It was my first crossing of the Alps. The experience was not what I had been led to expect.

The travellers I had met invariably spoke of the Alps in terms of dislike tinged by fear. But when I reached Como on the lake, and there for the first time in my life felt the presence of the high mountains, I was touched by an emotion of quite another kind. It reached a climax as I came out on to the summit of the pass, and the ice-bound peaks spread out before me, glistening like jagged jewels in the sun. At the sight, I was pierced by an intense feeling of contentment; as if a shaft of some mysterious emanation was glowing within me. It was the feeling normally produced by the Eucharist alone.

I felt as if I were worshipping God through His works. I know this is perilously close to the heresy called pantheism. But I am in good company. St Francis did the same. The crossing of the Alps opened a vision to me, and since then I have been constantly seduced by natural beauty. It is not the kind of feeling I can easily share: questions of orthodoxy aside, it would be hard to find anyone who understood what I was talking about. I had discovered yet one more thing that set me apart from my fellows.

But the circumstances were scarcely conducive to elevated thoughts. It was the pilgrim season, and all along the pass, I had to battle against an oncoming rabble on the way to Rome, I was in constant danger of being pushed to oblivion over the edge of the anything but well maintained road. I could not bring myself to stay at the hospice at the top of the pass, since it housed the poorer class of traveller. Instead, I spent the night in an expensive inn on the other side, at a village called Hospenthal. I am not sure that it was much of an improvement.

I had often heard it said that making a pilgrimage these days has remarkably little to do with piety, and much to do with showing off. I now had the opportunity of confirming this. The company at the inn was clearly in need of respectability; so they were going to Rome.

But that night at Hospenthal was memorable; for it was then I first saw printing. It was on the indulgences being hawked by one of the guests. I was so fascinated by the novelty, that I bought one.

'You'll find everything quite in order,' said the vendor. 'I have Vatican approval, and every copy has the Papal seal; none genuine without.'

'Do you really believe you can buy remission of sins?' I asked. 'I've always understood you've got to earn it.'

'I daresay you're right,' the man answered confidentially, 'but it's a question of supply and demand. The public believes it can buy itself out of Purgatory. It wants indulgences - I have 'em. It may be wrong, but don't blame me, blame the Popes; they thought of the scheme. I'm only an agent; a wholesale traveller, as it were.

'Marvellous invention, printing. D'you know, I was the one who told the Curia to use it for indulgences? I immediately saw the possibilities. It's quick and cheap, I said, and they'd never regret it. I'm glad to say they listened to me. Indulgences were the first printing job in Rome; and it's all due to me.'

I also remember that inn for an unbelievable Swede who looked like an eagle, but spoke like a goose, and appeared to think that his arrival was the Second Coming. He delivered a lurid but rather tedious and entirely unsolicited harangue on the iniquities of mankind. He seemed to have appointed himself conscience to the world. He had to endure a lot of teasing; but I suspect most of the humour was lost on him.

The mounting cackle of raucous voices announced an alien way of getting drunk; and I grew thoroughly depressed - my usual state in boisterous company, for there is a limit to my capacity for watching other people enjoy themselves. I retired for the night long before the Swede had had his say.

Happily provided with the means, I had managed to secure a room to myself, two or three guests, I believe, having been turned out to make way for me. I was able to make an early start, having slept well.

The road followed a valley for some miles, and then plunged into a gorge. Suddenly, I was out of the world, and in what seemed to be the gates of Hell. The mountains, which had been distant bright peaks glistering in the early morning sun, now turned into dark evil jaws of rock threatening to devour me. I felt fear being kindled.

When I crossed the Devil's Bridge over a narrow chasm I was consumed by the horror of falling. The rocks seemed to be waiting to swallow me. And then suddenly I emerged into the sunlight at Goeschenen, at the foot of the pass; the Alps were behind me; the worst was over. I reached Basle after an untroubled canter across Switzerland. But I had taken a full three weeks to travel from Genoa. I was later than I ought to have been.

XVI

BASLE did not seem to favour my quest. My introductions, without exception, turned out to be miserable failures. I drew blank with businessmen, booksellers, university professors and bitterest disappointment of all, even with my local Tertiary colleagues. So much for 'The Discoverers' Club'. Pareto's map, if it ever existed, seemed to have vanished into thin air.

Weeks passed. The prospect of a wild goose chase raised its

ugly head. As a last resort, I went back to Pestalozzi & Co., the bankers whom Carmogli at the Bank of St George had so highly recommended. Someone there suggested that the map might have had something to do with the Council of Basle. I could not see the connection between discovery and a Church Council but, by now, I was willing to try anything, however far-fetched.

Although it was over thirty years since the Council, the records, to my considerable surprise, were still in Basle, more or less intact. So I went to see the archivist. He was an elderly Augustinian called Father Garesio. He also happened to be Genoese, and the price of his help was merely a discussion on the state of Genoa, for the good Father was a true Italian, taking his politics with him wherever he went.

'Do you know,' he said, 'you're the second person within the past eighteen months who's shown a burning interest in the proceedings of the Council.

'I'm a little amused at this fascination with the records of boring debates conducted by excruciatingly prolix gentlemen, most of whom are by now dead and forgotten,' continued Father Garesio. 'Basle was just so much wasted time. It was supposed to reform the Church, but as far as I could see, all it did was to stir up a lot of bad blood.'

I explained what I wanted, apologizing for troubling him with a fool's errand.

'Not at all. Your informant was very sensible. These Councils don't confine themselves to the official agenda. Everything under the sun is ventilated in the corridors. And Basle was a monster of a meeting. All the King's horses and all the King's men were here and their documents.

'But it really is most extraordinary. That other visitor was also interested in a map. I found it too, so there won't be any difficulty. I know exactly where it is. I hope it's what you want.'

He led me along a corridor, and into a room crammed with bookshelves on which were ranged row upon row of bound volumes and bundles of documents, each neatly docketed.

'All my own work,' he said, 'my life's work. I came here as a young friar with the Italian delegation when the Council opened in 1431, and remained ever since. I saw the Council fade away by 1442. I saw two Popes come and go - Martin V and

Eugenius IV, to be precise. In its full glory, the Council had five hundred delegates at a time. But they were nothing compared to the hangers-on. There must have been thousands of *them*.

'It was in 'thirty-six or 'thirty-seven . . .' and he consulted an enormous ledger. 'My catalogue,' he explained. 'My own system too - ah, there we are, as I thought, 'thirty-seven. Some Franciscans came to the Council. They weren't exactly an official delegation; they had come for their own purposes. They wanted money for missionary work in the Far North. They didn't get it, as far as I remember. They had with them a most suspicious Dane - or was he a German? I can't remember which - it doesn't matter. Anyway, the point was, he wanted to be bishop of Greenland, and beyond, and nobody was quite sure where Greenland was, not to mention "beyond". The deputation had brought a map with them to prove that there was a diocese and that there were people to do mission work among. And that's what we want to see.'

In the meanwhile, he had got hold of a ladder leaning against a wall, put it up against a certain row of shelves, mounted to the topmost one, selected a bundle of documents, and untied it, talking all the while.

'Right first time,' he said with amused triumph, as he extracted a piece of vellum and handed it to me. 'I think this is what you're looking for.'

It was an ordinary map of the world. It was distinguished only by an unfamiliar island out in the Atlantic at about the latitude of Scandinavia. It was labelled 'The Island of Vinland discovered by Bjarni and Leif in Company.' A legend above the island said:

> By God's will, after a long voyage from the island of Greenland to the south toward the most distant remaining parts of the Western ocean sea, sailing southward amidst the ice, the companions Bjarni and Leif Eriksson discovered a new land, extremely fertile and even having vines, the which island they named Vinland.

This was tantalizing. I was faced with what was obviously the record of a great discovery. And it was useless to sail by. It was not a proper chart; it was too obviously a sketch. Latitudes were missing, so that it was impossible to judge the position of one place in relation to another. It was not what I had hoped for, and I said as much.

'Do you know,' said Father Garesio, 'that's almost exactly what the other visitor said.'

I asked who this mysterious other visitor was.

'Somebody called John Cabot. He was a Venetian.'

The answer ripped up within me the same emotion I had felt on learning that the Equator had been crossed. That someone else had been searching for the same map less than a year before was more than a sinister coincidence. That he was Venetian made matters even worse. It almost certainly meant a seaman, a cartographer or a cartographer's agent like myself.

'And I suppose,' continued Father Garesio, 'that your next question will be the same as his: do I not have a proper mariner's chart, with compass roses?'

I could only nod my agreement.

'I give you the same answer: no. That deputation to the Council only wanted something to illustrate their petition. Any authentic-looking sketch would do. It's quite possible, of course, that they might have brought other documents, more explicit. If that was the case, they've disappeared from the files - if they were ever put there. I know. I made a thorough search at the time - Cabot asked me to do so. I suppose you were about to ask the same thing?'

I admitted that such was the case.

'It's wasting your time - and mine.'

I offered him 50 guilders to make another search. He agreed. A week or two passed. A few scraps of circumstantial evidence turned up, but nothing conclusive, and of another map, there was not a trace.

I left Father Garesio with plans to remove the Vinland map from its file, and have it bound with Vincent de Beauvais' *Mirror of History* or some other encyclopaedia.

'If it is becoming sought after,' he said, 'I might as well have it conveniently available in a book.'

I could not share his simple satisfaction. I was convinced that the Vinland of this map and Scolvessen's Terra Nova were one and the same place. I had literally held in my hands proof that the country which had fed my imagination existed in reality, but it brought me no further. And I had a rival ahead of me: for all I knew, he might already have been out on the Atlantic by now.

But I had one advantage. I knew Scolvessen, where this Cabot presumably did not. What I now had to do was to make my way to Norway and find Scolvessen, or at least unearth sailing directions to Terra Nova, Vinland, or whatever it was called. Everything pointed in that direction. I was across the Alps, and on the Rhine. I merely had to go down to the sea and take a ship to Bergen.

PART THREE
Terra Nova

XVII

I COULD have sailed from either Amsterdam or Lübeck. Since Lübeck was in the Hanseatic League and, on that account, reputedly hostile to strangers, I chose Amsterdam. I rode there from Basle in just over three weeks; a courier, with all his advantages, could hardly have done better.

In Amsterdam, I found a ship ready to leave. I barely had time to sell my horse, and make a few necessary purchases. I needed blankets, warm clothes, and even fresh linen, for I had travelled light, and was quite unprepared for a voyage.

I sailed on the 27th August. A fresh offshore wind made the departure painless, and we scudded up the curious flat coast of Holland before a steady sou'-wester. The air had a bite, and the water a grey tint with which I was totally unfamiliar. But it was not until the following day, when we left the shelter of the Frisian islands, that I felt the surge of an alien sea, and grasped the enormity of what I was doing.

At least I had not been entirely devoid of forethought. Upon Pareto's first approach, I had seen that the journey to Basle might enable me to set out on my own. From the outset, I had made plans to take advantage of the opportunity thus offered me. I had scraped together every penny that I possibly could. Financially, at least, I was ready for anything.

But, as twilight cast its gloom over the waters, while the last smudge of land dissolved into a clouded horizon, I understood for the first time what it meant to be out on the open sea, and I was overcome by a strange nightmare of lingering remorse.

It was now almost the beginning of September; autumn was approaching; for all I knew North Atlantic sailing might have finished for the year. I ought to have sailed directly from Genoa, instead of dawdling across half the continent. I was late, too late! And I had only myself to blame.

I was burdened yet further by the knowledge that I had wilfully betrayed those who trusted me. It was not only that I had taken Pareto's money; I had stolen my father's as well. The £50 intended for my family's support was with me.

Guilt made me miserable, until I realized that perhaps my feelings were a punishment from Heaven. It must then follow that they would act as a penance. From this consideration there emerged a kind of grim pleasure in my own suffering, which I now sought consciously to intensify, so as to be doubly sure of avoiding future retribution.

My craving for self-mortification was answered by the ship. She was a carrack and, at the best of times, a carrack is an ungainly thing. This specimen was a monstrosity. She looked, and behaved, like a basin. She was a floating insult to St Anne, after whom she was named. She wallowed and pitched and yawed and rolled, and scarcely answered the helm. Luckily, I was not seasick. But others were. It was not pleasant. And, to make matters worse, we had a following wind, which hurled the vessel into every wave, so that the spray rose in torrents, and I learned at first hand the precise meaning of the expression 'a wet ship'. But that same following wind curtailed my misery. We took only twelve days to reach the Norwegian coast, supposed to be one of the fastest crossings that season. We could easily have taken a month.

Norway grew out of the water like the jaw of Leviathan. The first signs of approaching land were black swirls of the sea running over submerged teeth of rock. Farther on, columns of white spume showed where waves broke on reefs just awash. Then came black skerries jutting over the swell. Sucked this way and that by current and vortex, helplessly making leeway when the wind approached the beam, the ship threatened to founder at every turn. The skerries gave way to islands, and we threaded our way through the labyrinth of a windswept archipelago. I, familiar with the concentrated dangers of the Ligurian coast, found the suspense hard to bear. Mountains loomed up ahead; they seemed to open up before us, and we sailed into a long, protected inlet, at the end of which Bergen lay, hemmed in by a ring of peaks.

The entrance to the harbour was guarded by a castle built of stone; the rest of the city appeared to be of wood. The first mate pointed over the port bulwarks to ships crowded before a row of gabled buildings. 'That,' he said, 'is the Hanseatic Quay.

Not for us - only for Hanseats.' We had turned to starboard, and were making for the other side of the channel.

The first mate talked a kind of Catalan, which he had learned while serving in Flemish galleys on the Majorca run. He was the only person aboard whom I understood. He had come over to point out the sights as we entered port.

A most horrible cacophony of drums and bugles now floated across the water.

'You're lucky,' said the first mate, 'you'll now be able to see one of the Hansa initiations.'

The noise came from a procession of rowing boats that had put out from the Hanseatic quay. They crossed our stern, and in the leading boat there sat a number of gaudily dressed gentlemen whipping a naked youth. The 'music' stopped, and so did the beating. The executioners then plunged the youth overboard, holding him submerged while cymbals clashed. When the cymbals stopped, the figure was dragged aboard, whipped and ducked again. This was repeated several times, the victim finally being hurled into the bottom of the boat, from whence another, naked figure was extracted, and the same procedure carried out. They were still at it, when a hawser was brought on board the *St Anne*, and we were warped alongside.

'If they're still alive,' said the first mate, 'those lucky fellows are almost journeymen now. They've only got to be put up a chimney over a fire, and then they're through. It's the way the Hanseatics celebrate the end of their apprenticeship.'

'It seems a bit brutal,' I suggested.

'That's putting it mildly. We also have our little customs in Holland but nothing like this.' There was a cry from the bows, and he hurried forward to superintend some business with the warps.

I had, in the usual manner, paid the balance of my fare the evening before arrival. When he berthed therefore, the captain had completely lost interest in me. I was unceremoniously dumped ashore, like a piece of cargo, and left to fend for myself. Only the first mate had a word of farewell for me. Heavy clouds rolled close overhead, and everything was grey, from the water in the dock to the figures passing to and fro on the jetty. The howls of the Hanseatic initiates were still ringing in my ears, and over all hung the smell of fish. I seemed to have come to the end of the world.

My travels had so far taught me one lesson: in a strange city, start by seeing your banker. In this case, it was a Dutchman called Jacob Buyze, on whom the new letter of credit was drawn that I had obtained in Basle. He was not at all the grand kind of person one normally associates with his profession. He was roughly dressed, and the first object that I noticed on entering his office was a large dried fish, with a bulbous head, hanging from the ceiling.

'King Cod,' he said, noticing the direction of my glance as he greeted me. 'He keeps the wolf from the door.' Buyze laughed, as if it were the joke with which he regularly greeted visitors. As I had been told in Basle by Pestalozzi & Co., he spoke passable Italian; learned while on some commercial expedition to Florence. He was not really a banker in our sense of the word: he was a fish merchant, with banking a subsidiary occupation. To judge by the commission he took on changing my bill - 16 per cent instead of the usual 8 per cent in Switzerland and Italy - it was a highly profitable one. But at least he was as well informed as a thoroughgoing banker. When I mentioned Scolvessen, he grew serious.

'I'm not sure it would be a good idea to meddle with *that* gentleman,' he said. 'However, I suppose you know your own business. He lives on an island somewhere to the north of Bergen. He is supposed to be the leader of some Greenland pilots who have their headquarters there.

'To tell you the truth, nobody seems to know a great deal about them, except that they do most of their trade through the Hanseats on the other side of the port. They do very little through us Dutchmen on *this* side. You've noticed the quay at which you berthed was called "The Quay of the Hollanders"? - well there's a lot of bad blood between the two sides. Only last year we had riots, and the Germans have shut themselves in their quarter. It would be as much as your life's worth to venture there now.'

I mentioned the advice I had been given about keeping away from the Hanse.

'Very sensible,' said Buyze. 'I doubt whether you'd have got much beyond Lübeck. They're desperately afraid of losing their monopolies. They're in trouble, you know, what with the Dutch and the English beginning to trade on their own, directly. I expect that explains their nervousness.'

'About Scolvessen,' I said. 'I can't help it, but I've simply got to see him. Could I hire a boat to take me to this mysterious island?'

'Not a hope. There isn't a sailor would go within a mile of the place. Too many inquisitive boats have unaccountably disappeared. There've been some odd doings around that island, I can tell you.

'But Scolvessen's people sail in to Bergen periodically with trading goods from the island - and they're a villainous looking crew, I must say. Some of them are extraordinarily dark. They don't look Norwegian at all. Scolvessen himself very rarely appears. Why don't you go and see his agent? He doesn't live far away. I'll give you an introduction - we do some business together. He's a Norwegian - about the only one among the merchants. His name's Jesse Lauritsen. He speaks some Latin.'

It was now late in the afternoon. Driven by some odd sense of urgency, I had gone straight to Buyze from the ship, and I now set out to find Lauritsen, without waiting to consider where I was to spend the night. Leaving my belongings with Buyze, and guided by one of his porters, I walked through a maze of narrow cobbled lanes lined with wooden houses into a long, gloomy warehouse on a quay. There, at least, King Cod did not reign. Furs and tusks were stacked along the walls, together with a miscellany of iron objects.

Lauritsen was a squat, granite-faced man, whom I found in a little office at the back of the warehouse. He received me with a notable lack of enthusiasm.

'So you want to see Scolvus,' he said, using the Latin form of the name. 'Why?'

'Because I've met him before.'

'Who are you?'

I explained.

'And so you have come all this way simply to visit a childhood friend?' He paused, and then - 'Master Colombo, what is the real reason for your visit?'

'I've already told you,' I replied.

There was an uneasy silence, broken only by the distant shriek of a seagull.

'I don't think you have,' said Lauritsen finally. 'But it doesn't really matter. Tomorrow, you will be taken to Scolvessen.'

I thanked him, and rose to go.

'In the meanwhile,' said Lauritsen, ignoring the hint. 'You will remain within reach.'

'But I've got to find somewhere to stay the night.'

'That will be arranged.'

'My luggage - '

' - will be fetched. We are prepared for you.'

He crossed over to the door, half opened it, and called out. Somebody approached with a lantern - for the light was now failing.

Lauritsen now prepared to leave, inviting me to follow. I saw the glint of steel. 'Do not attempt to escape,' he said blandly. 'We are armed.'

And I, alas, was not. Perforce, I obeyed. I followed Lauritsen on to the quay, the man bearing the lantern - and the weapon - bringing up the rear. The doleful little procession trudged through the drizzling dusk over wet cobbles, and entered a house in a steep lane which seemed to climb up a mountainside. I was kept in a dark corridor, while Lauritsen went into a room leading off it. I heard voices: Lauritsen reappeared, and I was led up a narrow flight of stairs to a small room in the attic, and the door locked on me. I had the uneasy light of a single candle to see by. The only furniture was a chair and a bed.

The inexplicable turn of events, coming on top of too little sleep on board ship, made a sudden fatigue come over me. I slumped on the bed, and fell asleep in my clothes.

I was woken peremptorily by Lauritsen. Again an armed servant, and again the bleak silent trudge through cobbled streets. The first faint hint of dawn showed that I had slept through the night. We stopped on a quayside before what I recognized as the warehouse of the day before. I heard the water lapping evilly at the stones. What, I enquired, did they propose to do with me?

'Didn't you ask to see Scolvessen?' asked Lauritsen. I nodded. 'Then down there, please.'

'There' was a boat, hidden from sight by the low tide until we approached the edge of the quay.

'Your luggage is already stowed away,' said Lauritsen curtly, and gave an order. I was helped, or manhandled, aboard. Lauritsen's figure on the quay receded, the harbour slipped away, and the boat set sail in what I took to be a northerly direction.

We passed through a maze of rocky islands, with the mountains rising straight out of the water to starboard. Hour after hour we went on. The crew, as Buyze had remarked, looked villainous. They were also well armed, not to mention uncommunicative. Deprived of conversation, I could only review the various possibilities ahead, until I was numbed by repetition.

At least for the moment I was being well treated. In the middle of the morning, one of the sailors, a stocky, dark fellow, almost Italian or Spanish looking, gave me breakfast, consisting of bread, sour milk and cheese.

For two whole days we sailed on among the islands. At the end of the second day we entered a narrow sound and, when darkness fell, a light gleamed ahead. As we approached, it resolved itself into a torch spluttering on a quay. We tied up, and two sentries appeared out of the gloom. After some muttered exchanges, I was bundled ashore and marched into the night.

Soon we reached some lights, and I was taken into a long, low house.

Inside, a fire was burning, and a few people were sitting at a long, rough table, lit by a few candles. One of my guards went up to a man at the head of the table and handed him a letter. Everybody waited silently while he read it, and I had to submit to a battery of curious stares. I averted my eyes, and watched the dim light playing on the solid logs that made the walls. I had never seen such huge pieces of timber before.

Suddenly the man who had been reading the letter rose, laughing.

'It is - I thought it was!' he said. 'Still the same red hair and serious expression and,' coming up to me to examine me closely, 'the same freckles. It's young Cristofero - my dear fellow, you've grown up - but you're still recognizable.'

'You must be Scolvessen,' said I.

'Of course I'm Scolvessen' - and he shook me warmly by the hand.

I could not return the same spontaneous recognition. Although the difference between six and twenty-three is greater than that between twenty-three and forty, nevertheless it is difficult to recognize somebody who has lived only in childhood memories. The figure before me was not quite as I had imagined. It was shorter and not as powerful. But there was still the square face, which I thought I knew, and the shock of dark hair.

I was told to sit down; food was placed before me, explanations were given. The others at the table relaxed. For the first time since meeting Lauritsen, I felt the absence of hostility in the air.

'And what, my dear fellow, brings you here?'

'Exactly the same question that Lauritsen put,' said I, 'only less brutally. And I'll tell you frankly. I want to go to Terra Nova.'

There was a long, almost frightening pause.

'Do you know,' said Scolvessen, now speaking very slowly, 'exactly what you're proposing?'

'I know it's something that has a certain importance - at least judging by the way Lauritsen treated me.'

'Oh that. Well, he has to do his duty, and that's keeping inquisitive people away.'

'Was it really necessary to take me prisoner, which not to mince words, is what he did.'

'I'm afraid so. He took you to be a particularly dangerous person. I needn't remind you of the Genoese reputation in sailing and exploration. And you see there are other developments, of which you may not be aware. The King of Portugal is working with our own dear King Christian to send out an Atlantic expedition.

'And that's not our only trouble. You may wonder why I live in this Godforsaken place. It's a way of keeping our secrets to ourselves. We - that is myself and certain followers - trade with Greenland and beyond. We have valuable goods - ivory, furs and gold. Now I have incurred the wrath of the Hanseatic League by choosing to sell through the Dutch as well. And the Hanseatics, who pretty well rule Bergen - and the whole of Norway for that matter - don't like it. Three years ago they decimated us in a particularly barbarous raid. So you will understand we have to be careful.'

'You want to keep your secret, don't you?' I said.

Scolvessen nodded.

'But how much longer will you be able to? There are so many rumours about,' and I told him everything I had heard, from my early Genoese days to the traces of Cabot in Basle. 'One day you'll wake up to find some explorer on your doorstep. You can't keep the world away for ever.

'And eventually you will have to share it. Would you not prefer to do so with a friend than with a stranger - or an enemy? Show me Terra Nova and I will keep your secret as long as you want. But I want to be the person who reveals it to the world.'

While I had been speaking, Scolvessen stared at me: as I finished, he dropped his gaze, and sat long in silence before replying.

'Anybody else,' he said at last, 'would have regretted those words. But with you it is different. I owe you - or your family - too much. Nobody can say that I do not pay my debts. I am compelled to return to Terra Nova before the winter. You may come with me.'

XVIII

I HAD come to my point of departure. It was a bleak, grey, wind-smoothed northern island lying hump-backed in the water like a whale turned to stone. On top of the spine of rock a few low, wooden houses clustered round a watch tower, which commanded the approaches from all directions; from the channels of a desolate archipelago, from the jagged, sombre mountains of the mainland, and from the open sea glinting in the west. Ringed by reefs, the island was accessible only at a single point, close to one end, where a small cove formed a natural harbour. There lay the ship on which I was to sail; a drab, tarred, unprepossessing, low, narrow single-masted hulk with the unchristian name of *The Great Bear*.

I wondered how she would behave under sail. I was not long left in uncertainty. The boat that brought me from Bergen also brought certain items of cargo for which Scolvessen had been waiting. Now that they - and I - had arrived, *The Great Bear* could be made ready for sea. I offered to help: every hand was needed, for Scolvessen was obviously in haste.

All the time I was on the island, not a single vessel approached. The only sign of life outside was the occasional passage of a distant boat. It was like the lair of hunted men, and there was something furtive in the manner of our leaving.

Silently, *The Great Bear* slunk out of the harbour at dawn, a few days after I arrived. She passed stealthily between two sentinel rocks, traversed a panoply of uninhabited islands, and picked her way through the outer skerries. Unobserved, she slipped into the open sea.

Moving steadily, she rose to the swell. She neither yawed nor rolled, nor bobbed, nose downwards into the shallowest wave troughs. In other words, she was as different from the usual ship as it was possible to conceive.

It was all new to me - and yet familiar. I recognized much about the ship from the tale of *Leidarstjern* in the harbour at Genoa. In some peculiar way, I felt as if I had seen it before; it was almost as if I had come home.

I said as much to Scolvessen. He seemed amused or touched, I could not tell which. But he honoured me with a turn at the helm. 'See for yourself,' he said, 'that one of the few things which the Norwegians can still do is to build proper ocean-going craft, as I told you that afternoon in Genoa. I don't expect you to take anything on trust.'

Elegant and pointed, the stern had nothing in common with the blunted monstrosity to which one is accustomed. The rudder was mounted, not astern in the normal way, but a yard or two forward on the starboard side. The tiller lay athwartships, instead of fore and aft. I gripped it hard thinking that, in the usual manner, it would require all my strength to master. It moved at a touch, and the ship answered like a horse to the bit.

'Yes,' said Scolvessen, after I had returned the helm to the quartermaster, and finished loudly comparing the wonder I had just experienced with the sluggish antics of other vessels, 'the side rudder is an ingenious device. I don't know what good it's done us, though.'

Ashore, there had been little opportunity for conversation, because there was too much to be done. Now that we had put to sea the worst was over; with a steady nor'-easter, and a clear, bright sky – the best kind of September weather – the ship sailed herself.

'The trouble is,' continued Scolvessen, 'that we're so horribly out of date. Look at this ship: her design goes back to my Viking ancestors.

'There have been a few improvements since then: the freeboard has been raised, the stern built up and the hull decked over. But aside from that, she hasn't changed. She can't carry much cargo, but she can outsail anything else afloat. She is perfectly adapted to a life of piracy on a grand scale. But today, it is the respectable merchant who is in charge. And what *he* wants is size, not speed. Unfortunately, Norwegian shipbuilders have stuck to their old ways, and it is the Portuguese, the Germans, the Dutch and the English who now rule the seas.

'Those carracks and cogs and galleys may be clumsy abortions, but they can take bigger cargoes – and that's what counts today.'

'If that's the case,' I asked, 'why not use them?'

'Because they don't happen to suit my particular purposes. *I* don't need big holds; my cargoes are valuable and don't take up much space. But I must have a fast, nimble and seaworthy ship, because I have long distances to sail over dangerous waters. I need a shallow draught for difficult coastlines. And, above all, I've got to be able to handle ice safely. On all counts, *The Great Bear* beats anything else I know. You see, the point about this ship is that she's *perfect of her type*. Anything else is an ugly compromise. Shipbuilding hasn't yet caught up with the times; when it does, then we'll have the best of both worlds: speed and size in the same hull.'

XIX

UNCONCERNEDLY, as if negotiating a familiar channel, the crew settled down to the voyage. I may have helped: I usually bring favourable winds, at least outward bound, and so I did now. But the bland surface of everyday routine veiled a flood of discovery for me. It was not only that every inch we made was an inch more of the unknown as far as I was concerned, but the ship itself was a goldmine of the new and the ingenious.

The third day out, the wind shifted from the quarter to almost dead astern, and freshened violently to something like a storm. By all the rules, we ought to have shortened sail. Instead, every inch of canvas was crowded on, and *The Great Bear* leapt forward at fourteen knots, so they said.

I was willing to believe it; I needed no persuasion to convince me of those fourteen knots. The uneasiness at sheer, unaccustomed speed brought its own conviction. I could feel, as the figures proclaimed, that we were faster than the fastest ship I knew.

And this was achieved by a ridiculously simple rig. It was one vast, square sail mounted on a single mast amidships. Forward, there was a small staysail rigged from the top of the mast entirely for steadiness, I was told.

The wind whined through the rigging; the ship flung herself over the waves; showers of spume hissed across the deck. I had never seen such seas before, and what I now saw answered to the maritime inferno that the old salts down at the harbour in Genoa so graphically told of as the prelude to shipwreck and disaster. I kept repeating the 'Salve Regina' to myself, and made promise of penance and pilgrimage if only we were saved.

Yet the crew continued their business with undisturbed calm. A few seamen fiddled with the sail to extract the last ounce of speed, as if they were burdened with light and insufficient airs, and not threatened by a storm. A single helmsman still steered the ship effortlessly. Had I not seen on other ships how three sailors strained at a tiller in half the wind with a quarter the success? The side rudder was a stroke of divine inspiration: surely Scolvessen's mariners had been chosen for the special favours of Providence? But they seemed oblivious either of danger or of grace.

Scolvessen commanded me to feel the deck. Something rippled underfoot as we rose and fell with the waves.

'This,' said Scolvessen, 'is like riding on the back of some living creature in its element. It is the way a snake moves. My Viking ancestors didn't call ships serpents and dragons for nothing. Look at the sail: isn't it like the wing of a dragon, as one of our sea-kings said? Or:

> "The speeding serpent swathes the sea,
> Its mane sea-silver glittering."

to quote an old Norse poet.'

I had never before heard of a sea-captain who recited poetry: anybody who could do so in a storm obviously possessed monumental confidence.

Tenderly proud, as if exhibiting a favourite child, Scolvessen elaborated on the splendours of the hull. It was clinker built, which is to say that the planking was not flush, but overlapped from top to bottom like the tiles of a roof. I was shown how the strakes worked over each other as the ship moved with the sea.

'That's the secret,' said Scolvessen, 'suppleness. That's where we get our speed, and our safety for that matter. *The Great Bear* is very different from the usual modern ship. She's soft in every joint; I needn't tell you how stiff the ordinary vessel is. This ship is alive; she sails *with* the sea. A conventional ship is a dead object, which fights against every wave.

'And there's another thing. Below the waterline, the average ship looks like a box' - and how right he still is - 'but *we* have elegant and subtle lines that gently skim the water, instead of trying to plough through it. Naturally that gives us speed.'

But the ship seemed so insignificant on the waters. She was perhaps fifty feet from stem to stern, almost as long as a caravel, but scarcely standing one third as high. There was neither poop nor stern castle. Amidships, the full beam was occupied by a hold. What space remained had been ingeniously used. One cabin had been let into the stern, its roof forming the steering platform. Between it and the hold, lay another cabin, and a very cramped little one had been devised in the bows. The galley was in a tiny deckhouse forward.

I was inclined to believe Scolvessen when he said that his countrymen had remembered something of their ancestors' shipbuilding lore. The odd way in which *The Great Bear* swept up at bow and stern, like a swan's neck, utterly different to any other craft I have ever seen, was supposed to be like the old Viking ships. I had no way of judging that claim, but of the seaworthiness of the vessel carrying me across the Atlantic, there was no longer a shred of doubt.

XX

'Has it ever occurred to you,' said Scolvessen, 'how that particular constellation is unusually blessed with names? First, namesake of this ship - The Great Bear. Then, The Plough, The Great Dipper or, as you Southerners so literally say, *Septentrionis*, The Seven Stars. But best of all I like *Karlavagn*, as my countrymen often call it; Charles' Wain. Ah, we Northeners - Children of the Wain.'

We were standing on deck on an unclouded night, the moon not yet risen; the stars blazing with an unaccustomed intensity. The ship was rolling on the swell; the Pole Star pendulated violently above the masthead; higher than I had ever seen before. But the Great Bear it was that really blazoned an alien sky. The Pole Star was fixed, but with the other, I could see how it circled high, showing the celestial sphere canted by travelling from the south.

'Children of the Wain,' repeated Scolvessen. 'It means so much to us. It points the way to the Pole Star. In the dark watches of the night, it tells the time. But hang philosophy. We must take our latitude.'

Loath to abandon my favourite possessions, I had brought my instruments all the way from Genoa. I had produced them on board, and been allowed to join in the work of navigation. The voyage had become a training cruise.

For the first time, I was shown how to put theory into practice; a process not without its pains. It was, for example, one thing to take the altitude of the Pole Star on an immoveable roof in the Carrogio dell'Olivella; quite another on the deck of a vessel in the middle of the Atlantic. The procedure was to hang one's astrolabe from a special bracket on the bulwarks, wait for it to swing true and then, seizing a moment when the ship was comparatively steady in the trough of a wave to swing the alidate and squint through the peephole rapidly to get a sight. It sounds simple enough, but it took literally hours at the beginning before I could perform reliably, and the price was the crick in the neck that is conventionally supposed to be the mark of the professional navigator.

But much I learned that was in no books. As we sailed westwards, the compass swung, always west; at least a point every day, until it far from pointed north. And indeed Scolvessen and his shipmates had no reverence for the compass; to them it was an unreliable device. It was properly maintained, according to the rules: there were plenty of spare needles, regularly magnetized with the lodestone, but there seemed a general agreement to ignore it wherever possible. For example, the first two days after leaving the Norwegian coast, the helmsman steered a course, facing sternwards, apparently by guess and by God. But Scolvessen showed me how, for those with eyes to see, there was a mark on the seemingly featureless sea. To the east, in the sky above the land which had long since dipped below the horizon, there was a faint gleam: 'the loom of land', it was called. After much coaching, I was just able to detect it, but those seamen had no difficulty in seeing it, and by it they steered with astounding exactitude.

When the loom of land failed, the sun was preferred to the compass; every sailor aboard had the uncanny gift of telling time and direction from dawn to dusk. And even when the sun was hidden by cloud they were still able to steer by it. Scolvessen had what he called a 'sunstone', which told where the sun was. It was a rectangular crystal about the size of a man's hand. One waited until there was a gap in the clouds overhead, held the 'sunstone' up before the patch of clear sky, and rotated it horizontally. As it turned, it changed colour from yellow to blue. When the blue was darkest, the long sides pointed to the sun.

The compass seemed to be regarded as an insurance for emergencies alone. I can remember its being used only on cloudy nights or in thick fog and completely overcast skies, when the 'sunstone' was useless.

Scolvessen had a passion for accuracy, which was an education in itself. He explained that it was essential to keep precisely to the correct latitude, or one would assuredly run into trouble. There were, he contended, belts of prevailing winds across the Atlantic. It was out with the easterlies above the sixtieth parallel, and home with the westerlies around the fiftieth. We now had to keep north of sixty degrees - but not too far, because of storms and foul winds at high latitudes. There was not much room for error.

To Scolvessen (and, I think, his crew) this was a matter of course; to me it was revelation. So too was the behaviour of the compass. I had had two tremendous discoveries thrust upon me. If nothing else came of the voyage, they would be enough to make my reputation.

But already I could boast of another accomplishment. We had now been twelve days at sea, out of sight of land. No one else I knew of had ever ventured so far. The great voyages of discovery had so far been hops along a coast. Ca'Da Mosto had been wonderfully daring when he lost sight of Africa for a day. And here I had been sailing twelve times longer, and was still making for an empty horizon. It was something quite unbelievable. And still Scolvessen and his crew went about with the greatest unconcern, doing something for which the bravest of my contemporaries would have had to screw up all their courage.

One night, latitude settled; course and compass corrected, as usual, Scolvessen did not follow his habit and turn in. Giving some instructions to the watch, he remained on the steering platform. I too stayed up. The ship was lunging comfortably over the swell; we were running before a not too heavy wind; the air was cold and crystal clear; it was a wonderful night, and I could not bear to go below.

I leant against the bulwarks, in moonlight of an intensity

unknown in the south. I watched, while the angle of the Guards in the Little Bear showed the passing of the hours.

The sea was bathed in a cold unearthly glow from moon and stars. Quite clearly I could see the waves rolling by, shapes picked out, crests glistering. And then I saw something rise, like a monster from the deep, and I heard a long, eerie hiss. I cried out in fear, surprise, curiosity, I know not what.

'Whales,' said Scolvessen laconically.

I had never seen a whale before; but I saw them a-plenty now. Like a ghostly army of the sea, dim shapes darted round the ship, a school of whales playing in the moonlight.

To me, it was another wonder of the voyage. To the crew, it was something rather more. It was a sea mark; it gave them their position; it told them they were south of Iceland, over a third of the journey done. That was why Scolvessen had waited up. He knew we were approaching the place where the whales were usually found; he wanted to see them for himself, for it was the last fix before our destination, and the only certain guide to the critical point of the voyage.

That was where we had to change course. The whales told us when. We had been 'running down the parallel', and now we swung from west to south-west, to give the teacherous, stormy southern tip of Greenland a wide berth, and make the latitude of Terra Nova.

Now, the sailing was not as pleasant, and we ploughed along with awkward shifting winds on the beam, making far too much leeway for comfort. But, said Scolvessen, north-easterlies were quite common in these waters at that time of year, and with any luck we might pick up one. And, indeed, after a few days, a north-easterly gale sprang up, and held steadily. Now we romped along with a following wind. It would take some time to blow itself out, said Scolvessen and ought to see us over the worst: it might even take us all the way.

XXI

I KEPT a private log of the voyage. It is lost now; but I remember, each entry was very like the last. We did so-and-so many miles - usually between one hundred and one hundred and sixty - with such and such a wind on this course, in that kind of weather; the hackneyed observations of ocean travel. The accounts of successful journeys make dry reading, I am afraid.

We were not even visited with the conventional scourge of explorers; trouble with the crew. They were about fifteen all told - less than half the number usually found on comparable ships. One would have thought that the extra work would have brought insubordination in its train. Not a bit of it. Discipline was impeccable, and not once did Scolvessen, like so many captains, have to beg and plead to continue onwards.

'I don't see why I should,' said Scolvessen, when I raised the subject. 'They're all volunteers, and they know where they're going. They've every reason to be perfectly satisfied. And if the occasional malcontent isn't,' he continued, 'he's very quickly dealt with. We're all in the same boat together.'

He said this rather grimly. Indeed, despite the kindness he had shown me, and the debt he unashamedly acknowledged to my family, there was something forbidding about him. I took great pains never to contradict him, nor to intrude upon an interior reserve which he seemed bent upon defending. It was not until we had been almost three weeks at sea, that I plucked up the courage to ask about maps.

'Maps?' he said. 'What would I do with those things? The quickest way to disaster. How on earth do you suppose you can represent the curvature of the globe on a flat piece of parchment? Thoroughly misleading - that's obvious.'

'But in the Mediterranean - '

'Oh, that duck pond. It doesn't matter there, the discrepancy's so small. The Atlantic's another kettle of fish entirely, let me assure you. You're dealing with distances of a totally different order, and in that case the errors would be disastrous. One day,

I suppose, some clever mathematician will work out a way of getting round the problem. Until then, you can take it from me, maps are there to impress the ignorant - and make money for the map-makers. There's only one way to navigate, and that's by sailing directions - Admiralty Pilots, as I call them. Sorry, that's a private joke. If you knew Norway well, you couldn't in your wildest dreams imagine a Norwegian admiral today - let alone an admiralty. Anyway, here's my Admiralty Pilot.'

He now produced out of a sea chest a heavily bound volume wrapped in what appeared to be a waterproof bag. We were in the after cabin at the time. And there, under the yellow flickering light of an evil-smelling train-oil lamp swinging from a beam, to the accompaniment of a mocking commentary, I saw for the first time authentic records of Atlantic navigation; confirmation of all that I had heard and believed.

'My countrymen,' said Scolvessen, thumbing through the closely written volume, 'somehow lack the graphic sense. They are *literary* people. Even if maps were reliable - they would still prefer words. They can conjure up images from words, but a drawing to them - is just a drawing. Oh, I think this ought to interest you' - and he stopped at a page at the beginning of the book.

I could not read the superscription, since the language was Norwegian, but it was obviously a geographical index. It was divided into four parts. The first concerned Europe, starting with North Norway, descending through Nidaros, and Bergen, then to the Scaw in Denmark, and ports and landmarks along the Irish and English coast, and then all the way along France, Galicia and Portugal to Cape St Vincent; complete with latitudes; a list of land falls, in other words. The next two parts had similar information for Iceland and Greenland. The last was the other side of the Atlantic.

It started at the seventy-eighth parallel, farther north than others I knew of had yet dreamed of reaching, in a country called Helluland; then Markland; then Nyfundrland, and finally farthest to the south, Nynoreg.

Scolvessen pointed to Nyfundrland.

'Barbaric syllables to you, no doubt,' he said. 'It simply means New Found Land - your dear old Terra Nova.

'Markland,' he said, 'may have reached your ears as Labrador' – I shook my head – 'Anyway, it's what the Portuguese call it – but I *think* we've caught all who got that far.

'Now Nynoreg, being interpreted means New Norway – or Norvegia Nova if you prefer the Latin. I say this because you might have come across a corruption of the term in the form of Norumbega, again by courtesy of the Portuguese. You haven't? Oh, well, perhaps we've been lucky there too.

'Now these names, which seem so exotic to the uninitiated, are simply geographical descriptions – which doesn't say much for the sophistication of those who thought them up, you must agree. That' – and he pointed to something called *Langöy-Langöysund*, 'means Long Island and Long Island Sound, which is very literally true. That – *Torskodde* – is Cape Cod: the fisherman's paradise, naturally. And there, close to Cape Cod, we have our southern trading post, which we call *Nyhavn*. As you might have guessed it means New-Port. It lies on something called *Sundöy* – Road Island – I needn't explain that this is because it is liberally provided with roadsteads for our ships. My God, the *ingenuity* of my countrymen.'

XXII

'TOMORROW,' said Scolvessen, 'we should make land.'

We were standing on deck at sunset, watching the ship stood to for the night. It was the first time on the whole voyage that this had been done. We had now been at sea for over three weeks; and still there was no break in the waters. But for the past few days we had seen kelp and driftwood and birds flying out of the west; and that morning we had run into long shoals of cod. The signs could hardly be plainer. Even I could see it was journey's end at last. 'You must have been glad to give that order,' I said.

'Oh no,' said Scolvessen. 'Oh no. I hate destinations.' He then abruptly left me to go on his customary tour of inspection.

After some time, he joined me forward at the starboard

bulwarks, where I had gone to try and penetrate the darkness ahead.

'Looking for the Promised Land?' he said. 'You'll be disappointed, I'm afraid. Occasionally you can see fires ashore, but not this time. We're still too far out.

'But that won't stop you from staring. I know the feeling only too well. On tenterhooks the last night before sighting land. It's always the same, however well you know the route. The last few miles are always the worst.

'Especially when one is torn between two desires. After a long voyage, one hungers for terra firma again. And yet, somehow one wants to put off the evil moment of arrival because it only means disappointment.'

'The end of the game, in fact,' I said, thinking of the time I used to play at this very voyage in the harbour at Genoa. I knew the feeling all too well.

'Exactly. I think of the first men who came this way. Norway wasn't the fifth rate satrapy it is now; then it was the master of the oceans. The Norsemen roved as they liked from the Arctic to the Dardanelles. One of them discovered Terra Nova. His name was Bjarni Herjulfson - the Bjarni of the map you saw in Basle. It was almost five hundred years ago that he sailed from Iceland to Greenland, and was swept out of his course by a frightful nor'-easter. When the storm had blown itself out, he sighted the coastline which, all being well, we will see tomorrow.'

Scolvessen now told the story of Terra Nova. I cannot hope to convey the passion with which he spoke; how he talked as if he had seen what he described; how he swept me back to my childhood in Genoa, and seemed merely to be finishing the tale he had begun there as if it had been yesterday. I can only repeat the bare bones of what he said.

Over unknown waters, Bjarni brought his ship safely to Greenland in the end. Then a man called Leif Ericson - he too was mentioned on the map in Basle - sailed out to investigate Bjarni's discovery. He was the first to go ashore - for Bjarni had never landed. Leif was so impressed with what he saw that he called the country *Vinland hit Góða*, Wineland the Good.

After a year, Leif returned to Greenland. And then Thorfinn Karlsevni sailed out to colonize Vinland. He was one of Scolvessen's ancestors; he seems to have been an extraordinary person. He persuaded several hundred people to accompany him.

He landed at Leif's camp. All that was missing were the wild grapes which had inspired the name of the country. But Leif had explicitly said that they grew farther south. Karlsevni pursued his voyage along the coast, and eventually reached Long Island. There he found his vines. He had come to an altogether milder climate; the ideal site for a colony - except for one thing. The country was inhabited by hostile tribesmen, and his excursion became a running battle.

He decided to cut his losses, and returned to the comparative security of his northern landfall. As yet, he had it to himself, but he preferred to take no chances. He abandoned Leif's camp, which was hard to defend, and moved to a better site a few miles to the west. There he built a fortified settlement he named *Straumsvik*, which means 'The Inlet of Currents.'

Straumsvik turned out to be a goldmine. On land there were furs; also offshore in the shape of seals, not to mention ivory from narwhales. And in the barren lands to the north, there was the white falcon. Even in those days falconers paid almost anything for that breed.

Karlsevni's successors could not bring themselves to give up the south, however, and persevered with fortified outposts on Long Island and at Newport.

The colonies lasted three hundred years. They decayed with the home country. By the year of Grace thirteen hundred, the Norse had abandoned Vinland.

But the discoveries were not entirely forgotten. They were handed down by word of mouth and finally committed to writing by an Icelandic historian called Hauk, a descendant of Karlsevni. And Karlsevni's pilot book was preserved in the family, eventually making its way into the hands of Hauk's grandson, Paul Knudsen.

Paul lived in Bergen. In 1355, he sailed in search of *Vinland hit Góða*, and was never heard of again - officially at least. In fact he reached Straumsvik. He was the rediscoverer of the Norse Atlantic colonies. He was Scolvessen's great-great-grandfather.

Paul dubbed the country *Nyfundrland* - The New Found Land - or Terra Nova, which is how Vinland got its modern name. There was good reason for the change. The Vinland trade had been a royal monopoly, and Paul proposed to revive it illicitly for his own benefit. He had to cover his tracks. The new name would discourage associations with the old Norse colonies.

The land was empty no longer. The Beothuks (the wild tribesmen about whom Scolvessen had talked at Genoa, making such a deep impression on me) had now arrived. Paul, finding they were accomplished trappers, arranged to barter with them for their pelts. He rebuilt Straumsvik; he reached Newport. Once more the trade of Terra Nova flowed across the Atlantic, but now much increased, and far more conveniently for the colonists. Paul's fortune was made, but he found it advisable to avoid Bergen for some time. When he returned, he called himself Scolvessen, which was his wife's maiden name.

Terra Nova became the private estate of the Scolvessens. And when Jón returned from his travels, his father (Paul's great-grandson) asked him to go out and take charge.

He was only too pleased to accept. He found Norway down at heel, Genoa not much better. He looked forward to something new and fresh.

'I went out to Terra Nova without any expectations,' as he said, 'so I suffered no disappointments. Predictably, the place was dilapidated - just like the home country. But at least I could do something about it.

'I renovated Straumsvik. I put new life into the fur trade. I even managed to persuade more colonists to come over.

'I have settled in Straumsvik and raised a family. Only business compels me to visit Bergen from time to time. Otherwise, I would never go back. On *this* side of the Atlantic I am - almost - king.

'I ought to be safe for some time yet. Since Paul's day, the Atlantic trade has been run like a secret society. Of course, some of the news had got abroad. But most of it, I suspect, is comfortably out of date - like your Vinland map at Basle. My Bergen agents, as you well know - still keep intruders at bay. You don't realize how lucky you are. No, I'm still reasonably secure.'

But for the sigh of the swell and the creak of the ship, silence now fell. Something in Scolvessen's tale had touched an odd chord in me. After some time, I said:

'You have gone to extraordinary lengths to keep Terra Nova a secret - and yet you told me . . .'

Scolvessen waited before replying, and then he said, speaking very slowly:

'Yes, it's very odd. I've never told anybody else. But some urge made me do so. It wasn't just a facile trick to entertain a schoolboy; it was almost as if . . .'

And his voice trailed off.

'As if I had been chosen to know?' I said, completing the unspoken thought.

'You mean Destiny?' - Scolvessen smiled slightly; there was another silence. 'Perhaps, who can say? I often wonder how much longer this can go on. I say I am safe; but you know, there are omens. This voyage, for example; why do you suppose I am racing across the North Atlantic in October, when all sensible sailors are laying up for the winter? I am oppressed by a sense of change in the air.'

XXIII

IT was dark, with a presentiment of dawn. I stood at the bows straining my eyes to see. Somebody called out.

The cry of the watch - a smudge on the horizon; land!

'Terra Nova,' said Scolvessen, watching next to me. 'A sight that never palls - even after all these years: the first glimpse of land after an Atlantic crossing. What *your* feelings must be, I can only guess.'

I had crossed the Atlantic. There, before me in reality, lay what I had so often seen in my imagination. To tell the truth, the one ran into the other. For where does the spirit end and the flesh begin? I was allowed a moment of exultation before the familiar feeling of my childhood welled up from the makebelieve in the harbour of Genoa; dread disenchantment at the end of the game. In the moment of triumph, I was afraid of consummation. I wanted to put off the evil moment of landing.

I wanted the only true savour of achievement; I wanted to prolong the view from afar.

My unspoken wish was granted. For reasons not yet clear to me, we had raised land well south of our destination. For three whole days we now sailed, northwards, always with the dark ribbon of distant shore inspiringly in sight. I had been spared a sudden arrival; I extracted every ounce of pleasure from the reprieve thus granted me. It was one of the few interludes of contentment I have known.

On the last night at sea, Scolvessen took me aside.

'There's something I've been meaning to discuss with you,' he said. 'Tomorrow, all being well, we should make port. And before that, we've got to concoct a plausible excuse for your appearance.'

I was somewhat perplexed, and showed it.

'The trouble is this,' said Scolvessen, with a seriousness I had not noticed before. 'My colonists are a little suspicious of outsiders - especially if they come from the south. Rightly or wrongly they suspect that every foreigner is a spy, plotting to destroy their privacy, and take away their land. You see, to us, every explorer is an intruder.

'My crew does not wholly approve of you' - something that I had sensed on the voyage, but put down to a native churlishness - 'because they are not sure of your motives. I have explained *my* motives, and they understand the debt of gratitude I owe your family.

'The essential thing,' he continued, 'is to take the mystery out of you. You have told me that you are a Franciscan Tertiary. Now Terra Nova has been without a priest - I would hate to tell you for how many years - and if I could announce that at long last, I have brought one - that is to say you - everything would be settled, and I might even be praised for my initiative.'

I explained the enormity of what he was proposing. I was not ordained: I wasn't even a full Franciscan. I would be an impostor: worse than that, I would be leading innocent people to perdition.

'I doubt,' said Scolvessen, drily, 'whether they need any help with that. But I can't stand here splitting theological hairs with you. Could you say Mass and so forth with reasonable conviction?'

I had to admit that I could.

'And haven't you got an authentic looking costume with you?'

Again, I had to agree: there was after all, a full Franciscan's habit in my baggage.

'Then I suggest you put it on – in your own interests.'

So the next morning before dawn, I appeared in my habit, a genuine full Franciscan to the eye of the unobservant beholder.

'I have told the crew,' said Scolvessen, 'that you have been travelling incognito. I have explained that you yearned for the life of an ordinary mortal, and that now your holiday's over. I think they were convinced. Anyway, you can start your professional career now by leading a "Salve Regina". We're about to go into Straumsvik and finishing a voyage with a hymn, a custom I rather liked in the south. *These* heathens might as well be introduced to it – and it will show them that a new regime's beginning.'

I went to the mast, the bo'sun called the crew on deck, and somewhere or other I got them through the chant.

'Not bad at all,' said Scolvessen, after the last uncertain notes had died away over the swell. 'Not bad at all. In fact, thoroughly convincing. A genuine priest couldn't have done better. Obviously you've missed your vocation.'

Inwardly, I was shaking. During the prayer, every flap of the sail, each creak of the timbers, all the screeches of the gulls that were following the ship, seemed the herald of Divine retribution for my imposture. That the deck was still solid beneath my feet, I took as a temporary reprieve. But my remorse, I am bound to admit, was submerged by anticipation as we got under way.

The ship had lain to during the night. Now, as the full flood of daylight broke, we turned westwards, and entered a channel between a northwards-pointing promontory to port and a steep-sided island. Far beyond to the north-west, land showed well down on the horizon.

'Straumey,' said Scolvessen, pointing to the island, 'although Frenchmen I have met, call it Belle Isle. And this is Straumsfjord. We shan't be long now.'

We crossed a wide bay and continued westward through waters fouled with reefs and rocks among islets off a broken coast. Each corner brought only what had appeared before: land without sign of life. It was something utterly alien to me: I had only heard of similar places from those who had been to Africa. I watched mile after mile unfold, and no sight of anything but rock and water and trees. It was desolation without end.

And then we rounded a headland and I saw a watchtower on a bluff. The ship now sailed due south through a sound, keeping to a channel marked with posts. She rounded another headland, and ran into a little bay cradled by protecting arms of land.

On the shore at one end of the bay, there was a stockade, and through a gap I caught a glimpse of buildings beyond. The smoke of hearths streamed in the wind: Straumsvik and journey's end.

We berthed at a long jetty. I crossed the gangplank and set foot on Terra Nova. My first steps on the other side of the Atlantic! Against all my expectations, I was, thank God, spared the forlorn emptiness that I had believed must follow the accomplishment of my journey. But I did have to wait for time to give greatness to the hour. Only now, seventeen years on, do I feel its poignancy as I play the scene over again and again in my mind. Now and only now do I sense the splendour of the event. But if I was condemned to enjoyment in retrospect alone, at least my memory has been etched with the date: it was the 17th of October, in the year of our Lord 1475.

I went ashore about the hour of nones. I had been twenty-seven days at sea, and it was four months and twelve days since I had left Genoa.

XXIV

THERE was a small crowd on the jetty. It was hard to tell whether or not they were pleased to see us, for they watched us tie up in silence.

At Scolvessen's urgent order I was first ashore. I made no visible impression. Scolvessen followed, and a woman walked towards him. She put out her arms as if to greet him, but neither embraced nor kissed him, as one might have expected. Instead, she put her hands on his shoulders, and rubbed noses with him. I had never seen anything like it. And the woman herself was like no one else I had ever seen before. She had a brown skin, wide set black eyes, an oval face, and extraordinary high cheekbones which gave her the impression of squinting into the sun. But she was not unhandsome - she had long, coarse black hair gathered in a plait hanging down to her waist.

'My wife,' said Scolvessen, turning to me. 'I forgot to explain. She is of the country. Her name is Chegwaga, which means Trembling Water.'

She did not understand what we were saying, since we were speaking Genoese. But she smiled faintly when she heard the name, as if accustomed to such scenes of explanation, and shook hands with me. In the meanwhile, Scolvessen was greeting five children who had run towards him. They were clearly his and Chegwaga's. Indeed, fully half those on the jetty seemed to be of mixed blood.

Now Scolvessen addressed the little crowd. By his gestures it was clear he was introducing me. I was favoured by a few curious glances, but still I felt that the company was abstracted. Something appeared to be weighing on their minds.

A man, apparently in authority, now stepped forward and spoke urgently to Scolvessen. After a short conversation, Scolvessen gave a string of orders, and then turned to me, saying:

'No rest for the wicked. A strange ship has been sighted down the coast. Naturally, all our own ships are out somewhere. So we've got to unload faster than we've ever done before, and deal with it ourselves. We'll be sailing out again as soon as we can.'

'Do I come with you?'

'I think you'd better. There may be work for you.'

I do not know what I had expected of Straumsvik; something, I suppose, quite magnificent, a shining city on a sound. What I actually saw was something rather different.

I seemed to have come to a place in a permanent state of siege. The stockade I had first seen, although a solid affair topped with iron spikes, was merely the outer line of defence. Within, another stockade encircled the settlement.

Everything was crude and gloomy. Straumsvík consisted of a few dozen houses, or rather huts, with low walls of rough logs, and turf roofs with stunted stone chimneys from which there rose the smoke I had seen from the bay. After all my expectations, it seemed like hope betrayed.

But in one of these uninviting habitations, I was given a proper hot meal - an act of charity, since it was the first for some time: by the end of the voyage we were living on salt herring and sodden bread. And, whatever the surroundings, I was unbelievably glad to feel solid earth beneath my feet.

I was not allowed to enjoy it very long. Before the end of the afternoon, I was recalled to the ship, and we put to sea again, proceeding to retrace our track. By the time we had nosed out of Straumsfjord into the open sea, darkness had fallen. But we did not lie to for the night. Still following our incoming course, we turned south along the coast.

It was blowing half a gale from the south-east, so that now we had to beat to windward. It was not a comfortable night. Men and weapons had joined the original crew: we were crowded and slept where we could. One figure, I remember, wrapped in a fur, rolled in happy oblivion to and fro on the deck, as the ship heeled over from one tack to the other.

I, however, at first found it hard to think of rest. The erstwhile merchant ship had too plainly become a man o' war. What danger was ahead? Why Scolvessen's sudden, unwonted taciturnity and reckless hurry? I could hear how the breaking of the waves on the shoals grew uncomfortably close when we tacked to starboard and ran towards the land. In the end, worry and foreboding; the excitements of the past few days were too much for me. I was overcome by weariness, and fell into a deep sleep, from which I only awakened when a rough hand roused me.

It was already light. We had hove to in a small bay. Unruly waves jostled past us to beat on a desolate, windswept shore. The sole trace of human kind was a ship flying the Portuguese flag.

She was firmly aground. While I had been sleeping, Scolvessen had gone out in a dinghy and cut the intruder's moorings. He had only the light of the moon through the clouds to help him, but he had done his work well. Wind and tide had driven the vessel on to a reef. Tangled rigging and a half raised mainsail flapping aimlessly over the side told of a desperate, but happily futile, attempt to escape. That ship would be unlikely to see the shores of Europe again.

Scolvessen now ordered me into a dinghy and, together with the other ship's boat, we rowed towards the wreck. There was no sign of life on board. I was the first to become aware of movement ashore.

Not forgetting to praise me for my powers of observation, Scolvessen gave orders to investigate. In a cove, we found what was clearly the shipwrecked crew. They were gathered together on a narrow beach, some apparently unloading three or four boats drawn up out of the water.

We approached cautiously and when we were within about two hundred yards, a surge towards the water's edge suggested that we had been observed. It was then that out of the forest behind them, there issued, like hornets tumbling from a nest, a crowd of human figures.

They stopped; I was able to see that some were carrying bows; there was the recognizable movement of arms drawing bowstrings, a ripple as if arrows had been sent on their way.

Among the Portuguese crew, there was great agitation, as if they had been taken by surprise. I could see how they surged towards the boats, but their retreat had plainly been cut off.

I scarcely needed Scolvessen's explanations to grasp that it was the Beothuks who had attacked. Intermittently, with the shifting of the wind, I could hear the sounds of battle, the cries of the embattled, so that the figures, made unreal by silence, became living creatures in danger and mortal fear.

To my unconcealed revulsion, Scolvessen made no move to rescue the unfortunates on the shore. I too preferred the intruders not to return to Europe, but I could not stomach massacre in cold blood.

For an instant the fighting ceased; the ranks disengaged, and I saw three lone figures, a last pathetic pool of defiance. Then they were engulfed, and the signs of struggle died away. The attackers could be seen bending over here and there, as if examining their victims.

After a while, Scolvessen gave the order to row out.

'Surely you're going to go and look for survivors?' I asked.

'Not just yet: it would be as much as our lives are worth,' was the answer.

'But you have told me that you know how to deal with the Beothuks.'

'Normally yes. But the circumstances aren't normal. You see, they usually don't attack until I give the word. This is the first time they've acted on their own. I can't vouch for their behaviour any longer.

'It's a pity, I would have liked to get hold of someone to question. But I rather fear I'm going to be disappointed. I suspect they all went ashore together.'

He was right. We boarded the wreck and found it deserted. Jammed on her reef, she was listing sharply, grotesque witness to her crew's fate. Her name was *Mariagallante*; she came from Lisbon. I helped search her for books and papers; clearly the work for which I had been taken on this foray.

Meanwhile, Scolvessen had sent one of the boats back to *The Great Bear* with orders for her to approach. She came up, anchored at a respectful distance, and her crew started taking on board everything from *Mariagallante* that might be of value. This was firstly the armament: a few small cannon, powder and shot. Then came tools, navigational instruments, the compass and anything of iron. When the work was done, *Mariagallante* was set on fire.

'At least there won't be anything for them to loot,' remarked Scolvessen, as we stood on *The Great Bear*, watching the flames take hold, 'and not one of my men has got so much as a scratch.'

The crew seemed devoid of all concern for what was happening around them. They went about the business of stowing their new cargo as if such things were a matter of everyday routine.

'I suppose this isn't the first time that this has happened,' I suggested to Scolvessen.

'No. At least it isn't the first time that we've been visited by foreign ships, and that they've been dealt with in this way. You see, lives are our most valuable possession. There are so few of us, I can't afford to lose a single man - or even suffer an injured one.

'That's why I use these particular tactics. I depend upon the Beothuks, and they are only too pleased to help, because they want intruders no more than we do. They keep a lookout for us along the coast, and raise the alarm when anything peculiar happens. That's how we heard of this interloper. We drive the ship ashore, and let them get to work. They need us, because they are helpless on the water, and we need them, because we haven't the men to spare for skirmishes on land. They rather welcome these little outings. They always have the advantage of numbers, and usually manage to polish off everyone within reach.

'We have a standing arrangement that they are to wait for a signal before attacking. This enables us to get hold of those whom we want to question. But this time, as you observed, they didn't wait.

'Something has obviously gone wrong. When they have withdrawn, we will have to go and see what has happened. And you will come as well.'

I was not anxious to comply; I was quite frankly, afraid - but there was no way out. Late in the afternoon, when the beach seemed clear, we rowed ashore.

There were no survivors. At Scolvessen's insistence, I gabbled the office for the dead, and we hurried off without waiting to bury the remains on the beach. We rowed out, pitching past the *Mariagallante*, a flaming pyre now from end to end, like a macabre beacon on a rock.

Nobody spoke until we were almost alongside our own ship.

Scolvessen said something to the oarsmen and was answered by an uneasy murmur. Then he turned to me and said:

'I think there is no doubt that our friends have become anthropophagi - man-eaters. It's the only explanation I can see for the wholesale mutilation.'

I could not speak: I was still horrified at what I had seen.

'Did you see, there wasn't a single Beothuk in sight? But they were hiding in the forest: they weren't far away. There - look, now they're coming back!'

Figures were now moving towards the shapes on the sand. In silence we came alongside and clambered on board.

'That was a bad business,' said Scolvessen. 'We should never have gone ashore. Usually, we leave them alone after they've attacked. We knew there was something ritual about their killing, so that any inquisitiveness would be bad manners. But anthropophagi – I never thought that of them.'

The place had now become rather distasteful; there was nothing to be gained by staying. We sailed for Straumsvik almost immediately. As soon as we were under way, Scolvessen took me into the cabin to go through *Mariagallante*'s papers. They made distinctly unpleasant reading.

Mariagallante was not on that coast by accident. She had been fitted out as a joint venture by King Alfonso of Portugal and King Christian of Denmark and Norway.

'And a more dangerous combination,' said Scolvessen, 'it would be hard to imagine. There's Alfonso with his ships and his sailors and his money, and there's Christian, with his heritage of what the Norsemen knew. They met in Lisbon years ago, when Christian was making the usual Northerner's pilgrimage to Southern capitals. They became great friends: I might almost have predicted something of this kind.'

Mariagallante's captain had been worthy of such masters. He was a certain João Vaz Cortereal from Te-ceira in the Azores. He was frighteningly familiar with Northern waters. He seemed to have visited Labrador – Scolvessen's Markland. He had documents which might have been copied from Scolvessen's 'admiralty pilot book'. He knew by name a string of transatlantic places like Newport, Cape Cod, Long Island and Norumbega. He was looking for Straumsvik when we caught him.

'I think I know where he must have got his information,' said Scolvessen, and pointed to an entry in the roster of *Mariagallante*'s crew, 'Didrik Pining – another Bergen man. An old friend of mine. We were at school together. He became Governor of Iceland. Before that, he was at sea for years. He reached Greenland once or twice. I always thought he knew too much for comfort.

'And there's somebody else I recognize: Hans Pothorst. I see he's called Norwegian. But I happen to know he was really German. He didn't have a good reputation, I can tell you. He was a bit of a pirate, and I'm almost certain he was involved in a raid on my Greenland base a few years ago.'

Pining and Pothorst had been mustered as 'pilots' – presumably to tell Cortereal 'what the Norwegians knew.' Apart from them, *Mariagallante* appeared to have been manned by Portuguese alone.

I said I was sorry that we had not been able to save at least some of our fellow-Christians.

'Theoretically I agree,' said Scolvessen, 'but, I'm relieved that we encountered them in the form of their remains.

'It would have been rather awkward otherwise. What would we have done with them? We'd have had to get rid of them in the end, you know. Instead, the Beothuks saved us the trouble. We can console ourselves with the thought that savages did the deed, and our hands are clean. If you like, you can indulge in sorrow and regret. Either way, it's preferable to the alternative.

'And if you want more consolation, think of this. The expedition whose end we have just witnessed, was very well prepared. Its leaders are probably irreplaceable. I think you'll find that, when the ship doesn't return, Christian and Alfonso will be forced to stop their meddling for some time. No, believe me, what happened today was for the best.'

XXV

WE had a rough passage back, and I was dog tired when we returned to Straumsvik on the morning after the massacre. But I could not yet rest. An immediate meeting with the Beothuks had been decreed. The matter was urgent.

During the spring, the colony had run out of the wherewithal to barter. In order not to interrupt the fur trade, Scolvessen had persuaded the tribesmen to give him credit, and immediately sailed for Bergen to replenish stocks. He now insisted on settling the debt without any more delay.

The payment of the Beothuk account was a ceremonial affair. It required a procession of four horses loaded with bales of red cloth and iron cooking pots, and a dozen or so colonists carrying baskets with sewing needles, knife blades, coloured glass beads, brass wire, and cheap jewellery: the specie of this realm, so laboriously fetched from the other shore of the

Atlantic. At the head marched Scolvessen, unburdened, and every inch the commander-in-chief.

I too was in the procession, conscripted as an ornament to the ceremony. I had been placed after Scolvessen at a respectful distance - proper relation of Church and State! - and behind me came someone holding up a large, elaborate crucifix. I felt vaguely awkward at the ostentation of the Cross; my Cathar instincts stirring. On the other hand, my masquerading as a full Franciscan and a priest had ceased to trouble me.

A smoke signal was sent up, and when it was answered by another from the trees, we went through one of the gates in the stockade. We moved at a slow and stately pace across the meadowland surrounding the colony towards the edge of the forest about half a mile away.

At last, the meeting in the flesh with the phantoms of childhood imagination and the shadows of the distant view - out of the trees came men and in single file approached us.

Their faces were daubed grotesquely with scarlet dye. It accentuated their high cheekbones, making their already broad faces broader, and their wide-set eyes seem yet wider apart. It gave them an air of unmitigated savagery. It was obvious how they had acquired the name of Redskin.

When I had used the word, however, Scolvessen had not been pleased. 'It's a term of contempt,' he had said, 'which implies that you underestimate the tribesmen. And that's a dangerous state of mind. Remember, we're a pitifully few settlers in a huge country. It is absolutely vital to respect our neighbours. The correct term is Beothuk: kindly stick to it.'

We stopped about ten yards from the leading Beothuks. A man who, by his bearing, appeared to be in authority, stepped forward. After talking to him for a short while, Scolvessen stepped aside, and two colonists joined two Beothuks in the space between the parties. These were the book-keepers, as it were. Although illiterate, the tribesmen could keep accounts, I had been told, with fabulous accuracy. Their only aid was a stick hung with strings of beads, rather like a crude abacus, which was now produced. There seemed to be no disagreement between the two sides, and the process of tallying was rapidly completed. The goods were now placed in a row on the ground, Scolvessen exchanged a few words with the Beothuks' leader, and we retired.

'I'm glad that's over,' I said to Scolvessen as we walked back to the safety of the stockade. 'It was quite horrifying. I kept on thinking that I was face to face with the same creatures who had eaten those poor devils on the beach.'

'You almost certainly were. Nonosabasut, whom you saw me chatting with, is the local headman. It was he who first saw *Mariagallante* and raised the alarm.'

'You take it very lightly. How can you bear to associate with monsters who eat their fellow beings?'

'Only selected parts. Do let's keep a sense of proportion. And monster or not, a man's entitled to his money. But you're quite right. The meeting was a little strained. You see, we were late, and the delay was not appreciated.'

The understanding had been that the debt was to be settled on the fifth full moon after the original transaction. And it had already taken place. I pointed out that it was scarcely our fault, and, besides, we were only two days overdue.

'One day or a hundred, it makes no difference. Our friends have a somewhat rigid sense of justice. To break your word is, in their eyes, the ultimate crime. And they have no idea of extenuating circumstances, as Nonosabasut so clearly gave me to understand. He had sent a party to take delivery when the debt fell due; even although preoccupied with the little matter of *Mariagallante*, he had found time to make arrangements; why could I not have done the same?

'And what could I answer? I couldn't put the blame on anyone else. I was so obsessed with stopping the Portuguese that I forgot about the other matter. He could only see that I had broken my promise. I have been betrayed by two miserable days. What the consequences may be, I can only guess. Without trust, these people will be dangerous. To think – two little days, and God knows what I've brought on my head.

'And you know, there was something beyond the simple disapproval of an outraged creditor. Nonosabasut seemed, how shall I put it, to have lost his habitual respect. It was as if he suddenly felt stronger than I, where he used to feel the weaker. It has never happened before, and I can't explain it. Our whole existence here depends on being looked up to as the stronger and cleverer. I don't like what's happened; I don't like it at all.'

XXVI

THE Beothuks now vanished. They had migrated inland, so I was told, not to reappear until the spring. Bitter frost and icy autumn gales told of a winter bleak beyond anything I had known.

Nobody in his senses would go to sea in those latitudes at that time of year. I now understood why, at the outset, I had been told that I would have to spend the winter in Terra Nova.

To southern eyes, the prospect was at first scarcely pleasing. There was neither fruit nor corn; nor olive nor grape. Sheep and cattle were pitifully thin and few. And there were a hundred mouths to be fed.

But the North has its own bounty. Fish churned in the waters. Whales spouted far out in Straumsfjord. Cod, spread flat like fans, were crammed on long wooden racks along the shore, drying in the wind. I watched seals being flensed; I saw a stranded whale cut up, the men wading in blood as if it were wine running in the gutter from a cartload of overturned barrels. Although faced with a diet of an unfamiliar, and perhaps a nauseating kind, I would clearly be unlikely to starve.

So I settled down quite contentedly as the temporary vicar of Straumsvik. Scolvessen had solemnly conferred the appointment upon me. I was to prepare the resumption of the Christian life in the colony. I was a legate *in partibus infidelis*.

A church did in fact exist, but it was a rather peculiar one. It seemed more like a heathen tabernacle than a place of Christian worship. Inside it was dark and gloomy, the only light coming from a tiny window covered with a kind of parchment (glazing was unknown in the settlement). There was neither crucifix nor saint to be seen. On the other hand, dragons and serpents liberally decorated the place; carved and painted on the rafters, the wallboards, and even on a heavy wooden table I took to be the altar. Outside, two elaborate dragon's heads curved outwards and upwards from each end of the roof, like the prow of a ship. And the portal was in the form of a long serpent twining round in an arch.

'The Midgard serpent,' Scolvessen had explained. 'The world's support. It surrounds the world like a ring, biting its own tail, and keeps the outer cosmos at bay. It's not exactly a docile creature:

> "Smoke is spewed,
>   Flame roars,
>   From Midgard Serpent's
>   Gaping jaws."

according to an old verse.'

'I've never heard of it.'

'I didn't suppose you had. It's a kind of Devil. It's concerned with the old Norse Gods - Odin, Tor, and all that, you know.'

'It doesn't sound very Christian to me.'

Scolvessen shrugged his shoulders. 'Four hundred years ago,' he said, 'Norway was still heathen. I suppose it's Christian now - but we're a long way from Rome.'

'There's nothing here that resembles a church.'

'Oh, I wouldn't say that. You noticed that scrollwork on the eaves? It was all over St Sophia's Cathedral at Constantinople. I got somebody to make a copy. It's not very good, I admit, but all the man had to work from was a sketch I did from memory.'

Something else puzzled me. Scolvessen had said that no priest had been there for decades. But the church bore every sign of use.

'Oh, we've managed on our own, somehow. Of course, I can't answer for our orthodoxy, but no doubt you'll be able to put us on the right path.'

I said my first Mass on the Sunday after our return from the massacre of the Portuguese crew. It was a peculiar experience. The whole colony was there; a motley crowd with alien faces. My vestments were quite frankly of a pagan glory. They were made of some supple hide (deerskin I was told) encrusted with red and green and white glass beads worked into a pattern of leaves, and the ubiquitous snake - the Midgard serpent for all I knew.

Instead of candles, there were stone lamps fed with seal blubber, spluttering and smoking. Instead of incense, fresh pine branches were singed. They gave off the acrid fumes of burning pitch, which mingling with the sickly reek of blubber, filled the air with a nauseating stench. Instead of wine, there was some fermented brew of berries – very good in its way but, not being made of grapes, strictly inadmissible for the Sacraments. But Scolvessen had presented me with a Papal dispensation relaxing the rules in this particular case.

That was an interesting document. It was addressed to the Legate 'in Greenland and Beyond', permitting the use of other liquors 'considering the remoteness of the territories and the impossibility of obtaining wine.' It was signed by the Holy Father Martin IV, and dated 1282. I can only say that it looked its age, and may have been genuine.

After I had somehow got through the office, Scolvessen's only comment was on its brevity.

'Make it longer next time,' he said. 'Preach a sermon; read the Bible; swear at the congregation if you like. Do anything, but make it long. No one here knows a word of Latin, so it's all gibberish to them, and it doesn't matter what you say. Just stretch it out, that's all I ask. These people don't get anything out of a short ceremony; it's got to be substantial. And what's even more important; the longer it is, the longer they're kept out of mischief. Boredom's the great danger here, you know.'

I was having dinner with Scolvessen at his house when he said this. He and I were the only full blooded Europeans at the table. Besides Chegwaga, his wife, their three daughters and two sons, there was an elderly woman who looked after the children, and a young girl, who had been my guide when I landed.

Chegwaga, as I have said before, was a handsome woman. She was quite unlike the Beothuks I had seen. She was not even from Terra Nova, which, I now grasped, was a large island. She came from the mainland somewhere at the other end of Straumsfjord.

Her alien, yet unmistakably aristocratic, hawk-like profile was mirrored in the eldest child, a boy of about twelve. He stared incessantly and silently at me, like a sentinel ever on guard. It was like some inner eye of Scolvessen himself watching jealously over a sanctum to which he admitted no outsiders. For he seemed to nurse a core of privacy into which he would tolerate no intrusion. And the stare of the son was like a constant warning.

But I nerved myself to ignore it. I wanted to know all about Scolvessen's domestic arrangements; and I was prepared to take the risk of trespassing on forbidden ground. But I met neither resentment nor hesitation; the reserve which I detected lay in some other quarter.

'I married Chegwaga for three reasons,' Scolvessen said. 'Firstly, practical. It is very difficult to persuade my countrywomen to emigrate to a country which does not officially exist.

'Secondly, there is the political consideration. You might be tempted to assume that we live in a virtually uninhabited country. Nothing could be farther from the truth. And some of the inhabitants are sufficiently aggressive to make allies imperative. And what better way of securing an alliance than by marriage?

'Chegwaga's people are useful friends to have. They generally win their wars. They hold down some potentially awkward customers on the other side of Straumsfjord. They control the western mainland, where the best fur trade lies. And they supply us with flour.

'Grain doesn't grow here, but it does inland, where they live. They raise a kind of corn quite unknown in Europe. It has ears like peas growing on a cob as long as your forearm, and sheathed by big green leaves. The flour made from it, as you will have noticed, is peculiar, but it *is* flour, and having it on this side of the Atlantic does save a lot of trouble.

'And the third reason - well, there is a difference between woman and woman - and the Mohawk women, my dear Cristofero, are something quite out of the ordinary.'

I was prepared to believe him. It was not a subject that I particularly wanted to pursue.

'I meant to have a word with you on the matter,' he said. 'A small colony like this cannot stand jealousy - it's too demoralizing. We have rather strict rules. All the women you see here are - er - allocated. They're out of bounds.'

His warning seemed unnecessary. At the age of twenty-three, I had not yet slept with a woman; I think I was a little afraid to begin. I certainly had no intention of causing trouble. What I actually said was that playing the part of a priest, I could scarcely indulge in love making.

'Oh but you must,' said Scolvessen. 'I wouldn't dream of enforcing celibacy. The parishioners would certainly not admire you for it. All I'm saying is that you must have a little patience. Everything will be all right when our ship comes home.'

XXVII

FOUR Straumsvik ships were now long overdue, and Scolvessen was distinctly worried about them. Three were bringing flour. Stocks were low, bread was short, and we had begun to fear for the winter. One cannot live by meat alone.

To fetch new supplies, the ships had sailed a thousand miles to the west, up a huge river to some place called Stadacona. But what Stadacona was, whether city or village or camp, and what manner of men lived there, and what monstrous kind of country it was that could swallow such a voyage and still appear without end, I did not then understand. Nor had Scolvessen yet shown any desire to enlighten me. All I knew was, that Stadacona was his wife's home, and that the journey could be dangerous.

Scolvessen began to talk of a relief expedition, and I held a special votive Mass for the safe return of the little fleet. I also helped in manning the lookout posts. My religious duties were not arduous; my time was very much my own, and I too was affected by the anxiety now nagging the colony. I was goaded by the irrational feeling that to look for the missing ships would somehow ensure their arrival.

Early one Sunday in November, the cry of the watchman's horn cracked the air. I dropped what I was doing, and hurried to the watchtower on the bluff. I found Scolvessen already there: driven by an almost overpowering worry, he now spent most of his time trying to penetrate the horizon with a gaze.

Water and islands were laid out beneath me like a chart. A few miles away, at the end of the cape called Nordnes, which jutted out north-east to cut off a view of Straumsfjord, three ships were tacking towards us.

'The right number,' said Scolvessen, exultantly, as I clambered on to the observation platform, 'and from this distance they look the right kind.'

By the time they had run between the islets guarding the harbour channel, there was no doubt. I accompanied Scolvessen to the jetty where, together with what seemed to be the whole population of Straumsvik, I saw three replicas of *The Great Bear* coming into berth. The relief was general and obvious. Without them, Straumsvik would have been reduced to a single ocean-going vessel: connection with the outside world would have hung upon a thread.

The ships tied up; I stood back to let the colonists mill forward: at all times I dislike a crush.

Scolvessen scurried from one ship to the other, chattering like a schoolboy. He interrupted what he was doing to shout some instructions at me. I was to go and prepare for Mass; nothing would suffice, but that the safe return of the ships should be celebrated immediately. I was peremptorily sent on my way.

After the ceremony was over, and the church had almost emptied, a voice out of the gloom said:

'Not bad. Not a bad imitation at all.'

I froze in the chill of the unexpected. The words were Italian, but did not belong to Scolvessen. He spoke Genoese; this was pure Florentine, and the voice was that of a stranger. It was one of the new arrivals.

'You nearly convinced me,' continued the voice, 'but the last bit gave you away.'

Now the 'last bit' was a Cathar prayer, which I had added as a final touch. Whoever the newcomer was, he was uncomfortably knowledgeable. My thoughts naturally turned at once in the direction of some far-flung Papal supervisor.

But the figure who now moved into the dim halo of the blubber lamp belonged to another order of creation. His features were those of Scolvessen's womenfolk. His head was clean shaven except for a ridge of hair down the middle like a horse's mane. He was dressed in a long jerkin patterned like my vestments. This person, who spoke Italian and knew enough

Catalan to understand the Cathar prayer in the original, and was versed in points of orthodoxy, was no Italian, much less Norwegian. He was not even European. He was a full-blooded native of the country.

'And how is Florence these days?' this singular apparition continued. 'I hear the Medicis are still lording it over the place. Of course I knew it when old Cosimo was in power; what's this new man Lorenzo like?' I could only mumble that I had never been to Florence.

'Ah well,' said the stranger, 'you've got that pleasure yet to come.'

The conversation had very quickly reduced my thoughts to disarray. But now the voice of Scolvessen obtruded, mocking but mercifully familiar.

'I don't seem to have made the introductions. All that confusion on the jetty ... This is Deganawida, my brother-in-law. He's a *most* distinguished person. Amongst other things, he's the ruler of Stadacona. I can see you'll have a lot to talk about. There'll be plenty of time. He's going to spend the winter with us. But now, if you don't mind, there's work to do.'

He then drove us out of the church. The ships had to be unloaded, and the cargoes brought under cover. We were all required to be present; and the lord of Straumsvik brooked no delay.

XXVIII

THE ships had brought a cargo more diversified than I had been led to expect. There was the much wanted corn. But also there were furs and hides in a confusing variety. And there were passengers. Deganawida was the only man among them. The rest; a score or so, were women, intended for the solace of the colony. It was they, as much as the corn, that had worried Scolvessen while their fate was still in doubt. He was preoccupied with the needs of his men. He did not, as he said, want rutting bachelors driven berserk by the last stages of deprivation. In such a small community, that would spell disaster.

To meddle with the Beothuk women was to invite disaster too. *Ergo*, females had to be imported.

'A kind of slave market,' I said, surveying the new arrivals in the house where they were quartered.

'Good Lord no,' answered Deganawida with a pained look, 'they're all volunteers. *We* have no slavery. The girls come from enemy nations – Hurons and Ottawas, not that the names mean anything to you. They're prisoners of war. And we either kill our prisoners or adopt them. The choice is up to them. They decide whether they want to be adopted or not. I think every surviving female among the last batch wanted to come here. The work of pruning was invidious.'

'Rest assured,' said Scolvessen, 'they have been selected with a knowledgeable eye. And you, my dear Cristoforo, are to have first choice.'

I laughed, and made some facetious remark.

'I'm not joking. I'm perfectly serious.'

I pointed out that I was supposed to be a priest.

'What's that got to do with the case? I'm not asking you to marry; I'm simply telling you to take a woman. There's no virtue in celibacy here. Even priests are expected to use what God gave them.'

The conversation continued for some time in this vein: I maintaining the ecclesiastical proprieties, Scolvessen pressing the customs of his fief.

'I don't think you quite understand the situation,' he said at last. 'A man above a certain age must be normal – and be seen to be normal. That is an inflexible rule. We can afford no oddities here.

'One would have thought I was asking you to commit some hideous crime, instead of doing the most natural thing in the world. You don't want a woman, that's the trouble.'

Deganawida had been standing silently aside during the altercation. He now intervened.

'You're too harsh,' he said mildly. 'After all, if one is unused to women, to be faced with a robust cure for that state of affairs must be something of a shock.'

Why was it left to a heathen, a savage-born, to understand my feelings?

At the age of twenty-three, I was still a virgin; a woman was a dark pit waiting to devour me, a mountain waiting to crush me. She was also a soft cloud trying to envelop me. I was the battleground of dread and desire.

'What we might do,' Deganawida suggested, 'is to ask Chegwaga to do the choosing.'

'Rome has spoken; the case is closed,' cried Scolvessen; and the matter was turned over to Chegwaga.

She may have known that chastity was the greatest of virtues; but she must have known that to have faced me with it would have been to invite disaster. She selected for me a kind, almost motherly girl, a little younger than myself, but of some experience.

Otsego was her name; it means 'Clear Water'.

XXIX

THE pack ice filled the fjord; the harbour froze. The sheep, the cattle and the horses, unable to bear the frost outside, were kept in their barns. The ships were drawn up on shore, and sheltered against the bitter winds that constantly blew from the north. It was a winter such as I had not before been able to conceive; but it was comforting at the same time. The ice, impenetrable to ships, shut us in; but it also kept intruders out. As long as it lasted, we would be undisturbed. There, in happy isolation, on a shore whose very existence is unsuspected, Otsego now patiently taught me what St Paul meant when he said: 'if they cannot contain, let them marry, for it is better to marry than to burn.'

Daily, I walked the wooden battlements along the top of the stockade. I did so for a certain sight. It brought me out in all weathers; from the snowstorms that blinded me to the calm, crystal clear days on which I could almost distinguish the separate frost particles on the farthermost roofs.

At my feet lay Straumsvik: a score or so of buildings scattered within a fortified oval. But to me the colony was one particular house. It was near the centre, and it belonged to me. I had been sent there with Otsego at the proper time. And as I looked, I saw myself within, cradled beneath her. I thought of the simmering discontent she had sucked out of me.

Even now, through the veil of years, I can feel the tingling of the passion that welled up. It was a magnificent initiation into the rites of the flesh.

I make no pretence; it was at the shrine of pure physical love that I worshipped. And Otsego was an incomparable priestess. She was every inch a woman. She was voluptuous, sweet, comforting, yet animal-like and cruel as a lash. She was a creature of fire and water. She seared me like a burning flame; she soothed me like a running brook. She roused in me sensation so potent, it seemed to escape from the body and approach the spirit. In her I hovered between carnal pleasure and a mystic ecstasy of the soul.

What; am I wrong? Is this sacrilege? Is it really heresy to believe that one way to salvation lies through a woman? Surely it is at least a path away from hell. In thinking so I am in good company. 'Glorify God in your body' says St Paul.

And in Otsego I discovered what that meant. In her, I saw how the Two could become One. Sometimes the happy pain was almost too great to bear. But always she stopped when passion for the moment was spent; she satisfied me always, demanded never, and instinctively knew when she was needed again. I loved and was at peace, the hunger for warmth assuaged. So I walked the battlements that winter, and contemplated the field of my contentment. I knew I would never be able to enjoy another woman like Otsego again.

XXX

SCOLVESSEN had prophesied that Deganawida and I would have much to talk about. And that singular being did indeed appropriate my company to discuss European affairs.

'You wonder how a barbarian can possibly have such civilized interests,' he said at the beginning, with that enjoyment of another person's discomfiture which was recognizably Florentine, or should I say Italian? 'But if one may cross the Atlantic from east to west, why may another not do so in the opposite direction?'

Deganawida called himself a Mohawk. 'That means I belong to the leading nation on the western mainland. It sounds like boasting, I know; but it happens to be the simple truth. And it explains everything - or nearly everything.'

His story was a strange one; and yet listening to him was often uncannily like listening to an echo of myself.

'One of my earliest memories is the arrival of the first European ship.' He was forty-three when he said this. He was talking about the first Straumsvik vessel to penetrate the waterways of the hinterland.

Deganawida came from Stadacona. Until he started talking, it had been no more than a name to me, the mysterious destination of Scolvessen's overdue ships. Now I began to fit a picture to the word.

Stadacona was a town on a river called the Ganowägen. It lay about three hundred miles from the mouth, which is at the head of Straumsfjord. The place is also called Kebec, which is Mohawk for 'the river narrows here.'

It was when Deganawida was a tiny child that the Straumsvik navigators reached the far end of Straumsfjord; and found that it was more a gulf than a fjord, and discovered the mighty river flowing in from the West. The ship that he remembered had been commanded by a man called Guttorm Mattiasen, a distant relative of Scolvessen's.

Guttorm was the first European to sail up the Ganowägen, and he was the first whom the Mohawks had seen. He made a tremendous impression on Deganawida – as Scolvessen on me.

Guttorm left after a little while, but he returned the following year, and the arrival of the Straumsvik fleet became a regular event in the Mohawk calendar. For Guttorm had discovered a fur trade richer even than that of Terra Nova.

Deganawida's father was a tribal chief, and most business went through him. The Norwegians were in and out of his house. Deganawida became great friends with Guttorm and, over the years, picked up Norwegian in the mysterious way that a child learns without formal teaching.

His father had by now decided that it was essential for Deganawida, as his probable successor, to understand the colonists thoroughly. At the age of thirteen, he was sent with Guttorm to Straumsvik. In that distant and unprepossessing outpost of Christendom he received the foundation of a first class education.

There was then at Straumsvik a priest, the last before me. He was a Carmelite called Ivar Nielsen. He was clearly a remarkable teacher. He taught Deganawida, the unlettered native of a savage land, how to read and write; he taught him Norwegian, Latin, arithmetic and a little German.

But the most profound lesson that Father Ivar had to teach, was something of another kind. He planted in the impressionable mind of the growing Deganawida a fervid desire to see Europe.

Odd it is that two people on opposite sides of the ocean should be overcome by the same craving to see the other shore, and owe it to similar men. Father Ivar, in his own way, must have been a kind of Brother Niccolò; a traveller born, with the gift of inspiring those whom he taught.

In the end, he could stand it no longer; he asked his father to send him to Europe. His father agreed. They had long discussed the Norwegian connection; they deduced that there must be others, besides the Straumsvik colonists, who were capable of reaching Stadacona. It was probably only a matter of time before they did. There was no guarantee that they would be as easy to deal with as the Norwegians. It might be prudent to visit their homelands, so as to learn how to deal with them when they eventually came.

Guttorm approved, because he saw a means of preparing

Stadacona to repel future trading rivals. He undertook to make all the necessary arrangements. And so, at the end of that summer, Deganawida sailed for Europe in one of the Norwegian ships.

He reached Bergen in October 1455, barely eighteen years old. He spent the winter acclimatizing; not all the eloquence of Father Ivar could prepare him for the shocks of an alien world. By the spring, he was ready. He sailed for Lübeck, and his European tour really began. He spent a week here; a month there. Bruges, London, Paris, Augsburg, Prague, Venice and Milan passed rapidly under his review. He had to wheedle safe conducts out of surly Royal agents; he had to evade wars and flee from brigands. He was martyred by appalling roads. He was fleeced by inn-keepers everywhere. But why dwell on the minutae of European travel? After two or three years of this sort of thing, he finally reached Florence, more or less in a state of exhaustion. And there, he decided to stay.

He remained for six years. 'They were the best years of my life,' he once said: 'It was when I was transformed from a semi-literate savage into an approximation of a civilized human being!'

XXXI

CHRISTMAS came and the New Year went. I seemed to spend an unconscionable time arguing with Deganawida. At Stadacona, he was deprived of civilized company. He had taken all the trouble, he said, to undergo a not untrying voyage of near a thousand miles in order to spend the winter among people with whom he could converse.

This was true, but not quite the truth. It was characteristic of the atmosphere at Straumsvik that I had to wait for the real explanation of Deganawida's presence to emerge. He had come to discuss the future; more precisely the putative arrival of the Europeans in force at the narrows of Kebec. He wanted to know when: he thirsted after news from Europe and I was providentially there, to give news from the source. The interest Deganawida showed on meeting me was assuredly unfeigned.

'I find it significant, that you should be interested in such matters,' he remarked at the outset. 'If someone of your background is drawn to exploration, then it must, somehow, be in the air. No - don't take it amiss. I didn't mean to be rude. But you see, you aren't really the kind of person one would normally expect to take an interest in exploration. You haven't been to university, and you aren't really a professional deep-water sailor. By your own account, you've simply absorbed what has been said around you. I don't believe that Jón's tale would have passed beyond a childhood game, unless the circumstances were correct.'

I could not take umbrage because it was only what I had to admit to myself. I really was only one among many, although I have too often deluded myself that I was unique.

On that account, I was not quite at ease in Deganawida's company. He was friendly and talkative, but there lurked in the background some kind of uneasiness, or a tinge of menace. I was to him the personification of something he had noticed in Europe; a harbinger perhaps of trouble and discontent.

'In Florence,' he once said, 'I met a man called Paolo Toscanelli. He called himself a geographer. He had never stirred from Tuscany; he hardly left his study, but he knew all there was to know about geography, or so it seemed. He had conceived a burning interest in the Atlantic. He had even constructed a map, which he showed me with simpering pride.

'It was that map which brought home the danger so vividly. It was not that it was particularly authentic. In fact, it was a wild farrago of imaginary islands on the other side of the Atlantic. He had been listening to travellers' tales. It's odd how great learning often goes with great gullibility. And that was the frightening thing, you see.

'If a Florentine, a theoretician, an academic mediocrity, a landlubber who had never seen the sea, had gone to all the trouble of producing this amazing figment of the imagination, what then was in the minds of those who could actually sail? Now I saw proof of a suspicion that had begun to trouble me. It was that the Europeans would burst across the ocean sooner than I had thought. It wasn't just the Portuguese voyages along the coast of Africa - it was a kind of universal restlessness. Wherever I had been in Europe, I had observed it. I felt some invincible spirit moving over the Europeans. You could feel it among the English, who at the time could think of nothing better to do than smash each others' skulls in a messy civil war. You could feel it in the frenzied learning in Italy. Everywhere, I found energy, ambition and, this is the heart of the matter, *curiosity*.

'When I thought of my own people, they were placid, easily satisfied, and absolutely without curiosity. The next hill was the limit of their world. As far as they were concerned, what they could not see did not exist.

'But with the Europeans - ah, that was different. They were eaten up with curiosity. Curiosity had got them where they were; curiosity would drive them across the ocean, and give them the world. I had sensed all this, but it took Toscanelli's map to bring it home to me.

'It was Toscanelli, you see, who sent me home. Before I met him, I had settled down too well.

'I didn't want to go back. I had been seduced by civilization; I had half forgotten that I had come to Europe to help my own nation. Florence was so much pleasanter than Stadacona. I preferred silks to hides, stone houses to bark cabins, and stuffed partridge *al Toscana* to half cooked char *al natura*. And women - my dear fellow, at home I was just one of a crowd, with an occasional chance of worming my way into some mediocre sleeping rug, but in Florence - I was king. I was foreign, I was exotic. Women slobbered over me; I was supposed to be so *wild*. Think of it; I was spending my days doing my best to become civilized - and my nights profiting by my wildness. I found my way to some rather distinguished beds.

'Probably my choice of disguise helped me. Obviously my appearance was so foreign that I had to be prepared for questions as to my origin. The truth was clearly undesirable, so I had to contrive a plausible fiction. On the advice of Father Ivar, I pretended to be a Tartar. It was a clever choice, since it made me come from a place whose existence was accepted, but which few had visited. It was also a happy choice, since there was at the time - when is there not? - a fascination with things from the East.

'I was enjoying Florentine life, but at the same time, I could not get rid of a certain twinge of discontent. I didn't seem to be getting anywhere. I would never rise to the top of the tree. You had to be Florentine for that. I had become so far acclimatized so as to discover ambition, but not so far as to find the means to satisfy it. And I wanted to be at the top. "*Aut Caesar, aut nihil*", as I perhaps over-dramatically chanted occasionally to myself. I began to realize that only among my own Mohawks was I likely to live up to that inspiring maxim.

'The encounter with Toscanelli was the turning point. It showed me that there was less time than I had so blithely assumed. The spirit was pressing; the European invasion was closer than I thought. Self-reproach began to afflict me. My place – forgive the pomposity – was with my people.

'I rounded off my European stay by visiting Rome (and that was a disappointment) Provence, Spain and Portugal. I spent two years doing so. I learned Portuguese, Castilian and Catalan. And then, my studies, as I thought, completed, I returned home. It is an amusing thought that I had less trouble getting from Bergen to Kebeck than from Perpignan to Barcelona, although it is twenty times the distance. Europe, you know, is not uniformly tamed.

'I returned to Stadacona twelve years ago. It was the autumn of 1463. I had been away over ten years.'

We were on the Straumsvik battlements when he said this; we had a habit of strolling there to talk. I thought, as I had often done before, how happy must be the lot of a ruler in a country such as this. He ruled with an absoluteness impossible on the other side of the ocean. I suggested to Deganawida that he must have been happy to return.

He thought some time before replying:

'I enjoyed myself immensely in Florence,' he said. 'And I learned more than I can ever explain. I owe what I am to the city. It taught me one great lesson – perhaps the most important of my life – the discovery of *myself*. I seemed to be an individual, not, as I had been brought up to believe, a member of a family, a clan or a tribe.

'To you, this won't seem extraordinary at all – I daresay, until I mentioned it, you never even considered the matter. It's part of you; something taken for granted; something so intimate, you would have difficulty in identifying it.

'But to me, it was a revelation. The world seemed to have been turned upside town. I seemed to be brought face to face with new powers in myself, of which I had been totally unaware. I think I was a little drunk with the discovery.'

Until this point, Deganawida had related his European experience with an air of amused detachment. But now there crept into his voice a hint of passion.

'I looked into myself and I discovered ambition. And that will show you how thoroughly Florentine I had become. I had discovered personal ambition; that bitter-sweet consuming fever of the soul. I felt confined; as if there wasn't space enough in the world for me.

'By logical stages it drove me to the study which eventually became breath of life to me. I mean the business of ruling: some call it politics.

'And Florence under old Cosimo de Medici was the finest conceivable school in that subject. How he could rule! He played on human frailties with the sure touch of a musician familiar with his instrument. How I admired him; more than that, I envied him.

'And that was one of the reasons; perhaps the real reason why I finally went home. I had discovered I was a political animal. I wanted to be another Cosimo de Medici. And only among my own barbaric tribesmen could I be so. Let me at least be candid; it was ambition quite as much as fellow-feeling that brought me back.'

He was put to the test from the start. He found his father worn, aged and deposed. He had lost the right of succession. He very quickly rectified the situation. He took his rightful place as ruler of Stadacona. Within a year he was chief of the Mohawks.

It was a polished, bloodless conquest; very different from the crude violence of the Mohawk past. It had been accomplished by intrigue, cunning and playing on human weakness.

'I seemed,' he said, 'to have been raised above the obtuse creatures who made up the rabble called my tribe. I was almost frightened at the ease with which I had succeeded.

'I look upon myself as a Medici among the barbarians. I seem to have achieved some of the ambitions that were goading me in Florence.'

XXXII

FASCINATING it was in the beginning to hear Deganawida; the visitor from another world who had moved unnoticed through Christendom; echo of myself in *terra incognita*. But in the closed company of an isolated camp, thrown on the same few companions day after day, I grew restless, and impatient; overwhelmed by unexpected antipathies. There were times when Deganawida irritated me ungovernably with his appetite for conversation. The winter seemed to be dissolving into a dream-world of everlasting talk.

It was our custom to take our meals at Scolvessen's house, and one night, seeing him and Deganawida happily involved in a conversation of their own, I seized the opportunity to leave early. I called Otsego, and we went home, immediately going to bed. I had not yet overcome the animal novelty of entering a woman.

I woke unnaturally from a deep sleep. A light was burning, and the figure of a man was standing at the end of the bed. The mists of returning consciousness cleared, and I picked out a black mane on a shaven skull and eyes sunk above strange high cheekbones. It was Deganawida. Recognition did nothing to allay the uneasiness welling up within me. He lived with Scolvessen: he was an intruder here.

There was a wild look about him. I picked out the sickly-sour smell of berry wine. He had been drinking, and I knew by his own account that he could not stand much. I have a horror of drunkards, and fear mounted upon the gloom of interrupted sleep.

Deganawida stood still and silent like a statue; when he saw that I was awake, he spoke:

'What have I been dreaming?'

Now reason faltered. Answer died on the tongue.

'What have I been dreaming?'

His voice, at first low, controlled, was louder at the repetition. Otsego now stirred beside me, waking from her sleep. Deganawida spoke a few words sharply to her, in his own language.

Without a murmur, she left the bed, flung her dress over her nakedness, moved over to the fire, fed it and stoked it and when the embers flamed, she sat down in a corner impassively to watch.

Again the droning voice with its lurking native guttural invading the Florentine.

'What have I been dreaming?'

What did Deganawida want? Was this conundrum a price upon my head?

I saw no weapon in the half-gloom, but I supposed he was armed. I was helpless; he standing, poised for a blow, as I thought; I still lying down, frozen in naked fear, afraid that the least movement would provoke him.

Again the question, like a black litany. And now memory began to stir, pushing aside the curtains of dismay.

'You have been dreaming of a meal of human flesh.'

I could hardly speak above a whisper; and Deganawida could not at first make out the words. At last I managed to make him understand.

'Thank God!' he cried.

The recollection of a particular conversation had mercifully come to my succour. Deganawida had been brought up in the religion of dreams. They were supposed to mean calamity, and worst were those of eating human flesh. Somehow, fear had given me the strength to recall this, and deduce that it probably explained his agitation.

To prevent danger, the dream had to be guessed by an outsider. It then had to be acted out. It would be enough to offer a victim, who would then be refused and a symbolic meal eaten in his place.

'A Mass!' Deganawida cried, 'for God's sake, a Mass!'

Still shaking with fear, I rose and dressed hurriedly. We left the house, and went over to the church, walking in silence broken only by the creak of our footsteps on deeply frosted snow, self-glimmering under starless clouds.

And in that dark night, I celebrated a Mass for the solitary Deganawida. As I consecrated the Host, I heard a movement behind me. I turned sharply, fearing Heaven knows what. Deganawida was advancing; without a word he strode up to the altar, seized the wafer and crammed it into his mouth.

Without a word, he returned to where he had been standing. After I had finished the office, he said:

'The body and blood . . . *that* killed the dream.'

We returned to my house. Otsego was still sitting bolt upright in the corner where we had left her. Of sleep, there was now no question.

'Sacrilege?' Deganawida said as I tried to pacify my thoughts. 'No. I don't believe it.

'Is the Eucharist for the priest alone? Is the body and blood of Our Lord not for *my* comfort as well?

'Ah, the comfort of a ritual in which you can even half believe. And God knows, I need comfort. I am divided against myself. I don't know whether I am what I was born or what I have become. Am I a Mohawk or a Florentine? I wish to God I knew. There seem to be two people inside me - fighting, always fighting. Sometimes I feel as if I'm being torn apart. And the dreams! But to eat the Host; that drives away the last vestiges of criminal desire.'

There was a frightful silence; I could not trust myself to speak; and then Deganawida began again:

'Well, the devils have been driven out - for this time. Now listen carefully to me.

'You must by now have grasped that something urgent has made me come here. I have got to unite the tribes of the mainland. It's the only way of fighting off the explorers. But it's taking longer than I thought. I shall not be ready for the Europeans for at least ten years yet. And I am afraid that I have no time. It's preying on my mind; I am convinced they are already on their way. I have come to discover whether they are. Now tell me the truth: *who has sent you?*'

Something in his voice conveyed a dark undertone to the question; and a hint of panic. I had to make him believe every word I was about to utter; it was almost as if I was arguing for my life. I had no doubt that he had really undergone that dream; but I was equally in no doubt that the events of that awful night had their roots in what we were discussing now. Deganawida was still a heathen; he was ruled by superstition; he was unpredictable. One false step, and God knows what I would precipitate.

Gently then, as if pacifying a madman or an idiot, I presented my case with all the simplicity and persuasion of which I was capable. One thing was certain; I had to convince him that I had come on my own; that I owed nothing to any master. The words poured out; but the argument seemed to make no headway. In a kind of despair, I ended by saying:

'You want to keep the intruders out. But don't you understand that, whatever you do, the discoverers will come sooner or later. It would be far better, for your own sake, if the first were led by friends, instead of enemies or even strangers.

'You want to be unmolested as long as possible; well and good. But it is no use trying to stem the tide; you must divert it. It is no use fighting the Europeans; you must send them somewhere else.

'The first expeditions must be kept away. If I am in charge, I could lead them elsewhere. I could take them southwards. I could make sure that they missed your waters at the start. It would give you all the extra time you need.'

Deganawida stared at me unblinkingly. He did not reply immediately; he sat immobile while the firelight played upon him, turning him into the likeness of a brazen image. He seemed to be making up his mind. Then he said, speaking very slowly:

'Yes; you argue well. You are right. "Kick not against the pricks". You must be sent back - to keep the others away.'

Without another word, he left abruptly, and I was once more alone, with Otsego staring impassively before her.

XXXIII

DEGANAWIDA never once referred to what had passed between us; I could not decide whether he had been possessed by wine or some obscure devil, and something stopped my revealing to Scolvessen what had happened.

Otsego, although she offered no explanation, protected me from the worst anxiety with the warm cradle of woman-flesh. That almost persuaded me that nothing was the matter, and the aftermath of that eerie night dwindled to a vague sense of uneasiness that only occasionally troubled me. But it could not be entirely banished; and it was always there, lurking in the background, a new ingredient of my thoughts.

But superficially, life in the colony took its usual course. As before, there was little for me to do. I said the regular offices, but not much more besides. The colonists showed a disinclination to be born, to die or to marry. I now spoke a little Norwegian, but they were not particularly talkative – at least to me. I whiled away some of the time by taking astronomical observations and mapping the harbour – but it was too cold to find much pleasure in either.

All that remained was discussion with Scolvessen and Deganawida. We talked about the hinterland. I learned that beyond Stadacona the country rolled on westwards without end. First there were great lakes like inland seas, and then plains and then mountains. But most was hearsay and legend.

'You see,' Deganawida said, 'I am not Europeanized enough to care passionately about what lies beyond what I can see, or at least control. What concerns me are the people along my frontiers. I can tell you that my territory is bounded on the south by the Conestaga, on the east by the Algonkins, and on the west by the Hurons, the Ottawas, and a rather unpleasant crowd called the Ojibwas. My curiosity really doesn't go much farther.'

Scolvessen suggested that the Ganowägen was so big that it must rise in a huge country. Was it part of Asia? He thought not because, if it were, Indians would have been met with long ago. Deganawida believed it was, because the map he had seen in Florence showed the eastern extremity of Asia on the western side of the Atlantic. Both agreed that the desirable parts, that is to say Calicut, Canton, Hang-chow, Taprobane, Chipango, the rich ports of the East, must be thousands of miles away. We were probably as far from the fleshpots of Asia as if we had been in Genoa.

Our conversation now took another turn; again as if something had changed. We talked incessantly about how to organize Deganawida's empire. I joined in. One always knows how to improve the world; it is not always that one has the opportunity to do so.

'All those comings and goings among your Doges,' said Deganawida, on one occasion, after I had gone into the intricacies of Genoese politics. 'I must see that my people don't fall into *that* trap. We must have permanence among our rulers. No faction - no politics - stability shall be our watchword.'

We talked much about religion. Deganawida was fascinated by it. I found myself in an incomparable situation. I was a missionary to the heathen, with a whole world to convert. I pressed Deganawida to bring his Empire into the Church.

But that, he was unwilling to do.

'It's not that I disapprove of it,' he said. 'Father Ivar grounded me well in the Faith. And in my European days, I was observant beyond reproach. I found it a great comfort. But it doesn't hold here. I know my people; it won't do for them.'

I found this rather shocking, of course. I tried to persuade him that the Church held everywhere and for everyone.

'Wasn't there once a churchman,' said Deganawida, 'who proved that other continents couldn't be inhabited, because Adam and Eve could not have populated them? I fail to see how the Church can hold for people who, by definition, do not exist?'

That was good for a protracted argument of which, I hate to admit, I did not get the best. I did not, to be quite candid, try very hard. For I must confess, that *under those circumstances*, this lack of enthusiasm for the Church spoke to something in me. Deganawida was deeply interested in the Catharism I had revealed on the day of his arrival. And I expounded all I knew; turning on the instant from priest to heretic. But I was driven by conflict. I hated myself for treason to the Church; but I was proud of discoursing on that for which my forefathers had suffered. I felt, in a strange way, as if I were keeping faith after all.

'You may wonder,' Deganawida said, 'why I am so interested in your peculiar creed. Well, man does not live by bread alone, and unless I manage to introduce some regenerative religion, and see that it takes root, I rather fear my work will be in vain. Without goads for the spirit, men can't sustain their efforts. If you don't believe, you can't accomplish.

'But I am not so foolish as to believe that a faith can be transplanted. I don't suppose that orthodox Christianity would necessarily suit my people. On the other hand, there is something to be said for a heresy. Your Catharism has certain sides which ought to make it easy for the Mohawks to absorb.'

He was referring to the concept of a good and evil spirit, mutually hostile, dividing the Universe between them.

'It would be too much,' he said, 'to expect my simple tribesmen to grasp the subtleties of a God who is both good and omnipotent, but who nevertheless tolerates the existence of pain and evil. The Cathar view at least has this merit, that it fits the facts without forced explanations.'

How could I object? It was not an issue about which I had thought much, but now that it had been raised, I found myself unable to argue the Catholic view with conviction; Deganawida half-persuaded me that the faith of my fathers was the correct one. At least he convinced me that it was preferable for his people.

XXXIV

TIME passed; the month of March arrived. In Genoa, spring would be on the way; here the ships still lay useless under their covers on the shore. The harbour was still frozen solid. Straumsfjord remained a mighty field of glinting ice, swept incessantly by bitter storms that came whining from out of the north. Winter seemed to have no end.

I was haunted by a sense of impatience and disquiet. The colony began to feel like a prison. I longed for the sight of a fresh face.

I developed an aversion for what society there was. I took to going for long walks in order to get away from my companions. I was, however, not quite alone. I was accompanied by a dog; a huge black furry beast called Sam, belonging to Scolvessen. He had attached himself to me, almost as if he too, bored by the old familiar faces, was delighted to have found a new one.

We often sought the seclusion of the forest. But on our way

there one morning, Sam suddenly stopped dead in his tracks, growling tensely, his body stiffening in every fibre. The cause of his distress appeared to be something in the snow half hidden by the trees.

I walked forward to look closely, but the dog refused to follow. It was a man. He was lying on his face. Three arrows were embedded in his back.

I bent over to examine him. He was one of the colonists. As far as I could see, he was dead. I was rooted to the spot, staring uncomprehendingly. I was roused by the dog's insistent protests. He was now barking and whining; something of his urgency communicated itself to me. With a shock, I realized that if one man could be killed there, so could another.

I withdrew precipitately, hurrying back to the safety of the stockade, and hastened to report what I had seen. Scolvessen at first was disinclined to take me seriously, suggesting that I must have allowed my imagination to run away with me. But Deganawida, who had been observing Sam's behaviour, said drily that the dog appeared to have been imagining things too. After a brief altercation, they both returned with me to investigate.

Confronted with solid evidence, Scolvessen had the grace to apologize. He agreed that the man was dead. He had seen him alive and well only a few hours before. I suggested we postpone further discussion until we had retired beyond bowshot. Compliance was instant; almost comically so.

Collecting a patrol, Scolvessen immediately set off to track down the intruders. I watched them disappear into the forest. I waited all afternoon on the ramparts. At dusk I saw them return. Four figures straggled in across the snow. Six had gone out.

Scolvessen was among the four. His tale was short and unequivocal. He had stumbled into a Beothuk ambush and escaped by the skin of his teeth.

He was in a terrible state of despondency, which I put down to his having lost two of his best men. But when I tried to commiserate with him, he cut me short.

'That doesn't matter,' he said savagely, 'the casualties don't matter. The point is - the Beothuks have attacked - that's the whole point. It's never happened before. And it's the first time they've ever come back so early in the year. Don't you realize what that means? It means a deliberate, malicious plan to catch us unawares. The Beothuks have turned against us.

'We can't work among enemies. Our whole existence depends upon peace. And now we're faced with war.

'It's absolutely futile. We can't win. All we can look forward to is a battle just to survive. And there can only be one result: we'll go under. The Beothuk trade is finished. What's left then? The sole justification for the colony is trade; take that away, and what's left? - a military outpost, and that isn't worth hanging on to. It's the end of Straumsvik. There's nothing left to fight for.'

And Scolvessen, the old Guardsman, the commander of Straumsvik, the descendant of generations of warriors, was unmanned. He succumbed to the collapse of all his hopes, and lost the capacity to act.

In this emergency, Deganawida took command. I do not mean that he literally deposed Scolvessen, but he told him what orders to give. And Scolvessen unresistingly obeyed. There was something impressive about the Mohawk; he seemed endowed with a natural authority.

It was fortunate that he was there to act. The state of Straumsvik was a monument to criminal unconcern. Because the Beothuks had never been known to return so early, it had been assumed that they never would. During the winter, the defences had been neglected. Not even a proper lookout had been kept. Had it not been for Sam - 'that noble beast' as Deganawida called him - we might have had no inkling of disaster until it was upon us. There was no time to be lost. The Beothuks could not be so far off; and the settlement was in no condition to sustain an attack. Through Scolvessen, Deganawida set all of us, men, women and children, to repairing the deficiency. There was sleep for none; we worked through the night, under the fluttering flames of crude pine pitch torches. I was overcome by a sense of the forlorn to see the dark line of the forest against the night sky, and the silent fields of snow around the stockade. Terra Nova had turned from a wonderful discovery into a desolate, alien, hostile land.

Our main care was the protection of the ships. The founders of Straumsvik had had the foresight to arrange things so that they were drawn up for the winter within the settlement's fortifications. But the gap in the stockade through which the vessels were moved had been left open, because peace in the cold season had unquestioningly been assumed. Now it had to be closed. Theoretically, it was not difficult. Baulks had been cut and stacked ready for use; sockets had been dug in the ground. All that was necessary was to assemble the missing sections.

Unfortunately nobody had thought of keeping the sockets cleared, and now they were filled with snow and ice. They all had to be hacked clear. It took until dawn to finish the tedious work and close the gap.

With conventional preparation I expected conventional results. I assumed we were preparing for an orthodox assault. I imagined war as it is usually understood; the meeting of more or less disciplined men in an ordered clash of arms. The reality turned out to be rather different.

We were faced with an invisible enemy. In the forest he lurked, unseen, except by signs known to the initiated; a distant wisp of smoke above the trees; the circling of birds, the cries of small animals disturbed. He seemed in no hurry to attack; content to wear us out by waiting.

Night was the worst for us. The Beothuks were lords of the dark. They moved where they wanted. We could hear them prowling about outside the stockade. We lived in constant fear of being overwhelmed by a nocturnal onslaught.

But the original shock of discovering the Beothuk perfidy had passed away. We had before us a comprehensible, limited task: to hold out until the summer. And Scolvessen, now faced with the problems of sustaining a siege and the details of everyday military routine, ceased to brood on the future. He had recovered his self-possession, and was in command again.

I persuaded him one night to use artillery to frighten off the marauders. Straumsvik had about half a dozen small cannon. These were loaded with pebbles, trained at various points round the perimeter, and duly fired. The roars and flashes were suitably impressive, but I suspect that the hiss of the thousands of little projectiles through the air must have been even more impressive to those in front of the cannon's mouth.

The performance was repeated on succeeding nights and the Beothuks trod more warily than before. They kept away from the stockade, even during darkness now. So a random cannonade became a nightly ritual. I was modestly proud of my achievement.

'It won't do us much good, you know,' Scolvessen said.

In my innocence, I could not immediately fathom his attitude. Had we not discovered how to ward off a threat to our survival?

'Our weapons were supposed to deter. Now that they've been used, they've failed.'

XXXV

But, for the moment at least, our enemies still respected our superiority in arms; they showed no desire to match arrows against gunpowder. We were tolerably secure from massed attacks. Nor were we in danger of starvation. Winter in this country was a state of siege anyway; it was only a matter of contending with assailants of a different identity. Even without the Beothuks, food had been laid up as a matter of course; there was hay in the barns, the cattle were indoors and in safety.

But we nonetheless lived in constant uncertainty and fear. It was impossible to forget for one moment how we were ludicrously outnumbered. We were burdened by the realization that survival depended on the preservation of a brittle stalemate. Our territory extended as far as cannon range; say three hundred yards. The Beothuks were the undisputed masters of the forest. There they lurked, always out of sight, but always present; we held sway at sea alone.

Even that was to be an empty consolation for some time yet. I found the dead man at the beginning of March; the ice would not break up sufficiently for navigation until May at the earliest. Until then we would quite simply have to wait. I suffered from inaction and suspense, the twin tortures which my temperament is least able to stand. My existence was reduced to intoning a weekly Office to indifferent worshippers, and standing endless watches - for now we were on guard every minute of the day and night.

Otsego often kept me company in the watchtower on the bluff. She was pregnant now, and between us there had sprung up an animal affection. Towards the end of my watch one day in April, when it had been snowing with large, wet, heavy flakes, the weather lifted, and, for the first time since winter came, I saw, far out in Straumsfjord, the dark line of an open channel in the ice. It was the first sign of spring. Otsego then said something about our both going to live in Stadacona when the ice had melted.

Now we communicated by signs, rudimentary Catalan and even more rudimentary Huron. It was a charming, but necessarily limited medley, and we were prone to sometimes hilarious misunderstanding. On this occasion, I assumed that she had not made herself clear - or perhaps she had indulged in wishful thinking, since by now she was pregnant. But when I mentioned the matter to Scolvessen, he was oddly evasive.

I had to retire with doubts that fed upon each other. They converged into one obsessive fear; that I was going to be kept behind against my will.

A barrier had sprung up between Scolvessen and myself, so that I could not tax him with my suspicion. In the end I turned to Deganawida: since the events of that eerie night early in the winter had left a bond of unspoken, mutual confidence.

'This really is most unfortunate,' Deganawida said. 'I've told Scolvessen he must be open and above board. As he won't tell you, I will. You've got a perfect right to know. Our friend has decided to abandon Straumsvik. He is going to make his home in Stadacona. He intends taking all his followers - willy nilly. He thinks the thing is best managed by secrecy. I don't. And that's how matters stand.'

Although this was only confirming what I half suspected, I was nonetheless appalled. Scolvessen had promised to get me back to Europe; now he was preparing to go back on his word. I gave free rein to indignation; I may have overdone it. Deganawida heard me patiently to the end. Then he said:

'You must realize that Scolvessen is a very bitter man. He has taken the Beothuk affair hard. And, as you have had ample opportunity to learn, he is obsessed with the arrival of European discoverers. He thinks that if he prevents the return of anyone here, he will be safe.'

'But that's nonsense. I thought we'd settled that. Surely we agreed that it would be far better if you deliberately sent me back to lead the first expedition in a different direction.'

'Of course. That's precisely what I'm trying to hammer into the man. But you've no idea how pig-headed he's become. He's quite irrational.

'You're unhappy about the prospect of remaining. What about the others who came out with you? Some of them are native born Norwegians who're also anxious to return home. You'll have to be kept by force. Either you'll mutiny before we leave, or you'll cause trouble when you get to Stadacona. Either would be unpleasant. I certainly want no seeds of insurrection sown among my people. As for killing you off; I won't stand for that.

'So you see, I haven't changed my mind. Leave it to me; everything will turn out all right.'

XXXVI

IN spite of Deganawida's assurance, suspense dragged on. It had still not been resolved when, one morning early in May, I watched the covers being taken off the ships.

It was done with a curious reverence like a religious ceremony; almost a ritual greeting to spring. And, indeed, as the hulls emerged into daylight, they seemed as if they were being resurrected from a coma of the dark season, and they stirred sympathetic feelings within me. I, too, felt as if I were waking from a winter sleep. I left the ships to the music of sailors preparing their vessels for the sea. The acrid fumes of boiling pine pitch, the familiar incense of a living ship, filled my nostrils, relieving for a moment the oppression of the siege, and the uncertainties of the future, but immediately afterwards causing my interrupted gloom to return with almost intolerable force, because the promise of departure now held out did not necessarily mean escape. I returned to my house in a very bleak mood.

I found Scolvessen waiting for me.

'Do you think,' he said, as soon as I entered the door, 'that you could bring a ship back to Europe?'

It took a while for the implications of the question to sink in.

I responded by thanking him sarcastically for the favour of his visit. Even as I heard myself speak, I knew I was being churlish. But I felt a compulsion to hide the relief that seized me at his words; as if there were a danger of provoking him to change his mind.

'No, we've not seen as much of each other lately as we should have,' he said blandly. 'I've had so much to think of. Well, I seem to have put the cart before the horse. Let me explain.' And he told me substantially what I had already learned from Deganawida; how he had decided to make Stadacona his home, and never return to Norway.

'Of course some of you will want to go home; and a ship will naturally be made available. But unfortunately I can't spare the navigators. I need those I've got to sail to Greenland. I've got to send for some people living there; I can't leave them marooned. So you are, to put it bluntly, the only hope of those who want to go home. I suspect that you wouldn't relish the idea of staying here. Would you like to do the navigation? I think you know enough to cross the Atlantic.'

Not a word did he breathe of his original intentions. When I asked Deganawida about it afterwards, he said that 'it took some time to make our friend see reason. But when he did, he decided to put a good face on it, that's all.'

Of course, I accepted Scolvessen's offer. The task seemed well within my capabilities. It would simply be a matter of 'making our easting down,' along a certain parallel of latitude. And I knew my astrolabe well enough for that.

'I look to you,' Scolvessen had said, 'to keep us unmolested as long as possible.' Deganawida had done his work to perfection; as he himself said, Florence had taught him the art of advocacy.

With uncertainty removed, time no longer crawled. The ice became yellow with age and thaws; cracked and, bit by bit, drifted out to sea. The dark channel of open water spread across Straumsfjord, until only the innermost bays remained frozen.

I was now happily preoccupied with preparations for the voyage. I spent a great deal of my time copying into my notebooks what I needed from Scolvessen's 'Admiralty Pilot' for Terra Nova and the coast to the south. Without demur, he had given me persmission to do so; he was keeping to our original bargain. I almost forgave him for his spell of duplicity.

XXXVII

At last the day came when winter finally vanished. It all happened so very quickly. In the morning, the harbour was still frozen over, with no prospect of relief. Then the tide cracked the ice, it broke up, sailed out to sea like a fleet hurrying on its way, and by the afternoon the water was lapping the jetties. Straumsfjord was once more a dark, windswept mass of open water, broken only by scattered patches of old ice, like pancakes turned up at the edges, and icebergs drifting regularly by.

The icebergs, I was told, although I found it hard to believe, were the real signs of the reopening of the ocean. It meant the retreat of the pack ice, and it was the pack, unpredictable, insinuating, clinging, all enveloping that was the real danger; not the big isolated bergs, for they could be avoided.

Our retreat was now secured. The Beothuk threat also receded. As long as the ice held, they could, and did, occasionally make forays from the sea, but on open water they were helpless, and the harbour became an impregnable defence. The stockade facing the water was opened, and the ships were launched.

That same day, some of the colonists began making faggots with the firewood remaining from the winter, piling them against the stockade, and the buildings, including even the church.

'I'm not going to let those devils have a stick of it. They've turned on me; well and good, that's their privilege. They want their land back; but that's all they're going to have; the soil and no more. I shall destroy everything - everything. All they will have will be the ruins. If I could, I'd poison the meadows we've mown. Why should they enjoy what we've built up?'

Thus the lamentations of Scolvessen, as he watched the work of preparing Straumsvik for immolation. Now he had recovered some of his old decisiveness; he could not find rest until he had discovered why the Beothuks had acted as they did.

'How very European,' said Deganawida after one of these outbursts – for there were many more in the last days of Straumsvik than I have related – 'always torturing yourself with whys and wherefores, instead of simply accepting things as they are. Ah well, I suppose it's the dark side of curiosity; and without curiosity you wouldn't be Europeans: you'd be stick-in-the-mud, sordid, backward cisatlantic Mohawks and Beothuks.'

Scolvessen ignored this, as he now ignored the approaching departure. He left the preparations to his subordinates. He had decided to devote what time was left to solving the perplexity that tortured him. With a few chosen companions, he made reckless raids into the forest, until, three or four days before our appointed departure, he returned with two captives. One of them was Nonasabasut.

Now Scolvessen shut himself up in a disused house with the Beothuk chief. Nobody, least of all myself, was allowed to approach, and the final preparations for abandoning the colony had to proceed as best they could. All that day, and all through the night Scolvessen remained hidden with his prisoner. Then the following morning, the bulls belonging to the colony – five all told – were driven from their barns, and placed just outside one of the gates in the stockade. Nonasabasut was brought to join them. He had to be carried by the guards; he was clearly in distress and too weak to walk.

He was held upright, so that he could watch what was to happen. Four of the bulls were slaughtered, and their testicles cut off. He was then tied on to the back of the fifth one, whose legs had been lashed to stakes driven into the ground. The beast was then castrated under him, cut loose and driven off into the forest. And the other prisoner, who was apparently unharmed and had been forced to look on, was then freed. He followed the bellowing mutilated creature that carried his lord and master on its back.

XXXVIII

SCOLVESSEN said:

'I had to show Nonasabasut that I was leaving nothing for him. I could make him understand in no other way. At least he will grasp what I meant by the mutilation of the bulls.'

'But Heavens above!' cried Deganawida. 'Why this rigmarole when we had so much else to do? What a criminal waste of time.'

'I had to make him understand, don't you see? I had to. For my own satisfaction. I had to do so. I won't run away and let them think that I'm scuttling.'

I asked about the other prisoner.

'Oh him: so that there is somebody to tell the tale. Otherwise, what I did may be wasted. I'm not sure that Nonasabasut will be in a condition to talk.

'I wanted him to explain why he had turned against me. I was giving him the opportunity to tell me face to face what he thought of me. And he refused to speak. I tell you, he refused. So I tortured him - with my own hands - I tortured him, because I wanted to hear the truth. But he just stared in silence. It almost drove me mad.

'Well, I suppose he became my enemy because I didn't pay my debt in time. It's the only possible explanation - but I'll never know for certain. It must have been the promise - the broken promise.'

Deganawida answered:

'No, my friend. There was something else as well. Have you forgotten? The Beothuks are eaters of human flesh. When you turned them loose on the mariners you drove ashore, you were asking for trouble. You only eat a man to get his powers; well; the Beothuks felt themselves stronger than all Christians; so they were bound to turn on you sooner or later.

'I warned you this would happen, didn't I?'

There was a long silence, and then:

'Damn regrets, and excuses and recriminations,' said Scolvessen. 'We haven't come here for that.'

And suddenly he became his old practical and businesslike self again.

He deluged me with exhaustive instructions, both for the ocean crossing, and after. 'You must keep inquisitive explorers away from these waters. That is what I expect you to do. You must avoid my own dear King Christian. That ought not to be too difficult. He sits in Copenhagen, with continental preoccupations. Also keep away from the English; they are too familiar with northern waters as it is. They're impressive seamen; but ignorant navigators thank God. If ever a navigator gets among them, I'll be in deep trouble.'

No detail seemed to have escaped Scolvessen's attention. With my new responsibilities, it was a great comfort.

'But whatever you do,' he ended by saying, 'keep south on your own expedition. Keep well to the south.'

XXXIX

ON the day of departure, we were afoot long before dawn. The darkness was broken by the glow of scattered braziers, ready with fire for the end. For Straumsvik was to be burnt to the ground.

By daybreak, everybody, except for the rearguard, had embarked, and the ships moved out into the bay.

I had particularly asked to remain ashore for the final act of immolation. When the order was given, I set fire to the house where I had lived with Otsego, and the church where I had conducted my heterodox rituals. In both, I had known a kind of happiness, and I wanted my hands alone to send them to destruction. Had anyone else done so, it would have been a kind of desecration.

'A Viking chief's funeral must have been like this,' said Scolvessen as, waiting on the shore to be rowed out to the ships, we watched the flames take hold of the stockade and, fanned by a fresh breeze, grow into a curtain of fire, 'But then his servants would have been burned with him, a fair offering to Oblivion.

'I really ought to turn back and face my end with the colony. But I haven't the courage. Instead I stand here calmly, watching my life's work go up in flames. I've been tried on the balance and found wanting. It's taken this to show me that, after all, I'm a true child of my times.'

They were the last words he spoke to me.

We entered the waiting dinghies to row out to our ships, and I watched the final touches of destruction from the water. Straumsvik was to be picked clean, so that nothing would be left to those who had driven us away; they were to be offered desolation for a parting gift.

The cattle had been slaughtered; so too most of the dogs. The unwanted small boats - little masterpieces of the shipwright's craft, had been collected on shore, and were now burning on their own. The jetty alone could not be trusted to burn up. We had to wait while the rearguard completed the work of dismemberment. Prising and heaving, they sent the baulks rapidly tumbling into the water; in their feverish movements, they looked like fiends against the flames of Hell.

We were lucky to the last. The Beothuks kept out of sight, frightened by the fire, or perhaps by Nonasabasut's fate. The wind remained steadily in the north, so that the fire was held away from the ships.

At last it was all over. The rearguard rowed out. Straumsvik was now a woeful, blazing desolation. Of the jetty, nothing remained but the stone foundations upon which, so a vengeful fellow-fugitive suggested, Beothuk canoes might one day founder.

Our little fleet raised anchors, and slowly got under way. We kept company for a mile or two, until we were out of the harbour and beyond the bluff. Then *The Great Bear* swung northeast to make the open sea, and Scolvessen with his three ships turned north-west for the hinterland. Soon they disappeared behind a high promontory and all that remained of my winter's home was a pall of smoke above the land. The sight pursued me far out, tenacious reminder of the last moments ashore.

Deganawida's way of parting had been to say, flippantly, but with an undertone of wistfulness: 'You're going back to civilization; lucky man! Anyway - if you ever get to Florence, take a turn round the Piazza Signoria for me.'

As for Otsego, she put my hand on her belly, so that I could feel our child kicking in the womb. Without a word, she then gently pushed me away, turned and walked down to the vessel that was to take her to Stadacona. She never looked back.

'To every thing there is a season, and a time to every purpose under the heaven,' said the preacher: and if Otsego heard those, she would have understood. For our kind of love had to stop. She knew that her time was past; her rôle played out. And she saved me the futile pangs of an anguished farewell, a woman to the last. But I was heavy with lingering regret. She had rid me of the fear of women; she had taught me how to make love; I owed her more than I could ever repay. I knew that I would miss her, and in myself I carried a piece of her that would never leave me.

XL

WITH not too unfavourable winds, but bedevilled by a brutal succession of wayward icebergs, we followed the coast along which we had sailed before. But soon we left the familiar track of the outward voyage. We swung south-west round a cape which seemed to be the southern extremity of Terra Nova, turning our backs on Europe. For we were not going home just yet.

Scolvessen had said that first I was to find a southerly goal for a voyage of discovery, away from Terra Nova and the north. But I was not my own master. I was simply the navigator. The commander was a bo'sun called Sigurd Olavsen, promoted for the occasion. He had one outstanding quality. He was unswervingly loyal to his superiors. Scolvessen had told him that before heading back across the Atlantic, he was to sail south for sixty days. I could depend upon him to execute the order to the letter.

We had one mission before plunging southwards. We were to call at Newport on the way and search for the party that had failed to return the previous year.

Scolvessen's navigational instructions made that passage a romp, even although it was across waters totally unknown to me. We found the forty-second parallel, headed due west, raised the northwards-facing promontory of Cape Cod, which had been so graphically described for me, and then it was simply a matter of following the coast as it turned west. Towards noon of the tenth day after leaving Straumsvik, we raised a stone tower which I recognized easily from the descriptions as the landmark by which Newport was to be identified.

We turned to starboard, and slowly tacked against a fresh breeze into a shallow bay. I could see the tower quite clearly now; a round stone structure, built by Scolvessen's predecessors. Close to the shore, which was low, rocky and fronted by sandbanks, we found a wreck. It lay on its beam ends, a single mast fractured near the foot and resting crazily in the water like a branch of a fallen tree. It was unmistakably sister to *The Great Bear*, and Olavsen recognized it as the missing Straumsvik ship.

We anchored well out, and I went ashore with Olavsen and a few sailors. We were greeted by an anything but hospitable sight. A few charred remains showed where a house had stood before. The place had been picked clean; not an implement, not a human trace remained.

I had kept my promise. I had seen that Newport was abandoned. I did not feel called upon to investigate any further. My duty was to return safely to Europe.

Olavsen had the same views; if anything, he was even more anxious than I to leave. We remained just long enough to take on fresh water from a convenient stream and, long before the shadows began to lengthen, we were under way again.

We stood well out to sea, giving the offshore islands a wide berth, and avoiding the channels we had passed coming in. I had no wish to be ambushed.

So far, the country had scarcely proved to be hospitable. Beothuks, Mohawks and the attackers of Newport were clearly a ferocious breed. I could only hope for better things to the south.

XLI

Now came the real voyage of discovery. Newport was the last outpost of our own kind. The coast below existed only as scattered observations in Scolvessen's book of pilotage. As we sailed southwards and the land drifted past to starboard, the western contours of the Atlantic took shape under my very eyes.

I felt as if I were Gonçalves who had first crossed the Equator; but this was no imaginary line on the surface of the globe. It was greater than that. It was solid earth. It was what had been hidden from the sight of men. I was not the first to be led to it, but I seemed to have been chosen to reveal it to the world. Strange are the ways of the Lord.

But I could only look on the Promised Land. For days, weeks, we did not go ashore, because the coast was low, uninviting; sheathed in rain squalls, or dangerous to approach.

Olavsen kept a tally stick on which, every evening, he cut a notch for each of Scolvessen's sixty days as they passed. The tide of indentations inexorably mounted on the wood; time was running out; but I had not yet found what I sought. And then we were blown out to sea.

We were overtaken by a wind from the south-west against which there was no hope of beating. It was no ordinary gale. The sea was heaving in a way I had never known before, as if we were caught in the bowels of the deep.

Peculiar, low clouds overhung a sky from which all birds had suddenly disappeared, and the surface of the water became grey and oily. The chill of a terrible desolation came upon me.

Olavsen grimly predicted what he called a '*Havsgerding*'. I found it difficult to follow his explanations, but I grasped that it was some kind of extraordinary calamity involving both a storm and an earthquake.

It seemed somewhat far fetched, but I had little time to meditate on the subject, because strange things now began to happen. The wind mounted steadily until, screaming and tearing at the ship, it passed the worst flights of my imagination. It was as if the throat of Hell had opened. And, more frightening still, because I had never known the like, it blew not from one quarter, but shifted stealthily until it raged from the north-east.

'Praise God and hammer on.' There was no alternative but to drive before the storm. Slithering into the troughs of the waves, flung forward in the fuming crests, battered ever and anon by cross seas, the ship turned into a seaborne inferno. Green walls of water threatened constantly to engulf us; we were raked by torrents of spray. But why dilate on the horrors of those days? The miseries of a tempest are the same in all ages. It was all hands to the pumps and bailing buckets. In two hour watches, turn and turn about, we slaved to keep afloat.

By the end of the fourth day, the wave-mountains began to subside, and the unnatural wind to drop, leaving an ordinary north-easterly gale. The ship was showing signs of strain. We had lost a seaman, washed overboard. But I was grateful to the storm. It had blown us in the right direction; and without it, we would hardly have come so far.

We had been swept far to the south-west. We were still on an empty ocean, but I knew from Scolvessen's pilot book that the coast trended the same way and the birds, returning after the storm told that land was not far off.

But, shaken by what had happened, Olavsen wanted to turn tail now. I managed to persuade him to continue on our course since it would be prudent to go ashore soon and repair the ravages of the storm.

'Give me five days,' I said, 'and I will give you land.'

Ah, the authority of a learned man, and respect due to the clergy! Because Scolvessen had told them that I had mastered the secrets of navigation, because I still wore my full Franciscan habit, I was invested in the eyes of those simple mariners with the resources of profane learning and the infallibility of sacred office.

I had certainly not spoken in uninstructed hope. But my ideas were necessarily unclear. The unnatural dip of the Pole Star, the growing heat, announced the approach of the tropics; that was the only certainty. For the rest, everything depended on a guess of mine; I set a course to the west sou'west, and hoped that I had guessed correctly.

In the afternoon of the appointed fifth day, there was a cry from the lookout. Land. Or at least breakers ahead. And not too long afterwards, the line of a low island broke the horizon. A tortured eternity afterwards - the last mile is always the worst - we found our haven. It was a shallow, almost land-locked, bay.

'I promised you land,' I said to Olavsen, 'and I gave you land.'

But I was not quite as easy in my mind as I sounded. I seemed to have spoken with a tongue other than my own. I almost felt as if I had been possessed. The gift of prophecy, even in a small way, is not an entirely pleasant experience.

XLII

I seemed to have been cast up on one of the Fortunate Isles. There was no comparison with the harsh world of Straumsfjord. Ice was a bad memory. The sun burned brighter than those northern straits could ever know. The climate was like Andalucia, but less arid.

There was food and fresh water for the taking. The island was covered with luxuriant foliage. Birds and small animals abounded. Edible and nourishing fruit grew wild.

But fertility took strange forms. Nothing was quite what I was used to. The fruit looked, felt and tasted differently from anything I had known. The trees and their leaves were unfamiliar. The creatures were somehow alien. Life seemed to have been shaped by a strange hand. It was almost possible to suppose that I had been brought to the shore of a new world.

And I was unable to explore. I was obliged to help repair the ship and, when the work was done, Scolvessen's sixty days had expired. Olavsen insisted on sailing home immediately, and since he was within his rights, I had to make the best of it.

I managed to make the essential observations, determining the latitude of our landfall (and cursed the ignorance which will not allow us to calculate longitude), and I managed to walk across the island. It turned out to be about two miles wide, with a low sandy shore broken by little bays and lagoons. It appeared to be about ten miles from end to end.

We met nobody all the time we were there, although around the landing place there were traces of human beings. To me, this suggested the proximity of land. In fact, from a knoll near the ship, I was able to see distant smudges which hinted at other islands. The weather was clear, bright and almost cloudless.

I wanted to make sure of those islands. By the time we embarked, I had succeeded in persuading Olavsen to make a sweep to the South-West before pointing our bows homewards. But in getting my way, I acquired a bitter contempt for the men among whom I had been cast.

In vain, I had urged the honour of exploration, and the splendours of discovery. Even my pseudo-priestly power failed. It was only when I promised an exorbitant payment on arrival (how I was to honour it was another matter; but my ecclesiastical appearance clearly obtained me unlimited credit until the true state of affairs was revealed) that he finally consented to go beyond the limit prescribed by his master. But he made a grudging bargain. We were not to land, and we were to sail in the required direction for two days exactly - not a minute more.

We passed a cluster of islands in an emerald sea, like a garden of the Queen - and we sighted the mainland. But when the last hourglass had emptied, the ship remorselessly put about, I begged for a little more time. I urged that we were only a few hours away; that we could make land before nightfall; that the delay would be insignificant compared with what we would gain, but to no avail. These people were without curiosity; they were dead souls. A bargain was a commitment, from which one was not to deviate by a hair's breadth. Mutely I looked over the stern at the distant line of a low shore filling the horizon; a tantalizing glimpse of land I was not to be allowed to approach, let alone tread.

I ought not to have been surprised; Scolvessen had explained the limitations of this crew. The people who had gone to

Stadacona had lived long abroad. Most were of mixed blood, descended from Beothuks, Mohawks and Eskimos. Many had spent their whole lives in Greenland and Terra Nova. They were European in language alone, colonists in the true sense of the word. But Olavsen and his men were what in Straumsvik were called 'little Norwegians'. They had been born in Norway, had never stayed long elsewhere, and saw nothing beyond their own cabbage patch. They had come to Terra Nova almost by accident; their sole concern was to reach home with all possible speed.

When the mysterious shore had redissolved into the horizon, and I was once more faced with the naked sea, calm returned to me. I had discovered islands and mainland. They were preferable to anything I had yet seen. I no longer needed Scolvessen's admonitions to keep south; it was to these latitudes that I had decided to return. I knew what I had to show the world; all doubt had been removed.

Regrets for what I might have done on this voyage were suddenly irrelevant. I had taken the essential observations; I could find my way back. What I now had to do was reach Europe and return as quickly as I could to reveal the existence of what I had discovered. I became as anxious as any of the crew to get home without more delay.

XLIII

WE now had to pick up our westerlies once more, which meant regaining the forty-second parallel. Our point of departure was the twenty-fifth parallel. It was like sailing from the latitude of Cape Bojador, on the African coast, to that of Lisbon. Most of the way was an inferno of uncertainty.

It was not only that we were in unknown waters, but that I only had Scolvessen's word for those prevailing westerlies. Without them, we would be lost. We were, after all, where we were, because of a contrary storm where homeward winds had been promised. I had no way of knowing whether it was a freak, or whether Scolvessen had been wrong.

It took seventeen whole days to learn that he was right; seventeen days beating to windward or becalmed, tortured by a growing nightmare of never being able to make our way home again. And then we found what we had so ardently sought, but a little sooner than we had expected. To be precise, we picked up a wind from sou'west by west at the thirty-eighth parallel. This had happened once or twice before, but not for long, so that I still assumed the worst. But after two days with the wind in the same quarter, I began to believe that we might, after all, be saved. I think that the crew had by then almost given up hope. At all events, they joined in the Salve Regina with more than usual fervour.

The contemplation of difficulties overcome is the most satisfying of pleasures. One afternoon, I sat looking through the records of the previous weeks in my log. On the sunlit deck, with waves comfortably rolling by, and a following wind that, almost miraculously, now refused to desert us, I was able to smile at the suspense and anguish eloquently recalled by the disturbed handwriting and crabbed entries . . .

But, as I did, something started to tug at my understanding; something that seemed to be trying to escape from the untidy, stiff pages before me. Again and again I went through them; and then gradually I saw: *between the twenty-fifth and the thirtieth parallel of latitude we had met nothing but easterly winds.*

Of course, I had known it at the time; it was only now, after the event, that I grasped the significance of what I had written down. There stole through me a contentment so profound as almost to be pain. In that moment I knew what true discovery meant.

For I had uncovered a belt of easterly Atlantic winds. Finding the westerlies had merely confirmed what others had told me. But this was my own revelation.

'Hast thou entered into the springs of the sea? Hast thou perceived the breadth of the earth ' - thus spoke the Voice out of the whirlwind to Job - 'Declare if thou knowest it all.' - Ah, I could obey without vainglory. For who made me sail so that I should be caught in the storm? Who sent the tempest to reveal a mystery? It is not boasting to say what has been given by grace.

I had been driven before the storm so that the pattern of winds could be revealed. I had been shown that the Atlantic had to be crossed westwards from the Canary Islands and eastwards at the level of the Azores. Ignorance of that had kept the new lands hidden. The men of Europe had been shackled to their own shores by winds they did not understand. And to me it had been given to unlock the secret of the ocean. I had been shown that there was a meaning in all things.

XLIV

WE were now heading for Portugal. But a ship sailing in from the west would have invited dangerous curiosity, so I gave the Azores a wide berth, and made the crossing at one stretch. It was no hardship. We had fair winds nearly all the way, and enough food and water for comfort. What more can a seaman require?

But no voyage is over until the ship has safely berthed, and the last hawser has been secured. Before leaving Straumsvik, I had copied all essential navigational directions on a strip of parchment, which I had rolled up tightly, wrapped in seal gut, and inserted in a piece of hollow seal marrow bone, which I plugged with wax, and wore round my neck, day and night. I now opened the device and completed the information, to include the last landfalls and the voyage as far as we were. I then replaced the tight little scroll, re-sealed the cavity, and returned the contents to its place around my neck. Whatever happened, I would be able to find my way back to what I had discovered.

In a more conventional way, I also put my papers in order. Once we had made land, I would not have much time. Scolvessen's instructions were that I was to be put ashore in a southern port, after which the ship would continue to Bergen without delay. When I had brought *The Great Bear* across the Atlantic, my work would be done, and my presence on board, unnecessary.

When we had been at sea for five weeks, I ordered sail to be shortened, and soundings to be taken every hour from dusk to dawn. I felt sure we were approaching land but, not knowing the width of the Atlantic at that latitude, I was uncertain how far off we were. I had no wish to run aground in the dark.

It was an odd thought that when I returned to the unknown territories, I would be perfectly at home but, approaching my own continent, I had to feel my way like a stranger. But then I had seen Terra Nova, while I knew the Atlantic Coast of Europe from hearsay alone.

Two nights passed, and still no land appeared. On the third, the wind dropped, and we ran into a fog which clung to us well after daybreak. We now barely had steerage way, and I ordered soundings to be taken continuously. We had been making a steady seven or eight knots the previous few days, and I was now seriously worried about sea room.

About three hours after dawn, the lead found bottom. It showed a hundred and twenty fathoms. I knew this meant that land might be less than ten miles away. Since the fog still persisted, and visibility was down to a hundred yards, I did the only sensible thing in the circumstances, and immediately gave the order to heave to.

The morning wore on. The ship, like a blinded beast heaved aimlessly with the sea. The only sounds were the leadsman calling the depth - and Olavsen spinning a yarn. As the voyage had progressed, his reserve had melted. He had favoured me with his reminiscences. He was repetitive, but he had a picturesque way of using the defective Spanish at his command. He had made boasting into a minor art. He talked much of the times he had sailed to the Mediterranean, as if he had a sick longing for the south. But now he was talking of bigger and better fogs he had known in Norwegian waters.

I was running over to myself the various possibilities before me, scarcely paying any attention to Olavsen's insistent droning, when my thoughts were interrupted by what seemed to be a faint rumble. I commanded silence, and he and I listened carefully together, craning over the bulwark on the port quarter. At first all we heard was the lap of the waves and the creak of the ship's timbers. Then the noise came again, this time more distinctly. It sounded like distant thunder - or gunfire. I strained ears and eyes to penetrate the swirling greyness ahead. And then we ran out of the mist.

Not more than five miles away, a line of cliffs jutted out of the water. We were home. I had crossed the Atlantic - and come back!

I did not have time to savour the achievement. Not far off were the first vessels we had seen since leaving Terra Nova. They were many. They flew opposing colours. They were manifestly in warlike array. With all the waters of Christendom at my disposal, I had contrived to return to Europe at the precise spot selected by French and Genoese for a naval battle.

It seemed prudent to withdraw from the vicinity. I gave the order to head out to sea again. As we were putting about, we were surprised by a ship materializing at close quarters from a vagrant finger of the now dissolving mist. She was flying the French colours. Suddenly, she was bearing down on us with unmistakably hostile intentions.

This was the one eventuality for which we were not prepared. We could cope with all the rigours of the deep; but not with a man o' war. We had no cannon; we were poorly armed; we were not drilled in naval warfare. Speed was our only defence.

But the maurauder was to windward and under full sail. We were coming round and well nigh helpless. I became acutely conscious that *The Great Bear* was small, low and very exposed. Like a floating castle, the oncoming ship loomed high out of the water.

She took the wind from our sails. We wallowed helplessly in her lee. We could only watch while she came on remorselessly, ignoring our frantic attempts to indicate peace and goodwill to all men. On the puny oval of our deck, I felt like a rat in a trap.

When the attacker was so close that I could almost distinguish the features of the sailors on her deck, smoke and flames puffed from her gun ports, and my ears rang with the roar of cannon fire. One of the shots tore our sail; another splintered our port bulwarks. The acrid smell of gunpowder rolled over us.

On and on came the ship, foot by foot in the vanishing breeze, with barely steerage way. She towered monstrously above us and, high up in her rigging, archers were levelling their crossbows. We dived for cover; I flung myself to the deck in the lee of the hatch combing. A bolt buried itself in the bulwarks where I had been standing. At the stern, Olavsen, who had not been quick enough, was staggering about, hit in the chest. Near me, a seaman working the sail was pierced through the stomach. With a piteous groan, he collapsed, his hands slipping slowly down the rope he had been pulling, until they dropped uselessly away.

I felt a jolt; the attacker was alongside. From her stern castle, men hacked at our rigging. With a rent of parting ropes, the spar with our mainsail crashed to the deck. *The Great Bear* was no longer a living ship; she was a dead, drifting hulk.

There was the rattle of grappling irons. Men in armour were now swarming down the sides of the other vessel. There was no question of quarter being asked or given. The survivors of our crew had seized what weapons they could, some making do with boathooks and marlinspikes, and were heroically preparing to repel boarders. But we hadn't the ghost of a chance. As far as I was concerned, there was only one way out. I consigned *The Great Bear* and all within her to their fate and threw myself overboard.

I went under; I fought my way to the surface, choking, gasping, burning with the taste of salt water swallowed. I was struggling to keep afloat. It took a little while to realize that I was being dragged under by my Tertiary's habit. Somehow I managed to fight my way out of its now leaden, clinging folds. Clad only in my scapular, released from the terrible weight, I recovered my breath. Gradually the horror subsided. I trod water, and little by little my wits returned. When I had achieved some degree of composure, I looked around me. Not far off lay the attacker. She was still grappled to *The Great Bear*. I was overcome by an urge to get away as quickly as possible.

I heaved myself on to my belly to start the long haul. I am a good swimmer - how I thanked God for my boyhood lore from Genoa - and I was confident of reaching land. But, no sooner had I taken the first few strokes, than I was overcome by a horror of the deep. I was panic-stricken at the unfathomable dark beneath me. I started flailing about, possessed by sheer terror of being swallowed by the waters.

In that moment of extremity, I saw a piece of wood. I swam over to it. I don't think the distance was more than twenty yards. I cannot hope to explain what they cost me. I flung myself with my last strength on that God-given splinter of safety. It was part of a spar; it supported me, half submerged. I clung to it, shocked, immobile, numbed, whimpering and suffered the surge of the sea in my belly. Once more I had to wait while horror departed.

I grew conscious of the smell of burning. I looked up and saw *The Great Bear* listing and on fire. The Frenchman was clear, and making off in the opposite direction. Now I realized how fortunate I had been. I had lost everything. I was alone with a burning wreck. But I was alive. From the top of each swell, I could clearly see the cliffs ahead. The battle was to seaward; no obstacle, apparently, remained to block the way to land. Terror departed; will returned. At last I was able to set off towards the shore.

By now I was chilled, and it was not easy to move. But I struggled on and on, sometimes swimming with one hand, while holding on to the spar with the other; sometimes lying on it and paddling; sometimes just resting, allowing wind and sea to drive me where they listeth. Onwards, onwards, that was all I could think; onwards.

My world shrank to the dreary rhythm of the swell, the blur of the rough wood against which my face was pressed, and the ache of my limbs. I did not know how long my agony would last. I seemed to be lifted out into the void, looking down upon myself. I was alone on an empty sea. The dark night of the soul came upon me.

And then there came a Voice out of the cloud, saying:

'Courage, my son. I have chosen thee to be My messenger. Thou alone of all thy company shall be saved from the jaws of the deep, for thou shallt bring to men the tidings of new lands over the ocean. Thou and thou alone have been called to do so. Thou shallt go through the trial of water, that thou mayest be reborn, and become the pilot of nations, and the evangelist of The Word in another continent, beyond the islands of the sea.'

And then the Voice ceased, and I heard a rushing sound, and I cried aloud in my misery and exultation. And the sound continued, and I returned to myself on the surface of the water. And I recognized the beating of the sea upon a shore. The noise grew louder; I was underneath a cliff. With every wave, a shower of spume kicked up; no safety there; the land I so desperately sought, was waiting to destroy me. And then I noticed that each surge of the sea carried me *along* that inhospitable wall, not towards it. I was coming in on the tide. Hope hurled itself into me. From the top of the swell, I saw that I was being driven into a little bay, and somewhere on the left, there was a gap in the cliffs. I made for it, and soon I had come close enough to see a beach, with houses behind. Then I found myself among the breakers. One of the first tore my precious spar away, I did not care, for I knew the tide was bringing me in, and every wave was the throb of the sea pushing me onwards towards safety. Now I was in the surf, and the roar of the ocean grew louder, and I was lashed by water whirling and bubbling ever more confused. Once more I was swamped by a wave, and the breath was knocked out of my body: I had been flung against something hard. I tried to stand - and touched bottom. Another wave knocked me over and sucked me in its undertow. I stood again; for a moment head and shoulders remained above the surface, until I was overwhelmed by the next wave. Somehow, scrambling, paddling, gasping, I dragged myself out of the clutch of the sea. I was on solid ground. The ecstasy of it: ah Mother Earth, Mother of God, who saved me from Father Sea! My agony was over. It was too much. What remained of my strength withered, and I collapsed whimpering to myself. Through a cloud, I heard voices, and felt myself being picked up and carried. I remember my scapular being removed and warm liquid forced between my lips. My gorge rose, and blessed oblivion overcame me.

   I woke to find myself lying on a bed in a small room, and almost immediately I fell into a deep sleep again. Fitfully sleeping and waking, I gradually returned to consciousness. And then I saw faces around me. I managed to ask where I was. The answer was in an unfamiliar language. Eventually, it was somehow made clear to me that I was at Sagrés. Such was my return to my familiar continent; washed up on the coast of Portugal.

I started laughing uncontrollably. It must have seemed as if I had lost my reason. But I was laughing because my only error in the crossing of all the ocean had been to suppose at the end that we were a little farther north than we actually were; and God had made me do so in order that my ship should be destroyed, and my companions killed, so that I could return alone with my tidings.

PART FOUR

Lisbon

XLV

My landfall smacked of predestination, for Portugal, as I knew so well, was the home of discovery. I had been led to the best place from which to reveal what I had seen.

But it was only when I mounted to the Rock of Sagrés to look upon the site of my ordeal, that I understood fully the Divine care under which I must have been.

The Rock of Sagrés is a barren, windswept tongue of granite jutting out into the Atlantic. I stood at the edge, so high above the waves, that I was almost overcome by vertigo. To my right, picked out by the afternoon sun, I saw the grim outline of Cape St Vincent, dropping into the water. I was surrounded on three sides by sea that was a lifeless, sombre grey. The surface was lined by evil rippled streaks that told of currents sweeping round the headlands. I saw how I stood on the last promontory of Portugal - and of Europe - a Godforsaken place, indeed. Had time and tides been very slightly different, I would have been swept out to sea or dashed against the rocks. I had been guided to the one place within miles where I could crawl ashore.

The end of *The Great Bear* was also providential. She was destroyed in what has since been called the Battle of St Vincent; it ensured under honourable circumstances the disappearance of my companions on the voyage. This was a question that had been oppressing me for some time. I had seen that, to make certain of my secrets, I ought to contrive the disappearance of Olavsen and his crew. I had considered various more or less realistic plans, including the deliberate wrecking of the ship, but in my heart of hearts I knew I would lack the courage to act. The battle resolved the dilemma.

It was essential to conceal the truth about my voyage, and in that too the Battle of St Vincent was Heaven-sent. It offered a plausible disguise; I posed as a Genoese casualty of the fighting. The imposture was not difficult to maintain. A priest who came over from Lagos chose to believe my story; he also chose to be satisfied with my Franciscan credentials, thanks mainly to my medallion which had remained with me to the bitter end. When I explained that I wanted to go to Lisbon, he provided me with clothes, a passage on a coaster - and an account for services rendered. I settled it as soon as I could - to be rid of contamination by a person of such distasteful mercenary instincts.

The coaster was the first caravel in which I had sailed. In it, I reached Lisbon on the eighteenth of September, 1476; one month and three days after the Battle of St Vincent, and a year since I had sighted the shores of Terra Nova.

On the face of it, the circumstances were hardly propitious. I was being cast destitute, and alone among strangers in a foreign city. But the chilling grip of faint-heartedness lifted as the ship sailed up the Tagus, and docked, and I felt the bustle of men and ships and the rough paving of the quays underfoot. It was the atmosphere of a seaport, in which I had been brought up: it was Genoa all over again.

Moreover, I landed not without advantages. I was the only survivor of *The Great Bear*, so that the knowledge of Terra Nova was my property alone. And I still had the document that was worth more than the most lavish bills of exchange; the summary of Atlantic sailing directions I had worn round my neck.

It had survived the battle, my long swim; even more remarkably, perhaps, the attentions of my rescuers. The water had been kept out. The text was intact. All I needed now was the wherewithal to demonstrate the reality that lay behind the symbols. It was in a remarkably cheerful frame of mind that I left the caravel, and began to pick my way through the streets of Lisbon.

I did not wander blindly. I was looking for Brother João Carvalho. He was the Franciscan who had written to Brother Niccolò about the first crossing of the Equator. I found him without much trouble, still in the house to which he had then belonged.

I marched in and blurted out my tale. I assumed that my Franciscan connection would secure me the help I required. I had taken it for granted that I would be received with open arms. The friar before me, after all, was the man who, at some risk to himself, had reported one of the great deeds of our time.

If there was anyone in Lisbon who would understand what I wanted to do, this must be he.

Ah, the difference between a man and his writings! The letter which had made such an impression on me had been spirited and cheerful; its writer was crabbed, unenthusiastic and suspicious. His response to my tale was cool, guarded, reserved. To my explanations, there was no spark of sympathy. Even my Tertiary membership appeared suspect in his eyes. But at least in that, I was given the benefit of the doubt. I was allowed to stay in the house, while Brother João 'considered the matter.'

Time passed; I saw him regularly, but he did not volunteer comment on my business. To reminders, he was evasive. I did nothing but eat, sleep and walk the streets of Lisbon waiting for him to act. I felt the first pangs of the inaction that has become my *via dolorosa*.

Gradually it was borne on me, that Brother João must have written to Genoa, and that he was waiting for an answer to his enquiries before taking the next step. This was anything but pleasant. If Pareto had reported my misappropriation of his money to the authorities, and if Brother João heard of the affair, the consequences were unlikely to be pleasant.

I was oppressed by another worry. Scolvessen had written to Lauritsen, in Bergen, but his letters had gone down with *The Great Bear*. I had not seen the contents, but I was certain that he had ordered certain supplies to be deposited for him in Greenland. And I was equally certain that unless Lauritsen heard from Terra Nova, he would assume an accident and probably send out a relief expedition. I had, if possible, to prevent that. For my own good it would be preferable for Terra Nova to be dead and buried as far as the rest of the world was concerned.

So I wrote to Lauritsen, explaining that the crew had been lost on the homeward voyage, and that I was the only survivor. I also said that Scolvessen and his companions had perished in a sad disaster 'on land,' so that 'the business' was at an end. I took the precaution of writing in such a manner as to conceal time and place in case the letter was intercepted. Lauritsen, of course, would understand what I meant. I could only hope he would believe me. I had polished the truth because I considered that by persuading him that the colonists had been killed off, he would be less likely to act and the Atlantic traffic would cease - at least during the crucial period in which I would be arranging my own expedition. I delivered my letter to a ship bound for Antwerp, with a fervent prayer that it would eventually reach its destination.

After that interlude of what I suppose may be described as action, tedium resumed. Two or three months passed. Brother João favoured me with a little more civility, and gave me to understand that now he was satisfied with my Franciscan *bona fides*. He did not exactly say that he had heard from Genoa, but it was evident that he must have done. What he had been told, apart from the fact that I was a genuine Tertiary, I could only guess. But as he seemed puzzled rather than hostile, I had a feeling that he might not have learned the entire truth about the Pareto affair.

At last I could bear inaction no longer. I cornered Brother João one morning after Mass, and demanded an instant reply. Sometimes the frontal attack does pay. Coolly he said:

'You're not the first to talk about islands in the west. Most of them turn out to be clouds.'

'But I've been there; I've told you.'

'Yes, yes, they've all been "there". It's so easy to. I've had men sitting in front of me - like you - who've sworn to whole cities on the other side. Everybody's talking about discovery, so it's an understandable temptation.'

But I wasn't like these others; I had maps; had he not seen them? I had laboriously drawn a map of the Atlantic with the western side reconstructed from the information on the scroll that returned with me: there were local charts of Straumsvik, Newport, my southern landfall, compiled from my very own surveys.

'We see maps too. We have many people coming here on your kind of errand, you know, and all with the most impeccable evidence.'

I reminded him that he had promised to present my plans to the King.

'Well, these things have to be carefully considered.'

'Do you or do you not intend to help me get the ships I need?'

'Well, we think it's a good idea, but not just yet.'
'What you mean,' I said, 'is that you don't believe me. You think I'm a liar like the rest.'

The only answer was an eloquent shrug. As the proverb says: 'the truth is the cruellest jest.'

I wanted to shake the life out of this now loathsome, impassive figure, and scream at him that *he* was the impostor; he couldn't distinguish between the true and the false. But I was locked up in myself, silent, swallowing my bitterness and suffering the mortification of imprisoned fire. I could not afford to make Brother João more of an enemy than he already was.

But I would circumvent him. I tried the Royal establishment directly. I got no farther than a supercilious little clerk, who noted my errand, and promised to communicate with me in due course. 'Another one of 'em,' I heard him say behind my back, as I left.

The shock was almost unbearable. I became like a child, who, when things go awry, retreats into the world of make-believe. I paced the quays of the city, staring at the ships, seeking food for the imagination. Interminably I played over in my mind the course of my future expedition. The vision was so real that, sometimes, I felt that if I stretched out my hand, I would touch solid flesh. At the end of each repetition, I was overcome by an intense glow of satisfaction, almost like the aftermath of lying with a woman, so that the imaginary scenes felt as if they had actually been played out. Sometimes the feeling persisted so long and so violently, that I seemed to lose my grip on reality. I almost became the prisoner of my own fantasies.

But through the mists of pretence, I was yet aware of the world outside; dimly, but still aware. As the wounding tide of disappointment reached the flood, and started slowly to recede, reality began to return. In lucid intervals I grasped that I could not take refuge indefinitely in delusions.

I could not continue as I was. I was penniless. I was living among the Franciscans on sufferance. No one believed in me. I finally admitted to myself that my plans would take time in their fulfilment. In the meanwhile, I would have to stand on my own feet.

I turned to cartography, for which there was naturally a

great demand in Lisbon. I soon found a post as a draughtsman with a map-maker called Fernam Cortesão.

I left the Franciscan house, took lodgings, and went to work. I tried to convince myself that my stay in Lisbon must necessarily be short. It was the only means by which I could make my return to drudgery bearable.

For Lisbon was throbbing with the pulse of discovery. Ships and exploration ran like a fever through all conversation. The quays of the city were trod by sunburned sailors back from African voyages. In the little shops down by the port, exotic birds and crude trinkets, the petty spoils of the new African colonies, were on sale. There was a constant coming and going on the Tagus of ships Africa bound. Regularly, news would seep out of the Portuguese flag advancing, as explorers inched their way southwards, uncovering the African shore bit by bit. Terra Incognita was shrinking; the end of Africa was coming within reach.

Everywhere, discoverers and would-be discoverers were peddling their ideas. And I, burning with my islands, was excluded. I was on the margins, an onlooker. Day after day, I sat bent over my charts, inking in the coast that others were following; recording others' explorations, while prevented from accomplishing my own. I may be forgiven for being afflicted by the devil of despair.

Yet never, I can truthfully say, did I lose sight of my ultimate purpose. Always, I felt the discovery that had to be revealed. My saving grace was that not once was I tempted to blame others for my present failure. I considered the fault mine alone, and the remedy to lie in my own hands.

XLVI

BETWEEN my lodgings and my work there was a convent of the Military Order of St James. I made it my business to walk that way. I also took to carrying out my religious duties in its chapel.

There was good reason for doing so. I was looking for a wife; but I was a stranger; unknown; without introductions, and the convent provided a means of overcoming these impediments. It was an academy for well born ladies, and the chapel was open to the public. It was perhaps the only place in all Lisbon where I could approach the kind of woman in whom I was interested. To put it bluntly, I wanted to marry well.

I was not alone. The convent (colloquially known as 'The Saints') was an acknowledged marriage market. But my interest lay in someone distinguished from the crowd by almost total neglect.

Her name was Filipa Moniz Perestrello. The explanation for her singular plight was that she was poor, and the gentlemen thronging the chapel were interested in money. I, however, was exclusively concerned with rank and birth. In both, she was thoroughly desirable. Her family were one of the most distinguished in the Algarve. Her mother had friends at court. And, of great interest to me (but meaningless to my brother-suitors) she had Atlantic connections. Her father had been one of the colonizers of Madeira; her brother was the hereditary governor of Porto Santo. To marry her would be to marry influence, and pave the way for the accomplishment of my enterprise. For I had come bitterly to see that, in my present condition, submerged in a horde of common mariners importuning the authorities, I could not hope for patronage unaided.

It was therefore in pursuit of Filipa that I began to frequent the chapel at 'The Saints'. Stranger as I was, I did not entirely lack advantage. My height, my coppery complexion, my red hair, were distinctive among the dark heads of Portugal. And I made it my business to get a good tailor. I avoided the trap of looking like a beggar dressed up. I thought myself into my clothes, as it were; I convinced myself that I really was better than my origins; and I spoke and acted accordingly. I made will triumph over birth, and I held my own among the ostentatious gallants.

And, since I was no longer a gawky virgin, women, I assumed, would have ceased to be indifferent to me. I was not far wrong. Filipa duly took notice.

My primary concern, however, was not with her, but with the Mother Superior. For the Mother Superior, I had quickly learned, was judge of all would-be husbands, and her word was law among the families of her wards. I was not long in making her acquaintance.

On my second or third visit, when it was clear I was no casual worshipper, she intercepted me as I was about to leave the chapel.

'And what precisely,' she said, without any preliminaries, 'do you suppose you're doing here?'

I answered just as baldly; it seemed one occasion when the truth might pay.

'Well at least you're open about it. There's only one conceivable reason why a young - and not so young - man should suddenly discover a passion for hearing Mass in my chapel. And it's *not* a sudden onset of religious zeal, as they usually pretend at first.'

'I would never,' I said, 'try to deceive you, Reverend Mother.'

I meant it. This was no ordinary Mother Superior. Dona Ana de Mendoça was a splendid woman; a great lady in her own right, and the mother of the King's two bastard sons. I think that is the order in which she would have liked to be described.

She must have been over fifty; she was still handsome, with green eyes the years had been unable to dull. Upon her face was the look of one who regretted nothing.

Before this formidable figure I was for a moment in awe. She had a reputation for severity; even ruthlessness. She was certainly used to command. I had observed the obsequiousness with which my fellow-petitioners behaved towards her; I decided on an entirely different course of action. I seized the initiative; and I spoke out, plainly, without circumlocution.

But I did not talk about myself, like the others, I talked about my enterprise. That made a forcible impression. Instead of cutting me short with a combination of grandeur and mockery, as was her wont, she gave me a hearing: I was permitted to have my say while the chapel emptied.

I did not fail to draw suitable conclusions from that preliminary encounter. On succeeding visits, I took care to maintain the initiative. I did not wait for her to approach me; and I directed the talk.

One day, after we had met perhaps half a dozen times, she said:

'Let's not stand here; we might as well talk in comfort' – and she led me out of the chapel, through the inner recesess of the convent into one of her private rooms. Cell, it could scarcely be called; it was a vaulted chamber with an inlaid marble floor, furnished with intricately carved Moorish furniture, and hung with tapestries that revealed the finest of taste. To have been admitted into this sanctum was a victory, for ordinary suitors were interviewed in a little parlour reserved for the purpose.

'You know,' said Dona Ana, seating me on a cushion at her feet, 'I'm rather bored with empty-headed popinjays and their vacuous chatter. It's quite refreshing to hear a little sensible conversation for a change.'

I seized the goodwill of the moment to forestall enquiry and touch on my past, for I wanted my own version to be that on which she based her opinion. I had no desire to reveal my Atlantic adventures: I explained my presence in Portugal by pretending that I had been on the Genoese side at the Battle of St Vincent. I hinted at a better descent than my birth warranted. I took care to make it convincing by a casual approach, and avoiding the extremes of suspicious expansiveness and equally suspicious evasion. But most of the time, I kept to the sea; talking about the voyage I yearned to make in the west, and all I hoped to do.

'I've heard a great deal in this building,' said Dona Ana, 'about love and rank and money, but not about islands in the sea. I do believe you want this girl so that you can explore the world!'

She did not sound as if she disapproved.

I have always believed that God gives you what you think you are worth. Ask for little, and you receive little. But if you abstain from lesser rewards in the conviction that only the greater ones will do, you will eventually get what you want. So I had renounced inferior means of satisfying my urges. I did not patronize prostitutes, or sleep with low-bred women, so that I was distinguished from the general run of gentlemen at 'The Saints' by a freshness which a woman could not fail to notice. But, more than that, by living a chaste life, a kind of animal necessity lent passion to my speech and bearing, and this evoked within Dona Ana an answering indulgence. Perhaps this, added to her unconcealed pleasure in my conversation, made her disposed to accept the account I gave of myself.

I presented myself as being of good Genoese stock, temporarily in circumstances beneath those which were my due. 'I cannot pretend to a title,' I said, affecting a virtuous candour, 'but then, I come from a republic, where these things don't mean very much. On the other hand, it's not unknown in your country for explorers to be ennobled.'

'My dear boy,' was Dona Ana's answer, 'you're a thoroughly promising young man. I'm sure we'll all be proud one day to say we know you.'

I concentrate here in a few sentences the result of many conversations. For I spent long afternoons upstairs in that sumptuous apartment, talking to the Mother Superior; working on her feelings with exalted talk. And the time came when she responded with unqualified benevolence, and endorsed my courtship. I had discovered that I had a gift of inspiring confidence in myself.

In the course of these interviews, my position improved significantly. I left Cortesão's employment, and established myself as an independent cartographer. No longer entirely penniless, I now for the first time could waive all thoughts of dowry with conviction.

'That,' said Dona Ana, 'is a great point in your favour. The Perestrello household really is distressingly impoverished. To be quite crude, the family want to marry Filipa off, at almost any cost.'

When I had acquired a certain ascendancy over Dona Ana, I proceeded to address Filipa herself. She was not very much of a woman, although that may only have been by comparison with the Mother Superior. But she was pleasant to talk to, and talk I did.

Poor Filipa was already twenty-five; past the age at which a woman ought to marry, and haunted by the prospect of a life spent in the cloister. She wanted a husband for her manumission. So I quickly found favour in her eyes. There was a little more to it than that, however. She was still very much a virgin; she betrayed all the signs of passions too long thwarted. I was able to make convincing protestations of love, which she reciprocated with a sincerity that for a moment put me to shame. She added her entreaties to Dona

Ana's advocacy, and in the end we were allowed to marry.

I was not privy to all the negotiations, but I gathered that the Perestrellos required little persuasion. Since Filipa's father was dead, the head of the family was her brother, Bartolomeu, the governor of Porto Santo. His permission came by return of post.

'I'm not surprised,' was Dona Ana's comment, 'you'll be able to pay most of your wife's bills. What more can they want? Her mother's not displeased either; who wants a rake for a son-in-law when a clean, presentable young fellow like yourself is available.'

At her insistence, Filipa and I were wedded in the chapel of 'The Saints' - a rather unusual procedure, I gathered.

'To encourage the others,' Reverend Mother remarked.

To me she said: 'I shall watch your future career with the greatest interest.'

I did not forget that it was to Otsego my triumph was due; for without her I would have been unable to overcome the infirmity that had threatened to deprive me of my manhood. She it was who had taught me to lie with a woman. But I found it a task beyond my powers to work up the necessary feelings for Filipa: I was only able to consummate my marriage by pretending that my bedfellow was Otsego herself, and sometimes Dona Ana. *Amor Omnia Vincit.*

XLVII

MARRIAGE brought desirable changes. It is true, as Dona Ana had predicted, that I was expected to pay most of the bills; but on the other hand, I moved from lodgings over a bookshop to the Perestrellos' house, a pleasant place in a good part of Lisbon; the kind of establishment I could not have afforded to rent, much less buy.

My mother-in-law was away in Porto Santo, so Filipa and I were left to our own devices. She was a good wife, and introduced me to the consolations of domesticity, which worked miracles of self-confidence in the pursuit of my enterprise.

I assumed the Portuguese form of my name; I was now Christovão Colóm. I thought it would be advantageous not to appear too foreign, and also I wanted to relinquish my Genoese identity, as a precaution against possible enquiries about my misappropriation of Pareto's money.

But when all was said and done, I was not Christovão Colóm, or Christoforo Colombo, or anything else I chose to call myself; as far as Lisbon was concerned, I was Filipa Perestrello's husband, and the brother-in-law of the Governor of Porto Santo. It was enough; I penetrated circles hitherto barred to me. It was not long before I reached the *sanctum sanctorum*; I was introduced to the King's special adviser on geographical matters.

He was a controversial figure in Lisbon at the time. His name was Joseph Vizinho. He was rather conspicuous. He generally dressed in maroon or saffron. He had a large head with greying, tightly curled hair, a prominent nose, and the suspicion of a perpetual smile hovered about his face. He mixed with anybody and everybody; one day he was to be seen with some fashionable courtesan at the Royal Palace; the next, among seamen on the waterfront; always talking. He was not really a cosmographer. He was actually a surgeon. But he had displaced the corps of professional cosmographers who used to control policy. Of this, they were somewhat resentful. It was whispered that he had acquired an ascendancy over the King by curing him of a painful attack of piles. But there was no doubt of the doctor's wide learning. And in matters of exploration, his word was law. I could not have made a more profitable connection. One day he asked me to dinner.

His home gave the impression of a temporary camp from which the occupants were ready to depart at any moment. It did little to dispel the suspicions aroused when I found myself the only guest. Without any temporizing, he plunged straight into the business he wanted to discuss.

'I have heard rumours,' he said, 'that you have seen some new Atlantic islands.'

Now one of the conclusions which I had drawn from my unfortunate reception at the hands of Carvalho was that no shadow of suspicion must be allowed to fall on my tale. I did not, therefore, begin by answering his question directly. Instead, I decided to establish my *bona fides*, and so I said:

'You are waiting, I think, for news of a certain expedition to the North Atlantic.'

Vizinho said nothing.

'Let me elaborate. It was a joint enterprise with the Danish King. The purpose was to investigate the discoveries of the old Northmen in the west. The captain was João Vaz Cortereal; his second-in-command was Alvaro Martins Homem. They had two Norwegian pilots on board, called Didrik Pining and Hans Pothorst. The ship was called *Mariagallante*.'

'You say "was", "had",' said the doctor.

'Yes. The ship was lost' – and I saw again that terrible bay in the west, the waves rolling past on to the Portuguese vessel listing on her reef, the mutilated remains on the shore, 'lost with all hands.'

'When did this happen?'

'If you must know, on the twenty-fifth of October, in the Year of Our Lord, fourteen seventy-five.'

'How did it happen?'

Now I hesitated. The truth was unsavoury; it might even be awkward for me.

'Act of God,' I said.

If Vizinho noticed my hesitation, he gave no sign of having done so. He merely nodded. I had prepared the ground; now was the moment to strike.

Without revealing my voyage with Scolvessen, or details of Terra Nova, I said enough to prove that I had sighted new land, and that I could find my way back. I explained how, on that account, I believed I was uniquely qualified to pilot an expedition over the Atlantic. Once more I put my proposition; how I only wanted three ships, and a Royal licence for discovery in the west.

I ended my appeal by saying: 'I'm interfering with no one. *Your* explorers generally keep to the coast of Africa; *their* province is the south and the east; why not let me have the west? You've nothing to lose – and think what you stand to gain.'

I had rehearsed everything carefully. But, as the last syllables were uttered my heart sank. I had not said things quite as I had intended. Where I had sought fluency, I was merely glib. Even to myself, I sounded unconvincing.

Vizinho promised to 'look into the matter.' But he was a little bit too civil for comfort. I left with the unhappy feeling that something had gone wrong.

XLVIII

ONCE more the months went by, and I suffered in terrible suspense, waiting for the verdict that never came. I fought bouts of optimism to prepare myself for what I was convinced in my heart of hearts would be another disappointment. And duly disappointment arrived. My rejection at the hands of Brother Carvalho was confirmed.

It was done in an unexpected and roundabout manner.

One evening, I returned home from my work to find Dona Ana talking to my wife. They were rather subdued.

'I've been talking to Dr Vizinho, I gather you're suspected of being a corsair.'

This was so ridiculous, that I could only brush it off with some facetious remark.

'It's no laughing matter, I assure you,' continued Dona Ana. 'The point is, you have been talking about a missing ship with such intimate knowledge that you must have been involved. In plain language, you are suspected of piracy.

'You're lucky to have married a Perestrello, otherwise you might have found yourself behind bars now. As it is, suspicion will remain just - suspicion, at least for the time being.'

'But I'm not a corsair, I'm an explorer.'

'If I understand Vizinho correctly, the distinction is sometimes rather fine,' said Dona Ana. 'Well, whatever it is, I have the impression that you will not find the help you want forthcoming - not just yet, at any rate. I think it would be advisable for you to leave Lisbon for a while. That, to be frank, was the message I have been asked to convey.'

With that, she left.

Now I was overcome by a surge of loathing for Vizinho. He had raised my hopes; now he did not have the courage to announce my dismissal to my face, but had skulked behind an intermediary.

Filipa comforted me; whatever thoughts Dona Ana now nursed, she at least maintained the implicit trust she had put in me when first she saw me at 'The Saints'.

'It'll all blow over,' she said. 'But, now we must get away from Lisbon. We really must. We'll go and stay with my family in Porto Santo. We ought to go as soon as possible.'

It was a brave woman who spoke. Our son, Diego, had just been born; on the eighteenth of September, to be exact; it was the year of Our Lord 1479. Filipa was still weak from childbirth. Yet she insisted on the move. And I agreed; because I saw that it was necessary. So we shut our house in Lisbon, and sailed to Porto Santo.

XLIX

I SPENT almost three years in Porto Santo; three years marooned with my in-laws on a glorified rock out in the Atlantic.

Time passed in dreary exile in a sea-girt purgatory. I turned thirty: I felt the prison walls of inaction and wasted years piling up around me. My days passed in a cloud of emptiness. Often I cried in the words of the psalm:

'How long wilt thou forget me, O Lord? for ever? how long wilt thou hide thy face from me?'

The people around me seemed to retreat into the shades; it was as if they did not exist; neither Bartolemeu, nor Isabel, nor my poor Filipa, nor Diego, the strangely placid infant. I alone seemed to have a kind of existence, suspended between being and not being; between light and dark, between substance and shadow, between the land of the living and the underworld.

Sometimes I was reminded of the outside.

There came one day a letter from my brother; Bartolomé, the older one. I had written to him, seven or eight months previously; albeit with great reluctance. I wanted not to exist as far as my family were concerned. In my new incarnation – for after my ordeal by fire and water outside Sagrés, I felt as if I had been reborn – they had no place. It was not merely that they were of low birth, but they were failures, and I was still mortally afraid of their taint.

I had been moved to write to Bartolomé to discover if I had anything to fear from Genoa. This seemed the safest means of making enquiries. I counted on the ties of blood, and Bartolomé, who was now nineteen, would, if he had fulfilled his earlier promise, be possessed of some discretion.

I was not disappointed. That I had waited five years to write, he took as a matter of course. He gave the family news, a predictable catalogue of failure and ineptitude, but concentrated on essentials, notably Pareto's behaviour.

What he had to say, was reassuring. When Pareto failed to hear from me, he had assumed a mishap and, consequently, not reported me to the police. When subsequently, he discovered that I had at least survived, he still presumed that there was some reasonable explanation for my absence, and therefore refrained from having me pursued.

I had treated Pareto disgracefully, yet he seemed determined to think the best of me. It was astonishing, but reassuring, and I had no reason to doubt the authenticity of what Bartolomé had written. Shortly after I had left Genoa he, not being quite fourteen, had abandoned the family woollen business, and somehow got himself apprenticed to Pareto. It was not beyond the bounds of possibility that he had had something to do with the defence of my reputation, although he did not explicitly say so. But he appeared to be on particularly good terms with his employer, which was undoubtedly in character.

'I am informed,' wrote Bartolomé, 'that I show more talent than my elder brother – but then you, if I understand rightly, never intended learning how to make maps as anything more than a means to an end.

'And to tell the truth, that is more or less my idea as well. As soon as I've qualified – in a year or two I hope – I'm going to travel. I want to work in France and Portugal. There's no future in Genoa; you were sensible to get out when you did. Things are not too hopeful here.

'Perhaps,' he finished by saying, 'we might go into partnership some day. You don't exactly say what you've been doing, but I rather suspect that you've been going in for exploration. Well, I think I've got a better head for business than you, and between the two of us we might make a lot of money.'

I was not entirely happy with the tone of this letter. I wanted a little more than money. I hungered; my brother had an appetite. I was not sure that we were compatible. But he had reassured me on the essential point. I had nothing to fear from Pareto.

Shortly after receiving Bartolomé's letter, I had the one bearable interlude of my exile. I shipped as a navigator to St Jorge de la Mina, in Guinea. On that voyage, I learned two useful lessons. The one was that, whatever the theoreticians maintain, man *can* survive in the Tropics. The other was that the degree of latitude is shorter than is generally supposed. I proved this by taking my own measurements. It was to be of some importance later on.

Nonetheless, it was wasting time. I had no business making southward hops along the African coast: I ought to be sailing westwards over the ocean.

And then the old King Alfonso died. His son, John was on the throne and, by all accounts, the change of regime would be beneficial. The suspicions of piracy, under which I had been labouring, would probably by now have lapsed. It was a chance worth taking: I refused to bury myself in Porto Santo any longer.

I persuaded Filipa to return to Lisbon, and we arrived early in the summer of 1482. It was wonderful to sail up the Tagus and see the roofs of a city again. It was like returning from the shades.

L

ISABEL, my mother-in-law, had offered a piece of valedictory advice when I left Porto Santo. 'If I were you,' she said, 'I would dress what I have to say in a little philosophy. You've no idea the impression a show of learning makes.'

Now mine is a singularly impressionable nature. I am easily swayed by things said at fertile moments. And Isabel was the kind of person to whom I would naturally submit. She was well born, highly educated and self-confident; with a vocation, she would have ruled a convent; as it was she dominated Porto Santo. I took her suggestion as a command.

As soon as I was once more settled in Lisbon, I immersed myself in study to the exclusion of everything else. It was an antidote to the years in Porto Santo, when I had scarcely read a word, and frittered away the time. The golden mean is not for me; I am a man of extremes.

Isabel had not confined herself to generalities. She had prescribed a course of reading. I was to master the *Ymago Mundi* of Cardinal d'Ailly. It was the kind of book of which one hears, but never reads. Isabel however had insisted that I would find it the most useful geographical treatise for my purposes, although, or perhaps because, it had been written seventy years before. 'It will teach you,' she had said, 'how to dress new ideas in old familiar clothes. And that's the lesson you've got to learn if you're to impress the pedants with whom you will have to deal.'

'New ideas in old familiar clothes' - almost Deganawida's words. The same thought, worlds apart: among the unlettered savages of Terra Nova and the learned fools of Christendom. If it was universal, it must be true. I knew sufficient philosophy to grasp that.

So one of my first actions upon my return was to acquire the *Ymago Mundi*. It was neither difficult nor particularly expensive, because the first printed edition had arrived from Louvain.

'A very nice copy,' said the bookseller, 'legible from beginning to end, which is more than you can say for some of the stuff on the market today. Of course, a manuscript's much better; the real thing as it were - but you've got to pay for it. And this is quite a good imitation - from a distance it almost looks as if it was done by hand.'

He was not exaggerating. The last specimen of printing I had seen was the indulgence at Hospental, on the way to Basle. This was undeniably superior; the text was perfectly clear, so much progress in so short a time; an odd age we live in. I paid what was asked, and carried the three tomes back to the room at the top of my house - perhaps in all honesty I ought to say Filipa's - that I had arranged as a retreat.

I now embarked on an enterprise unique in exploration. I am surely the first to be in the position of knowing the result in advance, and having to make present theory fit future facts. But the intricacies of my situation did not end there.

I had to prove that I was more deeply read, better qualified, than the ruck of would-be explorers milling round the king. I had at least learned that much wisdom in Porto Santo. The new men come out of the desert.

The *Ymago Mundi* turned out to be a Godsend. Not for nothing had the writer been the Chancellor of the Sorbonne. He provided the authority of which I stood in such crying need. Often it was little more than an academically imposing form of words to correct a distressingly homely idiom; there lay the high road to plausibility. And d'Ailly led the way with all the spiritual and temporal authority of a University Professor and a Cardinal of the Church.

I had plenty of time to follow him; the change of reign did not imply that I was to see the King at once. But the delay was not entirely irksome. The glorious sensation of annihilating my own ignorance was so magnificent, that I did not want to stop. So I read on and on, neglecting most things around me. D'Ailly had so much to teach. From him, I learned that the Phoenix comes from Arabia, that the stone called asbestos, which once ignited, never goes out, is found in Arcady; that in Ethiopia there is a spring which freezes in the heat of the sun and melts in the cool of the night; and that dragons, monkeys ostriches and elephants live in Morocco. I must say, however, that I did treat some of the Cardinal's statements with reserve. For example, I cannot really understand how a white blackbird can exist. Nor can I quite accept that jewels come from the skulls of dragons; if that were the case, they would overrun the world.

Filipa was very patient with me. I was lost in my studies, and did not pay the necessary attention to my chart-making, upon which we still depended for our income. But she understood what my enterprise meant to me, for that I will ever be grateful.

Eighteen months went by, unnoticed, in the seduction of reading. But I did not entirely neglect life outside my books. I attended the Tertiaries' Sunday gatherings, although not with the same enjoyment as in Genoa. This was very possibly because now I knew more than the company about my chosen subject, whereas then I was still learning. Besides, I found the Lisbon brothers dull and uninspiring. They were all connected with the sea, but they were crotchety, secretive, self-important, and worst of all, repetitive. I usually left the meetings with a terrible sense of depression. But I persevered with them, in the hope that they might provide useful introductions.

I was finding it easier to get a hearing now, the result, no doubt, of my new-won learning. I pretended that what I offered might be a way to the East, although everything pointed to my discoveries being new country, the existence of which had never before been suspected. In search of verisimilitude, I studied Marco Polo, from him I got a little joke which I always included in my disquisitions. It was about the potentate *who made paper money*. That, I said was a trick worth learning; it would solve all financial troubles, and alone pay for a voyage. This never failed to raise a smile. I acquired a reputation for being someone who ought, after all, to be taken seriously.

Eventually Dr Vizinho interviewed me again. There was not a breath of accusation on this occasion; he was the soul of amiability. Isabel had known what she was talking about. At the beginning of 1483, I was summoned to meet the King.

LI

'My father was very interested in the North Atlantic. It was one of the great disappointments of his life that he did not see the results of the last expedition he sent out. It never returned, you know. The Commander was João Vaz Cortereal. He was one of our ablest seamen. I often wonder what happened to him.'

Thus did the King open the interview. And as he spoke, I seemed to return to that bloodstained bay in Terra Nova. I saw once more the ship with the Portuguese colours jammed up against the reef, the waves rolling past on to that desolate shore, and the mutilation on the beach. Did my manner betray the vision? I did not know. Was the King trying to trap me into some damaging admission? Again, I did not know.

The stories told about King John suggested a strong vein of cruelty and caprice. But Dona Ana, whom I had taken the precaution of consulting beforehand, had said that he was 'not as bad as he's painted.' As a former mistress of his father, his illegitimate stepmother as it were, she was intimately acquainted with the habits of his family. 'He will always give you a fair hearing,' she said. 'But he cannot bear dishonesty. There's a lot of that around him. If you're honest, you'll have nothing to fear. And remember, he's terribly shy.'

I took Dona Ana at her word: my only concern must be to put the king at ease. He was swarthy, slow-spoken, gross-featured, ungainly, and half a head shorter than myself; I supposed he would have liked to have been rather more prepossessing. I avoided the extremes of obsequiousness and stiffness, which would be due to his position, and tried to give the impression that I liked his person. I circumvented his reference to Cortereal, and took command of the conversation.

I began by talking about my Genoese origins. Then, quite deftly as I thought, I turned to my enterprise. I had planned my argument in two parts. The first was a general disquisition on geography, generously larded with quotation, in order to establish my accomplishment and general trustworthiness.

This was the necessary preparation for the second part, a guarded summary of what I had seen on the other side of the Atlantic. My experience had taught me that to be too fulsome was to invite disbelief.

'We are agreed,' I wound up by saying, 'that there are territories in the west within sailing distance of Lisbon. The only question is getting there and back with certainty. When Your Majesty mentioned the disappearance of Cortereal, it suggested to me that your navigators lacked the ability. Now I believe that I have discovered how to do so. I would like the opportunity to prove it.'

With that, the interview ended. The King had listened impassively; the functionary who conducted me out of the palace was noncommittal with, I imagined, a tinge of contempt. I emerged into the street already tortured by regrets in the conviction that I had ruined my case.

I had been too anxious to show off my philosophy. King John was the son of Alfonso V, who had sent out the expedition which had so inconvenienced Scolvessen. He was the nephew of the illustrious Prince Henry the Navigator. He had been trained to command explorers; as heir apparent, he had managed the Colonial Office in Lisbon. He had probably heard of Terra Nova; he almost certainly knew as much about Atlantic navigation as anyone living. And it was this man, whom I had tried to blind with my own paltry erudition.

I was quite miserable, and I hid myself at home, pacing aimlessly from room to room, in the certainty that I had failed again. Days passed thus, and then Dona Ana sent for me.

'You seem to have impressed the King,' she said.

I thought at first she was speaking with her habitual irony. But it was not so. The King, it seems, had really approved of me.

'He thinks,' she said, 'that you are a gifted mariner. He also enjoyed the interview. You must have behaved yourself splendidly. I think he imagined you to be some crotchety old sailor with a bee in his bonnet; he was surprised to find that you were a reasonable person. Anyway, he wants to see you again.'

LII

Now for the first time, I tasted recognition. The King saw me regularly. I was introduced to the Court circles concerned with exploration. I was admitted to the inner sanctum of opportunity. I enjoyed it all, perhaps too much. I was overwhelmed by the transformation overnight from outsider to initiate.

I had known beforehand that I was merely one among many exponents of discovery; I had been afraid of failure when exposed to their competition; it was with relief and then astonishment that I discovered I could hold my own with most of them. I felt the seductive balm of satisfaction (or vanity?) as I sustained an unfamiliar deluge of flattery for my knowledge and accomplishment.

This enjoyment gradually began to wither. I became uncomfortably aware of a suspicion that praise perhaps was expected to be its own reward. I noticed that acceptance in general was not followed by action in particular. I had assumed that my interviews with the King were a prelude to action. I believed that I would not have to wait long before being given command of an expedition for the rediscovery of my islands. But the weeks and months passed, and none of it materialized.

A day or two after a particularly irritating interview, I happened to be at a Tertiary dinner. I sat next to somebody called Bartolomeu Diaz. Today of course he is famous as the man who first doubled the Cape of Good Hope; then he was just one more Portuguese ship's officer trying to make his way in the business of exploration. He was rather pleasanter than the usual Lisbon Tertiary, so I struck up a rather less than usually stilted conversation. I mentioned my own difficulties.

'They can always find the tonnage if they want to,' he said, ' "We haven't the ships" is a hoary old excuse.'

Suspicions of duplicity, which I had been deliberately suppressing, now welled up within me. I left in a fit of preoccupation. Diaz, although he could not know it, had moved me to action.

For some time, I had felt that I was groping in the dark. I

realized that I would not get much farther unless I could discover what my interrogators knew. But in Portugal exploration, as I have explained before, is a State secret. To meddle with it is a capital offence, and I had shrank from the thought of the gallows. Now I no longer cared.

Filipa had not long before died in childbirth. I was sorrowing, lonely, afflicted by self-reproach. I saw that I had treated her callously; worse, I had taken her for granted. I had perverted the act of love-making. I had married in cold blood, like a mercenary. I had prostituted myself. I had sinned; I could not deny my guilt. I was beginning to perceive that what had happened was some kind of punishment. I could only lament that to punish me Filipa, patient Filipa, had to be carried off. But it is perhaps better not to question the workings of the Divine Will. I had been made the agent of my own retribution; with my body I had killed my wife. God had made me a murderer; I could not bear to think of it. My burden was heavy.

In that state of mind, I was capable of anything. When Diaz spoke as he did, it was the last little touch that opened the floodgates. I felt betrayed by men; deserted by God. I knew the abomination of desolation. In anguish and despair, I found the courage to act. I would find out what the Portuguese knew; I would steal their secrets. I decided to break into the archives where the navigational records were kept.

The archives were hidden in the innermost recesses of the Royal Palace itself, but not so hidden as to rest concealed from me. As a familiar figure in the crowd of mariners around the King, regularly admitted to the Royal presence, constantly interviewed by Vizinho, I had the run of the Palace. The sentries at the mysterious door revealed what I sought.

Now I knew where the archives lay. With little more trouble, I was able to discover their routine. There were two custodians, who arrived at seven in the morning and left again at dusk. They were Carmelites; for some reason, King John preferred not to entrust Franciscans with his secrets.

The approaches to the archives were choked with guards; but only, I was surprised to discover, during the day. At night, there was a single watchman for the whole wing. He never entered the vital room, because he was not provided with a key. My first action was to set about obtaining one myself.

The most accessible belonged to Dr Vizinho. It hung, I had discovered, in a cupboard in his office at the Palace. It was not difficult to remove, but I refused to take the risk of keeping it. I discreetly ventilated the problem among my acquaintances. I pretended to be engaged in a love affair, the audacious consummation of which required the ability to enter locked doors, the only keys to which were in the possession of a jealous husband. The solution was provided by someone to whom I had been introduced - by Vizinho himself! He was an Italian sculptor lately arrived in Lisbon and, being Italian, he was full of accomplishments he was eager to show off. He had learned some new method of accurately casting figures, which would precisely fulfil my requirements. Making the mould was quick, easily learned, and done *in situ*, using nothing more complicated than wax. I took the impression one afternoon, when Vizinho was out. Within a day or two, I had a beautiful shining bronze replica of the key. I had to pay a small fortune - the man was short of work, I suspected - but I had what I wanted.

It was laughably easy to remain in the Palace one evening, and try the key in the lock. It worked, but I did not choose to open the precious door just then. I relocked it, and left the Palace without drawing suspicion on myself. I could choose my own time.

It was about two months after the replica had been cast that I finally acted. I had waited until the King had called one of his periodical conferences on discovery, and the Palace was swarming with mariners, astronomers and cosmographers, genuine or false. I wanted a crowd in which to melt: there are occasions on which there is safety in numbers.

Everything was ridiculously simple. I hid in a room until after dark, and then slipped along the corridors which I had so carefully surveyed, avoided the sentry, and entered the mysterious chamber; I stood stock still for a moment to make sure that nobody had heard the grating of the key in the lock.

It was pitch dark inside. First, I plugged the keyhole with a piece of wax I had brought for the purpose. Then I lit a candle. What I saw was scarcely what I had imagined the greatest repository of navigational knowledge in the world to be. I was in a low, dingy room, reeking with the dank odour of mould.

There were two small shuttered windows at the farther end.

At first glance, I faced an impossible task. The walls were lined with shelves that were crammed with packets of documents. If a catalogue existed, it was out of sight. But to each packet was attached a small leather label hanging over the edge of the shelf. There was order in those labels, and I soon found what I was looking for. Most of the material; voluminous bundles, concerned Africa and the East; it was the section classified as 'The West and the North-West' that I sought. It was not large but, ominously enough, it lay well down in a particularly accessible shelf, and it had the feeling of being frequently consulted. I carried the files over to a table, and undid the tapes binding them together.

To begin with, I was faced with strings of reports of land sighted; routine, and doubtless apocryphal for the most part, and of no interest for my purposes. Then I came to a slim folder laconically docketed 'maps'. I opened it and the first map told me more or less what I wanted to know.

Before me lay a representation of the North Atlantic. But it was something rather different from the Vinland Map I had seen in Basle. This was no sketch by imaginative friars; it was a workable chart obviously produced by mariners who had seen what they described. There was Greenland and Iceland and Europe; and on the west a coastline that I knew so well - or partly so. I saw Terra Nova, with the northwards facing promontory containing Straumsvik, and the coast trending south-west to Newport. But the country was labelled '*Terra del Rey del Portugal*'. And north of Straumsvik, across Straumsfjord, I saw another coast, opposite Greenland; the coast I had heard of but not seen. It was what the Norwegians called Markland, but here it was designated Labrador, as Scolvessen himself had told me the Portuguese called it.

A memorandum attached to the map disclosed that it was based on the known voyages of Cortereal - the very man about whom the King had talked, and who had intruded upon the peace of Straumsvik. And there were detailed coastal charts ascribed to him.

From the memorandum, I also learned the whys and wherefores of the material before me. The maps had been commissioned - as Cortereal had been sent out - by Alfonso V, the

King's father. And Alfonso had been moved to do so by Christian, King of Norway and Denmark, an old friend. Christian had told him about the Norse Atlantic discoveries; Cortereal had been sent out to revive them. Christian had encouraged the enterprise, promising to provide, so the memorandum informed me, two unnamed pilots for another voyage, of which the outcome was uncertain.

If this was all, I had little to fear. Nothing I had so far seen told me anything I did not know. And one thing was crystal clear. After Cortereal's shipwreck, there was nobody known to the Portuguese who had crossed the Atlantic - except myself. I felt a surge of gratitude to the Beothuks; my position was stronger than I had suspected. Now I could face Vizinho and his henchmen with considerably more confidence. I felt remarkably comforted.

Now I turned to a list of cross-references on the whole subject of the Atlantic I had discovered in a file - and I saw my own name. I rummaged in the mound of documents and extricated my file. And there I found the pit of deception; there in the private repository of Royal privilege, between the sober covers of official records, I discovered the monstrous treachery which had been practised on me in cold blood.

Two entries alone were devoted to me - but what entries. The one was a concise summary of what my interrogators had extracted from me. They had been frighteningly skilful; they had learned nearly everything. The other was the report of a certain Fernám Dulmo who had been secretly sent out three or four months previously to test my way of crossing the Atlantic. He had been blown back by contrary winds a day or so west of Madeira. There was a comment by Vizinho: 'Dulmo does not appear to have been very resolute. It is possible, however, that we may have misunderstood C., or is he a fraud after all?'

I could tell them why Dulmo had failed. He had tried to sail westwards at the wrong latitude - the fool. That at least was a crumb of consolation, for it could only mean that I had not divulged the secrets of the Atlantic winds - that was still my own private property. But that had no effect on the fury and bitterness which now overpowered me. While Vizinho and the King had been so friendly to my face, they had been deliberately scheming to betray me behind my back. I was seized by a hatred so intense, I felt as if I were choking. I decided then to deprive those pernicious monsters of all their information. I would steal everything that could lead them over the Atlantic.

Until this mad urge came over me, nothing could have been farther from my mind. I had come to consult alone; now I had to remove documents, pack them and get them out of the Palace.

I now turned frantically to combing the material, extracting vital entries; the maps of Labrador, Cortereal's pilotage, and various other documents. I came across a name from out of the past: Toscanelli; the Florentine of whom Deganawida had talked. Strange it was to sit surreptitiously in Lisbon and be reminded of something I had first heard of thousands of miles away in Terra Nova. I found Toscanelli's file. In it there were three entries; a letter and map by his hand, and a note expressing the opinions of the King; the comments of a fool on the work of a fraud. For the map was exactly as Deganawida had described. It depicted the Atlantic, with the western shore a rash of dubious islands close to the eastern extremity of Asia. It was pure fantasy.

From the accompanying letter, it appeared that Toscanelli had sent the map to old King Alfonso as an unsolicited proposal for a westward voyage. He was so good as to inform His Majesty that by the cogitations of his own brain he could reveal that the way to the other side of the Atlantic was not as far as was commonly supposed, and that there were great things to discover. It said much for the discretion of the old king that he had ignored the document: it says equally much about King John that he had not only dragged it into the light again, but taken it seriously.

I had always supposed that the King of Portugal, reigning over the most accomplished mariners in the world, would be sated with the sensible advice of practical mariners. But in a turgid memorandum, the third component of the file, the Royal handwriting gave it as the Royal opinion that Toscanelli's was the definitive proof that the Atlantic was narrow at all points. John, the sea-king, the ruler of an Atlantic kingdom, turned for geographical advice to an opinionated impostor. But that impostor was a Florentine, a doctor of the university, and a professional philosopher, in that order. On those three counts, he was treated with more respect than a Colón or even a Cortereal.

I took Toscanelli's file; it would be useful to have before me. With it, I seemed to have obtained everything of interest, but I checked to make sure that I missed nothing. As I was tying up the documents I proposed to take, I heard the hoarse grating of a key being fitted into a lock.

Consumed by hatred, anger and jealousy, I had forgotten the passage of time. Too late, I now noticed a faint glow seeping through the shutters. I froze, the prisoner of panic. Something within me heaved, and I seemed to stand outside myself. I observed my hand, as if it belonged to someone else, extinguish the candle with a blow of the bare palm, and my legs flung me across the room.

There was a creaking of hinges, and the door began to open; by now I was pressed into the only conceivable hiding place, an alcove where the instruments were kept. Someone entered, and the door closed again. I made out a figure cross in the gloom towards the window. The shutters opened, and the gentle light of early morning flowed in. From my refuge, I heard a sharp intake of breath and a muttered exclamation of bewilderment. Whoever it was, had obviously noticed the confusion in the room.

The intruder now moved into my line of sight; but for the moment did not see me. It was one of the Carmelites who looked after the archives; he had come closer to inspect the tangle of documents I had left, and he was bending over the table with his back towards me. I cringed unthinkingly into my corner and as I did so, I made a noise. He stiffened.

My hand closed round a heavy object. As the Carmelite turned round, I swung out at him with it, and connected with his head. His hands jerked upwards in a grotesque gesture of surprise and, slowly collapsing, he slumped to the floor.

I stood where I was, gasping, trembling, unable to move. Now I saw that my weapon was a globe. It was one of those astronomer's models, made of solid brass. The edge of the flat ring representing the ecliptic had caught the Carmelite just above the temple. This was not what I had planned.

Unable to think I stared at the white and brown Carmelite

habit, limply crumpled on the floor like the fleece of a dead sheep. The cowl caught my attention - the cowl! - token of concealment. A corner of my panic lifted. I dropped my weapon and, bending down, stripped the habit off the lifeless figure and donned it myself. I seized my parcel of selected documents and walked out of the room. My only hope now was to brazen it out.

A guard stood outside the door. I had the cowl up, and he let me pass. Clearly, as far as he was concerned, a Carmelite had entered the room, and that same Carmelite had emerged.

Quelling an almost overpowering desire to run, I moved away as naturally as I could. I negotiated two or three corridors without mishap but, as I turned a corner, I met somebody whom I knew quite well. I drew into my cowl like a snail retreating into its shell; I averted my face; 'Good morning, Father,' he said.

And he passed without a sign of having recognized me.

But then his footsteps ceased. Had he stopped to look at me? I dared not turn round. I felt eyes upon my back, the surge of fear, and once more the mad desire to run. Then the footsteps resumed. Forcing myself into a semblance of composure, I continued on my way.

By now, I had left that wing of the Palace in which my presence was incriminating, and had reached the more public part. The work of the new day was beginning; I could not avoid people. I kept my eyes on the ground, trusted to my cowl, and arrived at the entrance still unmolested.

I had tortured myself with a horrifying picture of the perils of leaving the Palace. It turned out to be the safest part of all. The sentries never even glanced at me; the visitors going in were too intent on their own business to pay any attention. Before I had quite realized it, I was outside.

Still suppressing the compulsion to run, I forced myself to walk on trembling limbs until the Palace was out of sight. I dodged down some side streets and, in a deserted portico, tore off my disguise, throwing it on the cobbles. The Carmelite had disappeared and Colón it was who emerged into the light.

LIII

I FLED across the city, fear coldly mounting as I began to grasp what I had done. The documents I was clutching put me in the shade of the gallows. But I was guilty of something far worse than a crime; I had bungled. I had left my illicit key behind, which must inevitably put pursuers on my track. I had been unforgivably irresolute in dealing with the Carmelite. Whether he was dead or alive, whether he had seen enough to identify his attacker, whether I was a murderer as well as a thief, I had no way of knowing. I had compounded danger with uncertainty.

I reached my house, possessed by one thought; to save my neck, I had to leave the country. With that much certitude, I was able to fight the terror threatening to unman me, and regain sufficient calm to act.

Hurriedly, I packed my plunder, together with my own most precious documents, and a few necessary belongings. I then left, taking Diego, my son, having told the servants that I was going to visit friends outside the city. In fact, I went to the harbour.

There I looked for a ship. I found one bound for Palos. And that was an augury. I did not care where I went; all I wanted was to get away from Portugal as soon as possible. But now I suddenly remembered that poor Filipa had relatives in Huelva, which is near Palos. Her death had surely been a sign sent by God that I was to leave Lisbon; now she was pointing where I was to go. So I chose Palos, and secured a passage.

The ship was Spanish, which meant comparative safety. But she was not to leave until the next morning. The waiting was an agony. I saw in every passer-by an agent come to arrest me. I skulked around alleyways and behind warehouses; in fact I did my best to appear a figure of suspicion. But at the end of the day, I was still a free man.

Diego was mystified, for I dared not tell him the truth. However, he was delighted when, before darkness fell, we went on board. I refused to go ashore again.

I spent the night unable to sleep, expecting police to arrive at any moment and drag me off. But mercifully nothing happened. At last daybreak came. With Diego at my side, I watched through a dull drizzle as Lisbon drew away, and we began to sail down the Tagus towards the sea. Until we cleared Portugal, I was oppressed by fears of discovery and capture. But beyond that, I cannot pretend to any qualms over what I had done. I had uncovered the perfidy of Vizinho and the King; they had tried to deprive me of the rewards of my discoveries. Theft and even murder were under those circumstances justified. My interlocutors had put themselves beyond the law of God and man.

PART FIVE
La Rábida

LIV

Norway, Terra Nova, Long Island, my unnamed southern mainland, the Rock of Sagrés, Porto Santo; St Jorge de la Mina, I recited the litany of my landfalls as, once again, I approached another shore. I say another, and not foreign: Spain was in the offing, and I had a feeling of recognition, for still I retained the sense of being Spanish conferred by my upbringing. The coast now taking shape in a sluggish swell was the Condado de Niebla, which is in Castile; my hereditary allegiance was to Aragon. Nevertheless I lumped them all under the concept of Spanish, which somehow encompassed me, permitting me to identify Estremadura with Catalonia, because of - because of what? - a similarity of speech? As the voyage from Portugal drew to its end, I felt as if it were a kind of homecoming.

It was well that I did. I needed all the moral support I could muster. For the approach of land brought the depressing sight of sand dunes, marshes, sluggish channels, and mud flats glistening dully in an ebb tide. I jumped to the conclusion that I had chosen badly and the result was a familiar mood of dark hopelessness. It was 1484, the month November; I was 33 years old. An old man! - and nothing accomplished. I had failed in Portugal, and here I was slinking in uncouthly by a back door to try and make a new start in another country; a fugitive like my forebears. It was not the happiest first sight of Spain.

Even when we crossed the bar at Saltés, and entered the mouth of the Ria de Huelva, I saw little to comfort me. To port, the salt marshes were steaming in the rising sun; the low hills to starboard were barren and unpromising. An hour or so later, the ship rounded the Punta de la Arenilla, and turned into the Rio Tinto. Almost immediately, there came into view, on a hill to starboard, a large white building topped by a low cupola. I asked what it was; the answer, the Convent of La Rábida.

I had heard the name before. It was, if I remembered correctly, the home of an astronomer called Antonio de Marchena. The Father Superior was called Pérez, he too, was interested in navigation. It was a Franciscan house; that was the place for me. My steps had been kindly guided. I forgot most of my self-reproach. I had been presented with a priceless opening in Spain. I dismissed Huelva and the Perestrello connections: obviously I must go to La Rábida.

To one who has known Lisbon, or Genoa or even Bergen, Palos, engulfed in mud and marsh, is not, on immediate acquaintance the most impressive of places. And first impressions were scarcely helped by the monumental self-esteem of the customs officials.

Soon after the ship had docked, I set off with Diego for La Rábida. We walked all the way. I could have hired a horse, but I thought it would make a better impression on the brothers to arrive on foot. I had left my luggage at Palos in a warehouse: I carried with me only my papers and maps, with which I made it a principle never to part. I carried them in a pack over my shoulder; I must have looked like a pilgrim. I had taken care to arrive in my Franciscan habit; I rather enjoyed the sound of my sandals flap-flapping in the dust.

The way to the monastery was along a road skirting the top of a hill, retracing the ship's track up the river from its confluence with the Rio Odiel. It was two and a half miles, but the day was warm, even for an Andalucian autumn, and by the time we had arrived at the gates of La Rábida, I was very thirsty indeed, and poor little Diego was exhausted.

This suited my intentions. I wanted to evoke sympathy. I proposed waiting to reveal my true errand until it seemed politic. I presented myself at the convent as a simple Tertiary with no other desire than brief refuge between the trials of a coastal voyage and the tribulations of an overland journey.

'Make yourself at home. Stay as long as you like,' said the Almoner, taking me, I suppose, at my word. At all events, I took him at his. I got my luggage sent up. I accepted an offer to have a woman from the neighbourhood take care of Diego during the day.

I soon met the Brother Pérez of whom I had heard. He was Juan Pérez, and indeed the Superior. It did not take long to realize that the House over which he ruled was no ordinary convent. Conversation seemed mostly to concern the sea. Ships' officers from Palos were daily visitors. The Brothers were at pains to glean anything they possibly could about navigation. I seemed to have come to a kind of maritime academy. Palos, I now grasped, despite its unprepossessing appearance, was the home of accomplished deep sea mariners; a port from which ships regularly sailed out into the Atlantic and along the coast of Africa. The tales I had heard in Lisbon were not unjustified; I had chosen well, after all.

In these surroundings of professional seamanship, I had to move cautiously. I took care to cultivate Brother Juan's acquaintance and I unfolded what I knew at what I judged to be the correct pace to stimulate interest without arousing suspicion. Gradually, I worked round to my real purpose in coming to Spain.

The tale I told was rather different from that which had served me so ill in Lisbon. I had learned my lesson; I did not propose to repeat the same mistakes.

To nobody, would I disclose what I had seen and done; *nobody*, not even to my fellow-Franciscans. I repeated to myself, like a catechism, the necessity of observing an irksome reticence, for my nature is to speak about that which is uppermost in my mind.

Above all, I would present my plans as the consequences of theoretical deduction, because I wanted to be known as a geographer quite as much as a discoverer. I had seen enough now to realize that there were any number of mariners capable of crossing the Atlantic, but that something more than mere seamanship was required for a proper reputation. I had learned that the greatest respect was to be won in the study, not at the helm.

So my tale at La Rábida was all theory, with d'Ailly my sheet-anchor. I made one thing particularly clear. I was interested in the latitudes of the Canary Islands. This was not only on account of my promise to Scolvessen, to keep south, but because the climate was better than in Terra Nova, richer country was in prospect and also because I wanted to reserve the option of identifying my unknown islands with Asia, should that prove to be necessary.

Brother Juan appeared more sympathetic and trusting than those with whom I had had to deal in Lisbon. He was certainly an altogether pleasanter person; genial, kindly, and, as far as I could see, charitable. He decided we ought to hear Antonio de Marchena's opinion: that alone seemed to show that I had been taken seriously from the start. My Spanish sojourn had begun auspiciously.

Brother Antonio happened to be away when I arrived. I had to wait a month for his return. He heard me together with Brother Juan. The astronomer was thickset, taciturn, scholarly; listening to me in silence, fixing me while I spoke with a stare disconcerting in its frank severity. Brother Juan was much blander; yet behind his mildness, I began to feel an acute perception. He was not perhaps as credulous as I had at first supposed. In the quiet precincts of the monastery parlour, I was once more on trial for my credibility.

'If I am to understand you correctly,' said Brother Antonio, breaking silence for the first time, after I had finished my presentation, 'you have spent the past few years gazing out at the Ocean from selected points on the shores of Europe, and then by the process of your own cogitations deduced that there is land so and so many miles away in such and such a direction.'

'I thought I had made it clear that I based my reasoning on d'Ailly...'

'Quite so. You quote all the correct authorities. Of your orthodoxy there is not the slightest question. Normally, my immediate reaction would be to say "This man is a fraud" and dismiss you. But not in your case. For some reason or other, you do not give the impression of empty pretence, but of *a posteriori* reasoning.'

'I will be just a little more plain spoken than Brother Antonio,' interposed Brother Juan. 'I am after all a mere priest, while he is an astronomer first. I agree with him when he says that you're not the usual fraud; but why do you have to hide behind this philosophical rigmarole? It's well done - but it's unnecessary.'

I decided to exploit the situation by pretending to admit guilt.

'I omitted to tell you something,' I said. 'I have been to Iceland. It was in February, 1476. The sea was frozen. I can also tell you that the northernmost point of the island is seventy degrees, not sixty, as generally given.'

'Well,' said Brother Antonio, 'that has the ring of truth. But whether it *is* the truth, I'm not prepared to say.'

And that was all, on that occasion. Some time later, Brother Juan said:

'To carry out your expedition, you will have to secure the approval, if not the support, of the King and Queen - or at least the Queen. I know that the formula is The Catholic Sovereigns, Ferdinand and Isabella; but Isabella, in our experience has more to say; at least in matters such as these.

'She may quite well be favourable, but perhaps not just yet. We are still fighting the Arabs, you know. There is very little time or money for anything but the war. Until that's over, I can't see you getting the help you want.'

'Surely,' I said, 'the opposite must be the case. There's so much money and exertion in war; it is the ideal situation for enterprises of any kind. It must be easy to divert men and money already in circulation. I should have thought that peace only means parsimony and caution.'

'Your arguments,' said Brother Juan drily, 'are perfectly attuned to the circumstances.'

And on that impenetrable note, the interview ended.

Now began another trial of waiting. I could not breach Brother Juan's invincible benevolence; his intentions remained a mystery. I was virtually his prisoner, because I had scarcely any money left. I depended on his charity in all senses of the word. Sometimes Brother Antonio provoked me to argument, too obviously to test my knowledge of navigation and astronomy. Beyond that I was left very much to myself. Except for the pleasanter atmosphere, it was Lisbon all over again.

One day, after I had been at La Rábida six, seven weeks, two months, Brother Juan sent for me.

'I understand,' he said, 'that there has been a burglary in the Royal Palace at Lisbon.' Without waiting for a reply, he continued: 'Maps were taken. And somebody was killed - a Carmelite. The person responsible was almost certainly in Franciscan dress. Can you conceive of it? A Carmelite murdered by a Franciscan - it's been hushed up of course. A certain Christovão Colóm is suspected.'

I did not need to ask how he knew; he had been corresponding with the Lisbon Tertiaries.

'I may say,' continued Brother Juan, 'that this Christovão Colóm - whoever he may be . . .' - I reminded him firmly that my name was Cristóbal Colón. (I had reverted to the original form from the moment that I set my foot on Spanish soil; or should I say, returned to the land of my forefathers.) - 'Quite so. Well, this Christovão Colóm seems to have escaped with certain information which the Portuguese would have preferred not to divulge.'

After a pause, he continued, as if to himself: 'And a man who can penetrate the Lisbon archives - and live to tell the tale.' Another pause, and then: 'Perhaps you ought to put your case to Their Majesties. I have written to friends at Court.'

The revelation that I had killed a Friar did not weigh on me; I saw only that it had persuaded Brother Juan to believe in me. But I was not entirely happy. Getting your own way rarely seems to bring pleasure.

'I advise you to be patient,' said Brother Juan. 'Results are unlikely to be immediate.'

He was right. The months rolled by, and no answer came. I was told - and I had to believe - that while that year's campaign lasted, nobody at Court would have the time to spare for Colón. It was now the spring of 1485, and the war had flared up again. I waited at La Rábida, while Coin and Benamaquex and Ronda and Marbella fell to the Spaniards. Of course I too rejoiced at the discomfiture of the Arabs, but my pleasure was tempered by the delay these victories meant to me.

At last, even Brother Juan had to admit that officialdom was being a little too leisurely, so he invoked the aid of various noble acquaintances. One of them, Don Luis de la Cerda, the Duke of Medinaceli, responded magnificently: he was preparing to leave for the front (on garrison duty, because the campaign was now almost over), otherwise he would have been delighted to meet me. In the meanwhile, he promised to do what he could to get me a hearing.

'But I suspect,' wrote Don Luis, 'that your friend may still have to wait. I know only too well what that means. He has all my sympathy. As he seems to be someone worth taking care of, I am arranging to pay him a small allowance, so that he can keep body and soul together while Their Majesties make up their minds.'

'Don Luis doesn't cast his favours to the winds,' said Brother Juan when he showed me the letter. 'You seem to have a knack of compelling belief – even at second hand.'

About two months later, the order to present myself at Court finally arrived. After all the procrastination, now I had to hurry. I had been requested to be in Córdoba before the end of January, and the New Year had already arrived.

'Remember,' said Brother Juan, 'whatever happens, you can always creep back to La Rábida.'

I did anything but creep away. Soon afterwards, I rode out from La Rábida in modest glory. I was escorted, if you please, by a Royal messenger. I was of Royal interest, and subsidized by a Ducal purse. As I departed, I could not help thinking how different a person it was who now clattered out of the cloister above Palos, from he who had gone forth from the inn at Genoa.

I followed the road along the crest of the hill upon which La Rábida stood; down on my left, I saw the Rio Tinto, the ships dotting the roadstead, and Huelva and Palos nestling by the tidal flats. There was my kingdom; I seemed about to inherit it.

I swung inland, and the water vanished. For the first time for years, I had turned my back on the sea.

'Not for long,' I had said to Brother Juan, when I said goodbye, leaving Diego in his care, I was fond of my son. He was a sweet child, and my new barrier against the loneliness that always threatened to beset me. But the voyage from Lisbon had showed me that to have him with me was to be tied. Brother Juan had offered to find him a home and see to his schooling; thus was I granted the liberty I required.

'Not for long,' I had said. 'I won't trouble you too long. Only a few months at the most.'

'As long as you need,' the Franciscan had replied. 'With God and the Catholic Sovereigns, you can never be sure.'

LV

ALL the way from La Rábida, I was inspired by the prospect of imminent success. The daydreams were duly drowned on the twentieth of January, 1486 - when I arrived at Córdoba, to find that the Court had gone to spend the winter in Madrid.

I naturally proposed to follow, but the courier who had escorted me, a mulish fellow, informed me that his orders were to bring me to Córdoba, and no farther. I appealed to authority, in the shape of the senior official in residence, Alonso de Quintanilla, the Accountant General. But the verdict was upheld. I was to wait in Córdoba until the Court returned.

It was not an entirely profitless interval. It was then that I laid the foundation of the library that was to become one of my few solaces in the empty years ahead. There were *colporteurs* at Córdoba and, even my modest stipend (without the forethought of Don Luis, I would have starved that winter) enabled me to buy most of what I wanted. I acquired a Bible, a Ptolemy, and a brand new edition of d'Ailly to replace the copy left behind in Lisbon. And, while I waited for the Court, I read.

I talked also, perhaps too much, although little about exploration. Conversation was mostly about the war. The successes of the preceding summer had left behind an overwhelming optimism. One more quick push, and victory was ours. That was five years ago, and Granada only fell the other day.

That was a useful lesson about the people with whom I was going to deal. For although I considered myself Spanish, and thought of myself as half way home, yet I still felt among strangers, whose behaviour I had yet to fathom.

So, in idleness, talk, reading and observation, the winter passed. The Court returned at the end of April. On the eighth of May, the summons finally came. I was to see the Queen alone.

'We decided it would be best that way,' said Quintanilla, while I was waiting to enter the audience chamber. 'Ferdinand is a worthy character and all that but . . . between ourselves, he's a little unimaginative. The Queen is different.

And, for what it's worth, in my view, she rules the roost.'

My supposed resemblance to Isabella of Castile has frequently been the subject of comment. I maintain that it is a gross exaggeration. Admittedly there are the same blue-green eyes; there is the same auburn hair, and we are of a height and of an age. But there the similarity ends. Her complexion is fair, where mine of course is coppery and freckled. Her features are far more regular than mine; but the real difference lies in habitual expression. Hers is the embodiment of serenity, whereas mine seems to reflect the conjunction of worry and self assurance by which I am plagued.

I had been led to expect a potentate encased in luxury and pomp; the truth of which appeared to be confirmed by the sight that met me as I entered the audience chamber in the Palace of the Alcazar on that memorable day in Córdoba. The high walls were encrusted with elaborate draperies; the furniture was ornate; the Queen was expensively dressed.

But there was something at odds with the surroundings. Through all the ostentation the convent seemed fighting to emerge, and Isabella herself seemed a nun out of place. It was only a fleeting impression, and the next instant I saw the tableau as it was intended to appear. But the effect of the vision (for that is what I suppose it to have been) was exceedingly powerful, and it has never left me.

I grasped then, what I had occasionally heard, that the Queen had assumed this style to maintain her position. If it seemed overdone - but then perhaps I judge by Italian standards - I understood it was because Isabella had to govern noble underlings who perhaps are a trifle more barbarous than their Italian counterparts. She had, I divined, been forced to act a role in the achievement of her ends.

I felt the tug of an odd sympathy. I seemed not to have been introduced to a stranger, but to have been reunited with someone I knew well. Opening the audience was like picking up the thread of an interrupted conversation.

Isabella began by apologizing for having made me kick my heels during the winter. She also apologized for having kept me waiting since her return - although it had only been ten days and not, as I was subsequently to learn, particularly long by the standards of her court.

'It is terrible,' she said, 'to be forced to wait, unable to act, and allowed only to watch.'

'You understand my feelings very well.'

'Perhaps because they are my own.'

'But Your Majesty, look at what you have achieved. You have almost driven the Arabs out of Spain; you have already accomplished practically everything you set out to do. You must be free to act and decide.'

'That is what I'm told. But sometimes I think it's an illusion. Of course, I believe in free will. But then, my confessors who have gone to great lengths to instil that doctrine into me, try to impose their will on my actions. My advisers do the same thing in other directions. Very often, I doubt how much I'm really my own master - I suppose it's one of the penalties of power. Sometimes I envy the meanest private soldier; I imagine *he's* free to do what he wants.

'Or perhaps what I really want is to put myself entirely in the hands of my confessor, and forget that I have a mind of my own. How comforting it would be not to have to make decisions - let God decide.'

It was scarcely a conversation between sovereign and suppliant; it seemed more the exchange of confidences between sympathetic equals. Yet I was not at ease. The talk about the constraints on the will - how much was really philosophy, and how much a veiled attempt to undermine my defences by invoking sympathy for her plight? I was really put on my guard when the Queen abruptly changed the conversation by saying:

'We must make the most of this interview. Now please tell me exactly what it is you want. But remember, I'm a complete ignoramus when it comes to cosmography; so please be kind and make things simple.'

It was so artless, it smacked of guile. Then I suspected that the flattery which, in spite of my caution, I had felt at being treated as an equal, might have not been far removed from gullibility. And something else which, at the outset, I had taken as a compliment, now fed suspicion. We were alone, the Queen and I. I very seriously suspected a trap.

To this day, I do not know if I was right. But I decided then that there was a conspiracy to worm my secrets out of me. To gain time, in order to marshal my arguments and perfect my defence against the supposed attack, I began with an impromptu justification of oceanic exploration as it applied to Spain.

The Catholic Sovereigns, I said, were approaching the end of a long war. They would soon have expelled the last Arab; Spain was about to be master of its own house. But after that - what? Further conquest was desirable. But a land war was uncertain at best, and could end in disaster. It was far better to look to the sea. On the wide horizons of the Atlantic, there were few rivals and no obstacles. The Portuguese, admittedly, had gone far, but to the south and to the east. Let Her Majesty ignore Africa, that torrid wasteland, and let her turn west; there were new worlds to be had for the asking.

'Very well put,' said Isabella with the shadow of a smile. 'Most convincing - you almost seem to have missed your vocation: you would have made a good preacher.'

Was there a hint of irony in this? I do not know; I did not dwell on the matter; I had to plunge into my argument proper.

In my reading I had been led to the book of Esdras and this passage: 'Upon the third day, thou didst command that the waters should be gathered in the seventh part of the earth: six parts hast thou dried up.'

I now quoted this to prove biblical support for my contention that the Atlantic must be relatively narrow. Knowing how devout the Queen was, I judged it best to begin this way: faced with King John in Portugal, who was of an entirely different temperament, I had left Esdras alone. But I could see that I had approached Isabella correctly; and, the advantage mine, I now turned to my philosophic exposition. I presented myself as a theoretician who could *prove* the existence of new countries across the Atlantic, and who was only waiting for the opportunity to demonstrate his theories; Colón, cosmographer, mariner and explorer, rolled into one; a new kind of man.

For this was now what I wanted the world to believe, it was the ambition that would surely appeal to a generous-hearted woman. Merely to reveal what had already been discovered would be a mediocre reward for all that I had done. It may be argued that my intentions were dishonest. I can only reply that the outward forms are part of my reward; indeed, there is very little else left, I cannot make myself believe that I am the first to cross the Atlantic; at least I can compel others to do so.

To add travail to this conflict, my heart was bursting with what I had seen. I wanted the world to believe in my islands - and I had debarred myself from talking about them openly. I am certain that Isabella divined my anguish.

I talked about my agony in the waters off Cape St Vincent. I had not intended to, but I found myself compelled to do so. I told her how I felt as if I had been reborn. Something about this woman before me made me bare myself in a way I refused to do with anyone else.

I felt a silent response. I seemed to echo something within her, and she in me. She too had a vocation. She had been called to purify Spain and drive out the Moor, as I had been called to reveal the other shore of the Atlantic. And so I said, for it came upon me that moment as I stood within the audience chamber, that I had been sent to give Spain an Atlantic empire.

Then I unburdened myself - I was compelled to, even if only to maintain the authenticity of what I had said. I revealed who I was and whence I came; how I was of Spanish origin and how, if there were any place on earth away from a ship in which I could feel at home, it was in Her Majesty's dominions.

Isabella listened in silence and sympathy, interrupting me once only to say:

'There is so much enquiry into religion today, I'm sometimes rather perplexed. My very Cabinet Ministers are in trouble - and there is very little I can do about it. Let us agree that you are a good Catholic, and leave it at that.'

I sensed a kind of victory; but it was shot by remorse. I had left my son behind at La Rábida to fend for himself among strangers. Was that right? Perhaps I had sinned in doing so. At least I ought to repay him - and justify myself - by raising him from his father's mean estate. I thought of the Perestrellos and the hereditary governorship of Porto Santo. And then another vision rose up, from another sea, and another age. I seemed to be a child again, in the harbour of Genoa, offering to my imaginary Queen, the Terra Nova that was woven out of the rocks around the breakwater. And the image of that woman, that then lived only in the painting of the madonna in the Church, seemed to fuse with the real Isabella before me, and it was as if I saw myself as a child with a premonition of what was to come. And I said:

'I want the title of Don Christobal Colón, with the rank of Admiral of the Ocean Sea. I shall also be made perpetual Governor of the new islands, with a right to ten per cent of their revenues. The titles and income are to be hereditary, descending in the male line, in perpetuity.'

There once more was the half forgotten scene that I had often played underneath the lighthouse at Genoa. The game had come to an end; it was no longer make believe.

'You drive a hard bargain' - thus began Isabella, 'and you have an ear for a title. But perhaps you are not asking too much, considering what you are offering. I am not sure that I have understood everything you have said. But you seem to have those islands in your grasp, almost as if you had been there yourself. I am tempted to give you the three ships you want; as you say so persuasively, I have little to lose, and new worlds to gain.

'But I cannot give you a decision immediately. I am not quite my own master, you know. There are so many things to be considered, and I shall have to consult my advisers first. I must ask you to have a little more patience.'

And with that, the audience closed. I left in anything but a calm state of mind. I was sure that I had said too much and spoken too fervidly for the occasion. On the other hand, the Queen had been friendly and yet she had abruptly turned from a dreamer to a calculating woman of business. I alternated between hope and despair, according to the light in which this or that part of the audience struck me.

Days passed and then weeks and months, and I heard no more. I tried to cheer myself with plausible excuses for the delay. Then I pestered Quintanilla; I tried, unsuccessfully, to see Cardinal Mendoza. But all I got was perfunctory assurance that the matter was in hand. Then somebody in Quintanilla's office wrote informing me that I had been granted an allowance, out of the Queen's privy purse, of 18,000 maraveris annually. I was part of the Royal establishment, with the pay of an able seaman, no less.

Patience, patience, they said. I had ample time to cultivate that supposed virtue. I also had time to become intimately acquainted with the anger, gloom and despair, with which it is intimately related.

LVI

I AM born to fight lone battles. But before the twin demons of uncertainty and fear, I am helpless. Against them, I now hungered for a woman to protect me. Without one I do not believe that I could have survived the Spanish years.

She who answered my call is the woman with whom I still live. Her name is Beatriz Enriquez de Harana.

When I arrived in Córdoba Quintanilla introduced me to his circle of acquaintances. Among them was a pharmacist called Roderigo Enriquez de Harana. He was well read, we got on together, and he regularly had me round to dine. It was in his house that I met Beatriz.

She was an orphaned cousin to whom Roderigo had promised to give a home. At first, I scarcely noticed her. It was the happy time before the return of the Court and my first audience with Isabella. Possessed by unaccustomed hope I did not as yet crave consolation.

But the time came when I needed it. Waiting for the Commission that refused to appear, I at last felt my black mood descend upon me, and then I turned to Beatriz. I suppose it might be said that I seized the first opportunity that presented itself. It would be more correct to say that in all Córdoba she was the only woman I was able to approach.

She is not strictly beautiful, but there is about her a quality of softness that I had missed both in Otsego and Filipa. As the melancholy of my situation drove me to seek comfort, I became aware of its presence. And of pity she was full. It was to this that I appealed; and she answered. Words scarcely seemed to pass between us; without effort on my part or coquetry on hers, we moved insensibly through the various stages of desire until, as a matter of course, she came back to my lodgings one day and slept with me. In the best sense of the word, it was charity For I almost seemed to be attaining manhood for the second time. Otsego had taught me first, but half-contemptuously; what she achieved was eaten away by the strange, arid years with poor Filipa. With all my deficiencies, Beatriz was still generous with her feelings. She truly loved me; the only one who has done so.

To the everlasting credit of her family, I was allowed to enjoy her unmolested. Although twenty-two, she was still legally Roderigo's ward, and I had been guilty of the worst insult it is possible to offer a man; I had violated one of his womenfolk. He had every right to exact satisfaction; yet he did not.

Very likely the explanation was that Beatriz was no virgin, so that perhaps someone else had already paid the penalty. I did not pursue the matter, I was hungering for love, not honour. I needed a woman, not a girl, and I had no wish to destroy happiness with knowledge.

But even had the circumstances been different, I think I would have been forgiven. I was, after all, well introduced, had been received by the Queen, enjoyed a Royal stipend, and was altogether a man of some prospects. I would be entitled to a mistress, where an ordinary mortal would not - and I was taking Beatriz off her family's hands; no mean consideration this, for dowry there was none, and no husband in prospect.

But Beatriz was as a wife, and came to live with me. I moved out of my lodgings, and took the house which remains the nearest approach I have to a home. It is an old Moorish building, with a walled garden. There, I learned to make love again, and found the only contentment I seem to have known; for Beatriz is a true woman; she kept the world at bay.

With an unpredictable brutality, the outside breached the walls around me. Late one night, we were disturbed by a knocking on the door. Through a window, I saw three figures outside: when I asked who they were, I was told to open 'in the name of the Supreme Council.' By now Beatriz had joined me.

'Let them in,' she said, 'quickly; don't keep them waiting.'

I drew the bolt, and three nondescript men entered; they were obviously police.

'Go away,' Beatriz whispered urgently, 'let me talk to them.' I left the room, and waited for a long time outside while a muffled conversation took its course, terminating in the opening and shutting of the front door. I found Beatriz alone, half worried, half amused.

'You know,' she said, 'it's lucky I come from the right family.'

'What on earth do you mean?' I asked, 'I don't understand. Who were they? What did they want?'

Instead of answering directly, she pursued her own line of thought. 'There's something I've not told you,' she said, 'my full family name is Harana y Torquemada. I'm related to the Inquisitor General - you know, Tomás de Torquemada. My mother was the half sister of his father. These things count, you know. They wouldn't touch anyone in the family.'

'I don't understand,' I said. 'What have you done?'

'Nothing,' she answered simply, 'it's you they wanted.'

An icy squall seemed to sweep through the room. I had been long enough in Spain to realize that the intensity of religious passion was of an order to which I was quite unused; Genoa and Lisbon were easy going by comparison. And I knew what the Inquisition was. I had been repeatedly warned how dangerous it was, because it was so popular. There was much talk of Don Miguel de Iranzo, a nobleman and High Constable of Córdoba, who had been murdered by a crowd two years previously when he tried to exercise Christian charity by protecting some fugitives from the Inquisition. I had been advised to be very careful in my devotions, and not to give any suspicion of unorthodoxy. 'Even the Queen can't help,' Quintanilla had said, 'if they get hold of you,' and told a frightful tale of Cabinet Ministers dragged off for interrogation and punishment.

All this passed before me, as I stood feeling the coils of fear upon me, with Beatriz looking up at me that night.

'But I still don't understand,' I said. 'Why should the Inquisition be interested in me? I'm not a *converso*; I'm not a secret Judaizer.'

'No; but they say you're suspected of being a heretic.'

Now I had not told Beatriz about my Cathar antecedents; I had kept it an absolute secret, and still did. But I reminded her how I had been impeccable in going to Mass, and never swore or blasphemed.

'That's it,' she said. 'You're too pious, and that made them suspicious. Anyway, it doesn't matter. I told them you were a foreigner, so that means you can't be blamed. But it was the name that really did it. Of course they wouldn't touch a Torquemada.'

'I'm not one.'

'No, but as long as we're together, you're quite safe.'

But I was not willing to be convinced; not just then anyway.

'If your family connections are so useful,' I said, 'why did you drop the Torquemada from your name?'

Beatriz shrugged her shoulders. 'It's not something you usually boast about,' she said, 'especially when your friends have had dealings with the Holy Office.'

Now, for the first time I was struck by the habit which all my acquaintances had of referring to the Inquisition obliquely; it was the Supreme Council, the Supremo, the Holy Office, anything, but never the Inquisition; as if it were some evil spirit they were afraid of conjuring up by mentioning its name.

Beatriz was vindicated; I was no more molested. And I took great care to redouble my devotions; I heard the Office whenever I could; sometimes twice a day. I walked in fear, for the secret that I nursed was quite enough to get me into the most serious trouble. But the Inquisition was banished for a spell when, at last I was told that the Commission had been appointed to examine my enterprise, and that I was to appear in person before it at Salamanca. But although this was the promise of the consummation of my desires, I left Córdoba with a twinge of regret. Beatriz remained behind; and I now found that I depended on her. 'The husband hath not power of his own body,' says St Paul, 'but the wife.'

LVII

I APPROACHED Salamanca with all the reverent illusions of one who has never been to a university. I was rapidly undeceived. A day or two after my arrival, I heard the well remembered hiss and discord of a rabble. I looked out of a window of the inn where I was staying, and at first glance it was Genoa all over again. Heads were milling below me like a tidal race. I took some time to grasp that this mob was not made up of artisans, nor was it concerned with politics. It was the first time I had seen students on the rampage. It was also the first time I had seen a religious riot. Neither was a particularly pleasant experience. The pageant of disorder conjured up the family tales of past persecution, and my imagination planted me in Barcelona a hundred years before. I half expected to re-enact the Golgotha of my ancestors, and be savaged by this academic riff-raff.

They, however, were only howling for Christian teachers. I did not understand. Nothing in Genoa or Lisbon had prepared me for such a sentiment; nor had I been long enough in Spain to grasp what was happening. The innkeeper enlightened me.

'There's too many Jews and *Moriscos* among the professors,' he said. 'Vermin, the lot of them. The students've got the right idea. Clear 'em all out, and get some decent God-fearing Spaniards instead, that's what I say.'

As soon as it seemed safe to do so, I followed my instructions and went to report to the Governor's palace. There I was met with the announcement that 'pressure of events' had obliged the Commission to postpone its business.

'To put it bluntly,' said the elegant, but vaguely distraught secretary who received me, 'we can't start while the disorders continue. We're scared to death of the students. And I don't mean only the Commission: I include the University and the City Government as well. Strictly between ourselves, you see, the Inquisition is at the bottom of the trouble. And nobody can touch them. Anybody connected with the Inquisition is protected by the widest possible immunity. I don't only mean

Papal bulls - we can cope with them - but the Inquisition is of the people: and who can stand against them? *Vox populi Vox Dei* as those distressingly vulgar Inquisitors so smugly quote, although I should have thought *Vox Diablo* more to the point.'

I left with considerable food for thought. I was asked not to repeat the conversation; it was the first hint that my patrons themselves might not feel absolutely secure from the Inquisition.

I remained indoors for the next few days, while the disorder continued. I seemed to have been abandoned by the Commission. I had to depend for news on the students who frequented the inn. From them, I learned how the authorities put up a feeble fight, and soon capitulated. One evening, somebody at my table turned round to favour me with the information that:

'We couldn't get Old Christian professors; but we've got the next best thing. Tomorrow, we'll have some New Christians. Come along to the Cathedral and see the fun.' I had not the slightest inclination to accept, but something about the speaker induced caution. Always at the inn, a shade too friendly with the innkeeper, he had spy written all over him. It was safest to assume that he was connected with the Inquisition. For my own good, I would have to follow the crowd. So, the following afternoon, I joined the throngs in the Cathedral, and I watched the public baptism of the unbelieving professors. I stood among the students in the nave, and was submerged by their hoots and catcalls as each convert made a recantation of his errors.

It was impossible to mistake the embarrassment of the officiating clergy. A forced conversion as a sop to the rabble must be satisfying to no one in his right senses.

But the crowning discomfiture was when Professor Abraham Zacuto was announced. I had heard of him in Portugal, he was to be one of my examiners. He so obviously regarded the procedure as an act of expediency to keep his Chair; a more insincere Christian, or reprobate Jew, I doubt whether it is possible to find. And that showed how careful I would have to be in avoiding all suspicion of heterodoxy. If one of the most eminent mathematicians of our day was unsafe: what danger threatened an untried - and untrusted - explorer?

LVIII

It was an uneasy Colón who at last was told that, the students having been pacified and order restored, the proceedings could begin. By then I saw that my task was going to be harder than I had anticipated. Not only would I have to argue my case meticulously - for which I was prepared - but I would also have to fight at every syllable the danger unexpectedly shown to lurk under the double crown of the mob and the Inquisition. I began to understand that Spain was an awkward place for anybody with unorthodox antecedents.

Thus burdened, on the fourteenth of December in the Year of Our Lord fourteen eighty-six, I appeared before the Commission for the first time.

There are some people, who, from the moment of meeting, one senses are predestined antagonists. Unhappy premonitions of this kind assailed me as I was introduced to Brother Hernando de Talavera. He was the Prior of the Prado, the most learned of the learned Order of the Jeromites, the Bishop of Avila, sometime Confessor to the Queen. He was balanced, just and saintly. He had all the attributes of a reasonable examiner. And yet something about him cried to high Heaven of invincible antipathy. And it was this Brother Hernando who had been selected to preside over 'my' Commission.

The scene of that first session remains vividly before me; a stunted crescent of solemn figures seated on a daïs; a living repository of geographical and astronomical knowledge. There, on the left flank sat old Abraham Zacuto, fresh from baptism, still with the mocking half-smile he had worn in the Cathedral. I knew that he had submitted, only because he wanted peace at any price to finish his great work; the computation of new navigational tables. I devoutly hoped he would be able to, because bitter experience had shown how deplorably inaccurate were those in existence.

Next to him, sat Diego de Deza, every inch the Provost of St Stephens. Then came two sea-captains, Sebastian Rodriguez and Alonso de Riveras; there to judge questions of seamanship.

After them came two nondescript scholars called Vicente Sanchez de Segovia and Diego Perez who, to my cost, as I was to discover, between them had a comprehensive mastery of languages and the sources of geographical information. And next to them were two celebrities who by their very presence announced that I was being taken very seriously. They were an enigmatic, holy Don, very capable in worldly affairs, Juan de Fonseca, Archdeacon of Seville; a kind of business adviser to the Queen; and Luis de Santángel, Minister of Finance, no less. By Santángel's side sat Don Roderigo Maldonaldo, the very excellent Governor of Salamanca, who seemed to be thinking more of riots than of Colón.

Then came what at first seemed my one gleam of hope in that austere company; the only fellow-Franciscan, Brother Roderigo Navarez. It was not long before I grasped the danger he represented. He came from Galicia; he was a seaman's priest, and he specialized in collecting mariners' gossip. He knew as much as any man living about sightings of new land. Two sombre clerks brought up the end and, in the middle, slightly apart from the rest, sat my saintly taskmaster, Brother Hernando. I felt the thirteen pairs of eyes boring me with their interrogatory gaze; obscene caricature of the Inquisition which I am sure was so uncomfortably before our minds.

But why harp on that grim piece of mummery? For that sitting at St Stephens was the start of my Via Dolorosa.

Salamanca - Córdoba - Valladolid - Toledo - Ciudad Real - Madrid: thus the stations of that tribunal, nomadic, merciless and without end; memorial of the six years past, of my bitter wandering in Spain; of the torment of years thrown away. I have talked, listened and argued, while Africa was rounded and the ends of the earth were seen, I have been tortured by idleness while others made their gains on the sea. And to what end? - that the Commission of Brother Hernando, a monster begat by cupidity out of procrastination, might worm my secrets out of me.

I do not believe that this was Isabella's intention; I am sure that in all good faith she merely wanted to establish the validity of my enterprise before committing her support. But I had no reason to put the same trust in her domestics. Before me as a warning I had the ever-present spectre of the King of

Portugal who had all but stolen what I knew. Brother Hernando would not have the same opportunity.

I set out to compel the belief of the Commission, without revealing what I knew. I decided to argue from first principles; to present what I had seen as the fruits of logic, that ever-seductive false god. With hindsight, I can see that I must have made a fool of myself. One does not need interminable lectures on sultry, inland afternoons to prove that the world is round; we all agree that if you sail west you must necessarily (assuming no land is in the way) reach the east. Yet all this and more, the Commission suffered patiently from me.

My case was in fact reduced to one point; the width of the Atlantic. If it was 8,000 miles, as so many believed, then I would be unlikely to obtain the support I needed, because no ship, it was agreed, could survive such a passage. I had to convince my interrogators that it was narrow enough to be crossed.

It was there I turned to the Bible. I quoted the passage from Esdras that I had quoted to Isabella:

> 'Upon the third day, Thou didst command that the waters should be gathered in the seventh part of the earth; six parts hast thou dried up, and kept them, to the intent that of these, some being planted of God and tilled might serve thee.'

But faced with an assembly of qualified philosophers, instead of a mere sovereign, I now used the text to draw more elaborate conclusions. Starting with my own observations of land 3,900 miles out in the Atlantic, I took the most suitable estimate of the circumference of the earth, which is 27,000 miles. By Esdras, the Ocean Sea must necessarily be one seventh of that figure, giving the required 3,900 miles to the other side.

But the Commission refused to be impressed. They tried many ways of worming more substantial information out of me. They would adjourn, send me away, to wear me down in worry and idleness, and then recall me for another session of wearisome interrogation. There was an infamous sitting at Ciudad Real two years ago, when the Commission all but managed to bully my secrets out of me. They threatened me with torture; but I stood firm. Afterwards, old Abraham Zacuto - in many ways the most perceptive and dangerous of my interrogators-took me aside and said:

'You are too strong for us - you have *women* behind you.'

He is wise, old Abraham; in some ways the wisest of all my interrogators. I have women behind me. Beatriz, to whom I have been faithful, and she to me, all these years, has given me strength. Wherever I have been; in Salamanca, in Toledo, in Valladolid; in the extremities of Castile, Beatriz has been my support. When the agonies of the Commission were suspended, I hurried back to her at Córdoba, for I knew there was always solace in her loins.

But Beatriz was more than a bedfellow. I sent for Diego, my son, and she looked after him as if he had been her own. On the fifteenth of August, in the year 1488, she gave birth to my younger son, Fernando.

I have a home to go to. In Beatriz I have a refuge from my persecutors; I have an ever-ready cure for the ills of the spirit. And she knows how to wait. Abraham was right; I have a woman behind me: from her I had the strength to defy the world. Through her, and her alone, I have been able to keep my secret. But I am uneasy at the way I have been constrained to treat her.

Such respect as I enjoy in Spain is due to my antecedents, real or supposed. Because I was once married to a noblewoman, and because as a foreigner my origins may be garnished, I have been able to palm myself off as someone of good birth and well connected. To forfeit those advantages would be to make my path thornier than it need be. I would find it difficult to get hearing. I might find myself excluded from Court. A low-born wife would suffice. And Beatriz is not of noble stock.

To live with her is no disgrace; but to have her as wife would be a disastrous impediment. So, for the sake of my career, I have not married her. She understands perfectly and has never uttered a breath of reproach, but I feel it is a scurvy way of repaying all I owe her. In answering my call, she has become a burden on my conscience.

But beyond rank and relationship, there is another, and perhaps more powerful, justification for my conduct. It is due to the Queen that the Commission has been obliged to persevere with me. I know this from the audiences she has given me from time to time. I believe that I would have enjoyed none of her help if I had been married.

I do not mean to imply an affair of the flesh. I am not made to be the illicit lover of famous women. And Isabella is a paragon of virtue - at least in the physical sense. But there are many ways to consort with the opposite sex, and the most profound are not necessarily the most carnal.

On the occasions on which I have seen Ferdinand and Isabella together, it has been fairly obvious that they do not see the temptation of the flesh in each other. I know the rumour - among others - that under the mask of Christian chastity, Isabella hides a deeper, more troublesome coldness. I also know that Ferdinand does not stint himself in the satisfaction of his sexual requirements. It is obvious that some infirmity impedes Isabella in the enjoyment of physical love. Instead, she has to make do with her imagination; and I believe that she uses the men around her to give form to her thoughts. For some reason she appeared to be attracted to me. Perhaps it was because of our physical similarity. I know that she is supposed to possess incestuous leanings, and it is possible that she regarded me like a brother. I am sure that, in her mind, I was transmuted into an incubus.

This gave me, I believe, an ascendancy over her. It was invaluable in the prosecution of my aims. But it depended on my being unmarried. An attachment of the kind I am describing depends on the object being attainable. Once married, the person concerned is unable to arouse feelings because he has put himself out of reach. He has destroyed illusion, and can no longer be the stuff of fantasy.

Thus it was, that I had to keep the Queen in a state of suspense. Had I snapped the fragile bonds upon which her protection depends, I might have been defeated by now. I can truthfully say that for Beatriz' own sake, I could not marry her, but it is true, I have women behind me.

LIX

LATE in 1491, I received a letter from Brother Hernando requesting me to go to Valladolid. Something in its tone suggested that things were moving towards a crisis. The years had dragged on; the Commission had become virtually dormant. When I complained, I was reminded that 'there's a war on.' What was to be the final offensive against the Moor was now ponderously gathering momentum. Spain was possessed by a crusading fever approaching climax; there was an obsession with affairs on land: it was not the time for maritime enterprises. 'After the war,' they said, 'wait until after the war.' So I waited in Córdoba, while Baza fell and Málaga was sacked, and Granada, the last redoubt of Islam in Spain, was invested. Victory was finally within sight.

So I answered Brother Hernando's summons with more than the usual expectations. He saw me alone, by no means for the first time, but when I was ushered into his presence in the room of the Jeromite monastery where he was staying, I felt that something was wrong. He held a document which, as soon as I was seated, he handed to me, saying: 'Do you recognize this?'

It was a letter I had written. I did not need to ask how Brother Hernando had obtained it. The mails were regularly tampered with; and he doubtless had his agents.

'You're playing with fire, my friend.'

I preferred not to meet his eye. The letter was to my brother, Bartolomé, who was now in England. When my affairs in Spain had languished, I had written to him, divulging as much of my ideas as seemed safe, and asked him to go to London and try to interest the English King in my plans. So far, His Majesty, Henry the Seventh, had shown as little taste for action as Isabella the Catholic. This particular letter contained suggestions for better presenting my case; for Bartolomé, while he had immediately complied with my request, and was clearly enthusiastic on my behalf, was not the perfect agent. He needed coaching. And what I had written was decidedly incriminating.

'Let me remind you of one not unimportant fact,' continued Brother Hernando, with his habitual calm, but with an unaccustomed touch of contempt, 'you are being paid a royal stipend; so that you are a servant of Their Majesties; and at the same time you are treating with a foreign rival. There is an ugly word for this conduct; the penalty is serious.'

Brother Hernando took the piece of parchment out of my unresisting fingers, and put it deliberately on a small table next to him.

'Do you know,' he asked, 'why I am on the Commission?'

'It's always been a puzzle to me,' I said, finding my voice. 'You're no cosmographer, and you don't pretend to know a great deal about astronomy and exploration. Why put you in charge of men who do?'

'Exactly,' said Brother Hernando, in a tone of voice that disarmed my insults and made me feel rather foolish. 'But I may have other qualifications, you know. My work is to hold Brother Tomás de Torquemada at bay. In plain language, I am fighting the Inquisition.'

'Quite frankly, I don't see the connection,' I answered. 'The Commission is under royal patronage. Surely that's protection enough?'

'I think you take a little too much for granted. It may surprise you to know that I have to look after Abraham Zacuto.'

'But he's the most valuable member of your Commission. He's a brilliant mathematician, and he's the very Devil at cross-examination, as I know only too well. Besides - he's a Professor.'

'And a New Christian.'

'New or Old, what does it matter? I mean, I saw his baptism, and he does his best to conform. And he has become well versed in Catholic theology.'

'But he continues to avoid pork, and he generally manages to avoid lecturing on Saturdays.'

'Oh yes; "as sick as Abraham on the Sabbath," has become slang for malingering. It's a standing joke.'

'It's no joke, I can assure you. I admit you can't expect an old gentleman to abandon the habits of a lifetime. Probably old

Abraham does observe the law of Moses in private - and Christian charity suggests that it's nobody's concern but his own. But we live in odd times. Professor Zacuto faces a charge of secret Judaizing.

'And that is the worst imaginable crime today. Murderers are reprieved to satisfy the compassion of their judges, witches are nursed as the unfortunate victims of delusion, but Heaven help the New Christian who lapses, be it only a temporary aberration.'

'This is all very interesting,' I said. 'But I don't quite see what it's got to do with me.'

'The question is,' continued Brother Hernando, ignoring the interruption, almost as if he were speaking to himself, 'the question is: how much longer can I fend off Torquemada? The Queen dislikes the whole idea of the - the Inquisition,' he said, half reluctantly pronouncing the word. 'Like me, she disapproves of coercion. We both believe that the only worthwhile conversions are made by kindness and argument.

'But Brother Tomás has the monks, the parish priests and the populace behind him. When he speaks, he speaks for the carpenter at his bench, and the peasant behind the plough. When he tortures, they are behind him at the rack. Who can stand against a man like that?

'I have been hard pressed, I can assure you, to keep Professor Zacuto out of Brother Tomás' clutches. But protecting Abraham has not been my sole concern. I have had to devote considerable attention to the task of seeing that the reason for which the Commission was created does not disappear in the flames of Torquemada.'

'I don't quite understand what you're driving at,' I said. This interminable harangue was beginning to weary me.

'No? Well, in plain language, Colón has to be defended from the Holy Office, *and his safety depends on Talavera alone.*'

'I see; you're trying to threaten me now.'

'You never speak before the Commission,' Brother Hernando continued deliberately, 'without quoting holy men and sacred texts.'

'And what of it?' I replied. 'I know the dangers of the *Supremo* as well as anybody. I'm quite aware that it is essential to show unimpeachable orthodoxy at all times and in all places.'

'Quite,' said Brother Hernando. 'But the Inquisitor has a highly developed nose. Too much attention to the Faith is as dangerous as too little. Indifference suggests the backslider; but ostentatious zeal turns suspicions in the direction of heresy.

'When somebody - supposedly a foreigner - arrives in Spain clearly speaking Castilian, or at least Catalan as his mother tongue, and in an old-fashioned form, one does begin to wonder. There may be a perfectly reasonable explanation. But some people tend to think in terms of a religious refugee returning. There have been heretics in Catalonia - in Aragon - on Majorca too.

'Well, I won't press the point. I was able to satisfy the *Supremo* on that matter. But when you insisted on bringing faith into the Commission, you made my work much harder.

'You see, you have completely misjudged the nature of the Inquisition. It is not concerned with thought, as you seem to imagine, but with belief. To assert that the earth rotates while the sun is fixed, instead of the other way about, won't necessarily be punished. You may safely profess the most daring ideas, provided you respect the observances of the Faith. You have failed to grasp that elementary truth. To have dragged theology into the Commission was the worst possible thing you could have done. It was worse than dangerous; it was unnecessary. And so transparent.

'We have several times been on the point of dismissing you - '

'I know,' I said. 'The Queen has stopped you.'

'Don't delude yourself. It was not only Her Majesty, although I daresay you would like to think so. We have wanted to dismiss you, not because your idea is fundamentally unsound, but because you insist on behaving like an impostor.

'Although we who are on the Commission are of vastly different training, temperaments and backgrounds, we all agree in not taking your reasoning seriously. But we also agree that there is about you an air of authenticity. You seem to bear the mark of someone with secret knowledge in his keeping. That is why we have not sent you away long ago. But time is running out - '

'I don't need *you* to remind me,' I interjected with the accumulated bitterness of the years. 'Indeed, time is running out. Everyone is an explorer now. Anyone may stumble on my islands tomorrow – '

'*Your* islands,' cried Brother Hernando, his voice trembling with the first outburst of emotion I had ever seen in him. '*Your* islands! You've let exploration go to your head. No – don't misunderstand me. I'm not condemning exploration. It's a branch of learning. But in your hands it almost seems a perversion. You are not humbled by the wonders of which you speak; you treat them simply as a means of self-aggrandisement. You are riddled with spiritual pride!'

Sorrow, blended with scorn, pervaded the words lashing me. For Brother Hernando mortified himself with self-abnegation. There was a story that, when he first was offered the see of Avila, he had refused until the Queen, whose confessor he then was, had said: 'I have always obeyed you, are you not going to obey *me* this once?' Such was the man whom I now faced.

'I noticed it when I first met you,' he continued. 'You are consumed with vanity and self-seeking. If you want to destroy yourself, that is your affair. But when you waste my time, it is very much my concern. Time and again you have stood before the assembled Commission, pretending to be a philosopher, a geographer, a biblical exegetist; all things rolled into one; demanding preposterous rewards. And in fact, you're only an explorer; you're not even a proper seaman.'

Now I felt a wave of loathing; the loathing for someone who had seen too well. Or was it self-loathing that came from having made a fool of oneself? Whatever it was, Brother Hernando obviously divined my disarray, for immediately he leapt to the attack.

'If you insist on showing off your faulty erudition, well, I am prepared to overlook it. But when you flaunt your religious irregularities, I am bound to take notice. You quote Esdras; an apocryphal prophet, which leads thoughts far beyond delinquent New Christians to the Cabal, magic, Black Masses, ritual murder; in fact the perilous regions of the occult. You talk far too much about bringing the Faith across the Ocean; as if you believed yourself divinely appointed to do so. You may have been trying to avoid the Inquisition; you have only succeeded in drawing its attention. You have presented yourself as a most original candidate for the stake. And I have been put to considerable trouble to save you from that uncomfortable fate.'

'I seem to have been living in a fool's paradise,' I said, with as much irony as I could command.

'A pity you didn't realize it sooner.'

'I have not been told sooner.'

'Well, I decided it would be better if you didn't know. I'm not sure I was right. However, I am sick and tired of all this contention. We have shown exemplary patience; we have given you every chance. Now I want the truth; tell me exactly what you know; perhaps what you have seen.'

'How do I know that you won't want to steal my ideas? How do I know that you aren't still scheming to deprive me of my reward' - I was on the verge of losing control of myself by now.

'No,' said Brother Hernando, 'that won't do. I want the truth.'

'Under the circumstances, I don't see why I should oblige. I want my ships first; and my contract; afterwards you can have your explanations. And remember; I'm not entirely in your power. Believe me: I and only I can give you new land across the Atlantic.'

'Let me be more explicit,' said Brother Hernando, now displaying his habitual calm. 'This is your last chance to speak. Unless we have the whole truth, immediately, you are to be dismissed, once and for all; and I withdraw my protection.'

'In plain language,' I said, with difficulty controlling myself, ' " Do as we want, or we throw you to the Inquisitors: talk or burn!" '

There was no answer.

'I won't stand for that,' I shouted. 'Don't think you can frighten me' - and I jumped up, to leave In so doing, I knocked over the candle, and I felt my way out in the dark, for now it was late. At the head of the stairs, Brother Hernando appeared with a lighted taper.

'I'm deeply honoured,' I said, 'to be shown out by a bishop.'

'It is the business of prelates,' he replied, 'to light the way for those who err, and you might fall down those steps.'

His parting words were: 'You seem incapable of speaking the truth. Perhaps you can write it.'

I did not trouble to reply. I was by no means as easy in my mind as I had tried to appear. I was in truth exceedingly frightened of the Holy Office, because although I was a good Catholic, I was only too aware of the heterodoxy in my background. And the Inquisition, in one form or another, was so much a part of my family history.

Flight seemed the only course. Early the next morning, I left Valladolid, and rode as fast as I could back to Córdoba, half believing that the Inquisition was already on my tail. But soon after returning home, I was presented with another and, as it turned out, more substantial threat. There arrived from the Court this note:

'I am directed to inform you that your case is to be suspended until further notice. Her Majesty is now compelled to devote herself to the prosecution of the war, and cannot deal with any but the most urgent matters. She will be pleased to recall you when she is once more in a position to favour your application with her undivided attention.'

This tempted me to despair, for Isabella by this communication seemed to have deserted me. But Beatriz suggested that it was out of character. If the Queen had really wanted to write to me, she said, the Queen would have done so herself.

'I don't believe Isabella knows anything about it,' Beatriz said. 'It's signed by some secretary. Don't you think that man Talavera's got a finger in it?'

Although Beatriz lacked formal education, she was full of common sense and a shrewd judge of people. I had found that it usually paid to listen to what she had to say.

'Perhaps your Brother Hernando wants to frighten you properly.'

'You mean an ultimatum in disguise?' I said. 'You may be right. But supposing that it is, what am I to do?' for now I had reached a point where I had succumbed to self-pity, and was virtually incapable of thought.

'Well, if I were you, I'd pretend to leave the country and take my plans somewhere else. Why don't you go to La Rábida? It's near the border, and that'll give them something to think about. Brother Juan is sure to tell them where you are and what you're doing. You'll get your way all right. But you must show you're not going to knuckle under.'

Beatriz did not know everything about me; neither my Cathar antecedents, nor the truth about my Atlantic voyages; for with secrets, I felt I could not trust even her. But her advice seemed sound and, leaving her to look after the children, I immediately acted on it.

LX

PRECISELY how I was to act at La Rábida, I had only the haziest idea, but when I arrived, my mind was rapidly made up for me. Brother Hernando had spoken truer than he knew, when he said that time was running out.

Brother Juan was still Father Superior. He greeted me without a trace of surprise, as if expecting my arrival. But he was concerned with another would-be explorer. This was a sea captain from Palos, called Martin Alonso Pinzón.

Pinzón, thank God, was a fool; he did not conceal what he knew. He was full of a map he had seen in Rome, whither he had been on a pilgrimage. It showed 'new lands to be discovered,' and he wanted to sail across the Atlantic, to search for what it showed. So I was spared uncertainty; the threat was kindly identified.

I was faced with the awful prospect of seeing my life's work destroyed. Unless I could claim priority, what was left? Somehow, I had to prevent Pinzón forestalling me; and yet I refused to forgo one iota of my claims. My difficulties were considerable. Pinzón was a true mariner where I was not; he had Brother Juan's confidence. Somehow, I had to prove that I knew more than this abominable rival. Desperation pointed the way.

I wrote out a summary of my Atlantic voyages, with copies of the charts I had saved and the necessary observations to prove I was at last revealing the truth. I held back only one piece of information; the system of prevailing winds, so that I still kept the sailing key to the Atlantic to myself. But I wrote enough to convince any of the qualified gentlemen on the Commission.

I then went, document in hand, to Brother Juan, and asked him to confess me. He showed some surprise, for I came abruptly at an awkward hour. He took me to a little white-washed cell, leading off the convent chapel; we assumed the positions of confessor and penitent, and I said:

'What I now tell you is under the seal of the confessional.'

'Of course,' was the reply; not in irritation, but perhaps with a trace of mystification.

'You will not divulge what I have to say to any *profane* person.'

'Is there any need to state the obvious?'

'But you could communicate what I reveal to someone else in Holy Orders. A bishop for example.

'Brother Cristóbal, you are acting very strangely.'

'But you could, if you wanted to.'

Brother Juan made a gesture of exasperation.

'I have been told,' I said, 'that I cannot speak the truth; but perhaps I can write it. Very well, here is what I have to say' - and I handed over the document. 'We agree that the contents are under the seal of the confessional.'

The surprise which came over Brother Juan was almost comical; I prompted him to complete the more customary part of the confession, and then I went out.

Brother Juan did not refer by so much as a word to what had happened. But I made it my business to discover that he had written post haste to Brother Hernando. I therefore waited, not patiently, but with the comforting belief that I would not be left long in suspense.

And three weeks later, a Royal courier arrived with a letter recalling me to the Court. For the second time, I rode out of La Rábida, to meet the Catholic Sovereigns.

LXI

I HAD been summoned to the triumph of my own struggle and of a holy crusade. The King and Queen were with their army before Granada, last Moorish redoubt in Spain. They could not receive me when I arrived, because they were immersed in the parleys for the inevitable surrender of the enemy. But I was turned over to a senior official whose mandate was simply to settle the terms of my voyage. That I was to sail seemed now taken for granted.

Thus the news for which I had been waiting fifteen long years, came stealthily. Any awe I might have felt at the way the prison walls of insuperable difficulties had fallen overnight was discouraged by the person selected to deal with me. For he is a man who can make poetry sound like account books.

He is joint Secretary to Their Majesties. Ironically enough he is almost my namesake: Juan de Coloma. I would have preferred not to have faced him just then. For I was in great turbulence of spirit. After seven hundred years the Moor was about to be driven from the soil of the west. It was revenge for the Fall of Constantinople; consummation of the ardent desires of Christendom, the finest moment of the age; and I was merely a spectator. I had been so wrapped up in my voyage, that I had ignored what was happening under my nose. The name of Colón would not be inscribed among those who had defeated the Moor. But I wanted to hold my head high among those who had.

So I magnified my demands. I had claimed the title of Admiral of the Ocean Sea: but this was new, and not necessarily impressive to my contemporaries, although I believe that it will be sonorous to posterity. I now wanted the privileges and quarterings of the Grand Admiral of Castille. This is a celebrated magnate of the Realm, his significance grasped by anyone, even by the captains in the field.

Coloma was scandalized. The Grand Admirals are drawn exclusively from the very finest of the aristocracy; the present holder of the office is Don Alonso Henríquez, of the very blood royal. I was accused, in so many words of offering an unforgivable insult by daring to suggest that his privileges ought to be shared with a person of such undistinguished birth as myself.

I could not explain why I had asked for this particular honour; Coloma would be incapable of understanding. In his hateful manner, where arrogance and obsequiousness meet, he rejected my demand, suggesting that my other rewards ought to suffice.

But having come so far, I refused to renounce one iota of my claims. As I had maintained all along, the voyage was to be on my terms or not at all. I declined to make a mockery of all the years at the last moment.

Early one morning, I took my horse and, once more, left my tormentor with the intention of returning to Córdoba in another demonstration of defiance. Before Granada disappeared from view, I turned round to gaze my fill upon the scene; since I could not know for certain whether I would be recalled. In the distance, as if hovering in the air, ran the snow-capped ridge of the Sierra Nevada. The walls of Granada, and the minarets of the Alhambra were picked out by the rays of the rising sun. And at my feet on the plain, I saw the buildings of Santa Fé; the Royal town thrown up within a few months by a whole army turned artisans. It was laid out in the form of a cross, with two wide avenues intersecting at the centre, covered with substantial buildings of brick and mortar; erected in a magnificent gesture on the site of the original camp; to show the Moor that there would be no retreat; the only town in Spain, as somebody has said, 'never contaminated by the Moslem heresy.'

With intimations of regret, I left all this. But I was not allowed to go far. At the Bridge of Pines, after about an hour's ride, I was overtaken by a Royal courier bearing a request to return to Santa Fé. He conveyed neither promise nor apology, but I discerned the hand of God, so I turned back.

I was met by an austere and chastened Coloma. Would I kindly not repeat the performance? His reputation would be compromised. Their Majesties would be distressed to see me leave; they asked me to wait a little longer, and all would be amicably settled.

So I waited while the capitulation of Granada was signed and the final act of surrender prepared. It was a delay I could not grudge, for it permitted me to witness a scene that will be remembered as long as history itself. Yet what I remember most clearly is not the victors but the vanquished.

The ceremony of capitulation was on the second of January 1492. Happy augury of things to come, I was among the privileged spectators, able to see and hear what was happening. Armour glinting in the winter sun, Abdallah, the last Emir of Granada, appeared with his retainers in a ceremonial Spanish camp on the banks of the River Xenil, in front of Santa Fé. With inexpressible dignity, he rode between a guard of honour formed of the chosen officers of the Christian army. Dismounting from his horse, he made as if to prostrate himself before the Catholic sovereigns. But Ferdinand stopped him with a chivalrous gesture. And the Moor handed over the keys of the city, saying in perfect Castilian:

'They are yours, since Allah so decrees; use your success with clemency and moderation.'

I felt a lump in my throat at this: Ferdinand was unable to reply; nobody in that company was unaffected. I caught a glimpse of Brother Hernando among the Royal retinue: he had a look of infinite compassion on his usually impassive face. Sometimes there is nothing sadder than victory except defeat.

The following day I was received by Isabella, but on this occasion together with her husband. The Catholic Sovereigns had not yet moved into the Moorish citadel, remaining at their headquarters in Santa Fé, where they had spent the siege, as an act of humility, I suppose. And in a simple audience chamber still smelling of new plaster, I heard the announcement of my own victory.

Besides the King and Queen, there were Coloma, a clerk, and Brother Hernando. The King made some commonplace remarks; the Queen greeted me with her customary friendliness.

'I am glad,' she said with every appearance of sincerity, 'that the decision finally went in your favour.'

I caught Brother Hernando's eyes, and he gave me an enigmatic, fleeting smile. For one frightful moment, I thought that my whole secret had been betrayed. But it was soon obvious that the Queen knew only as much as I wanted her to know.

'You ask a great deal,' she said, 'but you have spoken well. You promise much, but you do so persuasively. And my advisers point out that you will only have what you want if you succeed. If you fail, you receive nothing.'

'I would have it no other way.'

'If I may say so, that is one of the strongest points in your favour. It's not everyone, you know, who can ask for honours - and get them. Still, if you do even a fraction of what you promise - you'll be worth at least a coat of arms.'

'Your Majesty will have no cause for regret,' I replied. 'You have just defeated the Moors. But what is Granada? The last Moslem sore on the face of Christian Spain, I agree. But it is only a decadent minor province; the miserable remnant of a corrupt infidel enclave; a patch of soil that will scarcely be noticed on the map of Christendom. I have much more to offer; I will bring you more than all your generals. And I will devote the profits from my voyage to the recovery of Jerusalem from the Turk, to the honour of Christendom and Your Majesties.'

'Come back safe and sound,' said Isabella with a smile, 'and we will be satisfied.'

And there, save the formalities, the audience ended. Afterwards, Coloma (rather more civil than before) enunciated the conditions under which I was to sail. When I suggested Palos as my base because I knew people there, he said:

'Most convenient. The City Council owes the Crown a lot of money. They can settle the debt by providing your ships.'

I was to have three, as I had requested.

I handed Coloma a memorandum of agreement which I had prepared well in advance, to be ready for the occasion. He read it impassively, made no objection, and promised to have it officially approved, warning me however, that it would take time. 'The Chancery,' he said, 'is in a state of chaos because of the end of the war. But in principle, your plans are approved, and you may start work immediately on your preparations.'

And so, once more I returned to La Rábida, in triumph at last. But my troubles were not quite over; it seemed as if God had decided to try me to the end. The elders of Palos knew how 'orders are to be obeyed, but not carried out,' as the saying has it. The ships were not forthcoming, my preparations were delayed. On Brother Juan's advice, I overcame this by inviting Martin Alonso Pinzón to join the expedition. In this way I obtained what was my due, by taking a local hostage, as it were. And in another way, it was not a bad idea. Pinzón is a first class seaman, and I may yet be glad of his help. Besides, he represents a danger of the very worst kind. He will always be capable of forestalling me, or threatening my reputation. It will be far better to have him under control; I want no rival of his stature at large. It's an ill wind that blows nobody any good.

I have also acquired reinforcement from a totally unexpected quarter. Their Majesties have finally expelled all unrepentant Jews from Spain. I have watched the fugitives pouring into Palos, to be packed into ships for transport God knows where. I must confess that I could not avoid feeling sympathy at the sight. And I have been frequently approached by the victims, asking me to take them with me, saying they are prepared to face anything if they can escape the life of a wandering exile in a hostile land. Most of them were highly qualified, and a cut above the kind of person I was being forced to recruit. Brother Juan, emphatic in his sympathies, persuaded me to accept some of these unbelieving applicants; 'An act of charity,' he said, 'that you will not regret.' In this way, I acquired a surgeon, an accountant, and an interpreter, without whom I would otherwise have been compelled to sail. They have promised to accept baptism just before departure, which will save their scruples, and avoid trouble with the crews.

As I finish writing this, Beatriz has arrived to bid farewell. She will follow me in a pilot boat until I have passed the bar at Saltés. The parting will not be pleasant, for it will be like leaving half of myself behind. What it will be to her, I can only imagine. But she shows indomitable fortitude, which is just as well, because in her presence I am overcome by melancholy and self-reproach.

'You mustn't worry,' she says. 'I know how to wait.'

There is indeed strength with such a woman behind one. And, God knows, I have needed all the strength I can summon for, besides the worries of the expedition, I have had to bear the recriminations of Brother Juan; he is worried for my soul.

'You got your way after all,' he said the other day, in what is bound to be one of our last interviews before I leave. 'I only hope you'll be happy. Do you really believe there is happiness in having all your prayers granted? My experience suggests the contrary.

'And once more I say: wouldn't it be better to admit publicly what you've done, and what you really are. Why have you chosen a lie? Can there really be honour and satisfaction in deceit?'

'Think of it as some recompense for all the suffering I have had to endure,' I replied. 'Think of all the years I have spent, bursting with the islands I could almost touch, but unable to talk openly about them; prevented from sailing out to them. I have been like one of the damned.

'And remember: discovery is a moment. The pleasure is fleeting. The very act of accomplishment is in itself a form of destruction. Afterwards, there is only anticlimax. The pleasure lies almost only in anticipation. I can expect happiness on the voyage alone. The only satisfying consolation will be to appear before posterity as I wish. It will balance the sadness of consummation; it will wipe away all the wasted years; it will wash clean the remorse I periodically suffer for the sins I have committed.

'I told you the truth under duress, in the privilege of the confessional. You have no right to break confidence, even if you think it is for the good of my soul.

'Under no circumstances are you to divulge one word of what I have confessed; if you do it will be a sin far worse than any I may be guilty of. No: I do not mean to threaten. I appeal to you as a Christian, a priest, a fellow-Franciscan, do not betray my confidence.

'Without reputation, there is no victory. I wish it to appear as if I had found my way across the Atlantic by the process of my own reasoning alone; as if I were explorer, philosopher, prophet all in one.

'I am only interested in the image of myself that posterity will see. I offer an empire; in return I am really asking no more than the privilege of deciding how I will appear to the historians.'

MEMORANDUM OF AGREEMENT BETWEEN DON CRISTÓBAL COLÓN AND THEIR INVINCIBLE MAJESTIES, FERDINAND AND ISABELLA OF SPAIN.
(Called The Capitulations of Santa Fé.)

THE things which your Highnesses give and declare to Cristóbal Colón in some satisfaction for what he has discovered in the oceans, and for the voyage which now, with the aid of God, he is about to make therein in the service of Your Highnesses, are as follows:

First, that your Highnesses as Lords that are of the said oceans make from this time the said Don Cristóbal Colón your Admiral in all those islands and mainlands which by his hand and industry shall be discovered or acquired in the said oceans during his life and after his death his heirs and successors, from one to another perpetually, with all the pre-eminences and prerogatives belonging to the said office and according as Don Alonso Enriques, your High Admiral of Castile, and the other predecessors in the said office held it in their districts. - *It so pleases their Highnesses.*

Likewise, that your Highnesses make the said Don Cristóbal your Viceroy and Governor General in all the said islands and mainlands which, as has been said, he may discover or acquire in the said seas; and that for the government of each one and of any one of them, he may make selection of three persons for each office, and that your Highnesses may choose and select the one who shall be most serviceable to you, and thus the lands which our Lord shall permit him to discover and acquire will be better governed in the service of your Highnesses. - *It so pleases their Highnesses.*

Item, that all and whatever merchandise, whether it be pearls, precious stones, gold, silver, spices, and other things whatsoever, and merchandise of whatever kind, name and manner it may be, which may be bought, bartered, discovered, acquired or obtained within the limits of the said Admiralty, your Highnesses grant henceforth to the said Don Cristóbal, and will that he may have and take for himself the tenth part of all of them, deducting all the expenses which may be incurred therein; so that of what shall remain free and clear he may have and take the tenth part for himself and do with it as he wills, the other nine parts remaining for your Highnesses. - *It so pleases their Highnesses.*

Likewise, that if on account of the merchandise that he might bring from the said islands and lands which as aforesaid he shall acquire and discover, or of that which may be taken in exchange for the same from other merchants here, any suit should arise in the place where the said trade and traffic shall be held and conducted; and if by the pre-eminence of his office of Admiral it may belong to him to know of each suit, it may please your Highnesses that he or his deputy, and no other judge, may take cognisance of the said suit, and thus it is decreed henceforth. - *It so pleases their Highnesses if it belongs to the said office of the Admiral, as the said Admiral Don Alonso Enriques held it and the others, his predecessors in their districts, and if it be just.*

Item, that in all the vessels which may be equipped for the said traffic and negotiation each time and whenever and as often as they be equipped, the said Admiral Don Cristóbal Colón may, if he wishes, contribute and pay the eighth part of all that may be expended in the equipment. And also that he may have and take of the profit, the eighth part of all which may result from such equipment. - *It so pleases their Highnesses.*

These are executed and dispatched with the responses of your Highnesses at the end of each article in the town of Santa Fé de la Vega de Granada, on the seventeenth day of April in the year of the nativity of our Saviour Jesus Christ one thousand four hundred and ninety-two.

By the order of the King and of the Queen.
I, the King.
I, the Queen.
Juan de Coloma (Secretary).

FROM THE JOURNAL OF CHRISTOPHER COLUMBUS ON HIS FIRST VOYAGE, AS GIVEN BY BARTOLOMÉ DE LAS CASAS IN 'HISTORIA DE LAS INDIAS', WRITTEN ABOUT 1527.

'Friday, August 3rd.
On Friday, the third day of August, of the year 1492, at eight o'clock, we set out from the bar of Saltés. We went with a strong sea-breeze sixty miles to the southward, that is, fifteen leagues, before sunset; afterwards, to the south-west and south by west which was the course for the Canaries.'

Thursday, September 6th.
He set out on that day in the morning from the harbour of Gomera and shaped his course to proceed upon his voyage.

Tuesday, September 25th.
This day was very calm and afterwards it blew, and they went on their way to the west, until night. The admiral [Columbus] talked with Martin Alonso Pinzón, captain of the other caravel, the *Pinta*, concerning a chart which three days before he had sent to him to the caravel and in which, as it appears, the admiral had certain islands depicted as being in that sea.

Thursday, October 11th. [The first landing]
He navigated to the west-south west; they had a rougher sea than they had experienced during the whole voyage. They saw petrels and a green reed near the ship. Those in the caravel *Pinta* saw a cane and a stick, and they secured another small stick, carved, as it appeared, with iron, and a piece of cane and other vegetation which grows on land, and a small board. Those in the caravel *Niña* also saw other indications of land

and a stick loaded with barnacles. At these signs, they all breathed again and rejoiced. On this day, to sunset, they went twenty-seven leagues. After sunset, he [Columbus] steered his former course to the west; they made twelve miles an hour, and up to two hours before midnight they had made ninety miles, which are twenty-two leagues and a half. And since the caravel *Pinta* was swifter and went ahead of the admiral, she found land and made the signals which the admiral had commanded. This land was first sighted by a sailor called Rodrigo de Triana, although the admiral, at ten o'clock in the night, being on the sterncastle, saw a light. It was, however, so obscured that he would not affirm that it was land, but called Pero Gutierrez, butler of the King's dais, and told him that there seemed to be a light, and that he should watch for it. He did so, and saw it. He said the same also to Rodrigo Sanchez de Segovia, whom the King and Queen had sent in the fleet as comptroller, and he saw nothing since he was not in a position from which it could be seen. After the admiral had so spoken, it was seen once or twice, and it was like a small wax candle, which was raised and lowered. Few thought that this was an indication of land, but the admiral was certain that they were near land. Accordingly, when they had said the *Salve*, which all sailors are accustomed to say and chant in their manner, and when they had all been gathered together, the admiral asked and urged them to keep a good look-out from the forecastle and to watch carefully for land, and to him who should say first that he saw land, he would give at once a silk doublet apart from the other rewards which the Sovereigns had promised, which were ten thousand maravedis annually to him who first sighted it. Two hours after midnight land appeared, at a distance of about two leagues from them. They took in all sail, remaining with the mainsail, which is the great sail without bonnets, and kept jogging, waiting for day, a Friday, on which they reached a small island of the Lucayos, which is called in the Indians, 'Guanahaní'. Immediately they saw naked people, and the admiral went ashore in the armed boat, and Martin Alonso Pinzón, and Vicente Yañez, his brother, who was captain of the *Niña*. The admiral brought out the royal standard, and the captains went with two banners of the Green Cross, which the admiral flew on all the ships as a flag, with an F and a Y and over each letter their crown, one being on one side of the cross and the other on the other. When they had landed, they saw very green trees and much water and fruit of various kinds. The admiral called the two captains and the others who had landed, and Rodrigo de Escobedo, secretary of the whole fleet, and Rodrigo Sanchez de Segovis, and said that they should bear witness and testimony how he, before them all, took possession of the island, as in fact he did, for the King and Queen, his Sovereigns, making the declarations which are required, as is contained more at length in the testimonies which were there made in writing.